THE RETURN OF SIGURD

THE DRAGON SLAYER

S. P. Grey

First published in Great Britain in 2008
by
Hall Publishing

Copyright © 2008 S.P. Grey

A CIP Catalogue of this book is available from the British Library

ISBN 978-0-9558220-1-8

Cover illustration by Dean Harkness.
Snickelway map by Mark Jones, author of
'A Walk Around the Snickelways of York'
and other interesting publications

Printed and bound in
Great Britain by Biddles Ltd,
King's Lynn, Norfolk

CONTENTS

Special thanks to

Pete, Colette, Jessica and Mark Jones
for all their help in producing this book

Prologue

The Return of Sigurd
the Dragon Slayer

The Return of Sigurd the Dragon Slayer is the second book in the Viking series. In *The Last Vikings...*

Peter leaves his home and his father in Wales and travels to York with his mother and grandmother. Before he leaves, his father tells him that "York is a magical city". In the middle of his first night, Peter is woken by strange sounds coming from the ancient church outside the flat he is staying in. As he watches in astonishment, a dozen ghostly Viking warriors appear and lay their swords beside a tall gravestone in the church's graveyard.

The following morning, Peter sneaks out of the flat before his mother wakes up and explores the graveyard, but he finds no trace of the Vikings or their swords. The tall gravestone appears weathered and worn. Suddenly a rainbow appears, illuminating the stone. As the light shines on it, the gravestone is transformed and Peter is able to read the inscription: 'HERE LIES SIGURD THE DRAGON SLAYER VIKING KING OF KINGS.'

Lying on top of the gravestone is a golden talisman in the shape of a dragon with his jaws agape and its clawed feet ready to rip and tear. As Peter puts it in his pocket, an old man appears in front of him, claiming to be a simple gardener, but it soon becomes apparent that the old man is Sigurd himself. "I am Sigurd, though I have not been called by that name for over a thousand years. I have come here to speak with you, Peter. Will you listen to me?"

Sigurd tells Peter that Vikings are still living in York. Long ago, they built their halls beneath the Minster where they found the root of Yggdrasil, the tree of life. Anyone who drinks the sap of Yggdrasil gains great strength and power, and the Vikings used the sap to understand magic and explore its limitless possibilities. York is the only place where any of Yggdrasil's three great roots rises to the surface. But the Vikings were double crossed by the powerful Necromancer, Maledict, who destroyed the root and drank all its sap before stealing the Viking Stone – the only seed of Yggdrasil - which contains the concentrated power of the tree. Over the centuries, the Vikings have slowly died out as Maledict has hunted them. Only a few remain, hidden in their Halls, unknown to the modern inhabitants of York.

Sigurd warns Peter that Maledict is returning to destroy the last remaining Vikings forever, and asks Peter to help them. He tells Peter to return to the graveyard that night at midnight, then he mysteriously disappears.

That night, Peter waits in the freezing churchyard as the distant Minster bells toll out the hour. Finally he hears a strange voice and watches in amazement as a short bald man seemingly steps out of the church wall! The peculiar man is a foot shorter than Peter, is almost bald and dressed in an old-fashioned blazer and tie. The man identifies himself as Dunstable, a Viking scout. Clearly terrified, he tells Peter that he has seen Maledict's troll army beyond the city walls and is urgently trying to find his way back to the Viking Halls to warn the Viking Queen and Prince.

Dunstable takes Peter through the magic snickelways - which are narrow winding passageways through York that hide the Vikings from the 'city dwellers' - to the Viking Halls beneath York Minster. After entering the enormous Debating Hall, Peter stands nervously beside Dunstable in front of all the Vikings, including the Queen and Prince, as he tells them about Maledict's army. The plight of the Vikings seems hopeless. They are vastly outnumbered by Maledict's army and there seems no hope of victory or even survival. Peter tells them he has seen Sigurd, and learns that Sigurd was the greatest Viking warrior, who vowed to return to the Vikings when their need was the greatest.

The Council is suspended to take in the news Dunstable and Peter have brought, and the Queen shows Peter the Candle Chamber – an enormous chamber beyond the Debating Hall that is full of candles representing the life of each Viking who has ever lived in York. Almost all are extinguished. At the back of the hall, the Vikings' eternal flame still burns brightly. Behind it is the root of Yggdrasil - a long black scar marking where Maledict struck his axe over a thousand years before. Beside it is a slender branch from which the Viking Stone once hung.

As Peter waits for the re-convened Viking Council to conclude, he meets the immaculately dressed Viking Princess, the daughter of the Queen. Haughty and arrogant, she barely speaks to him. Soon they are called into the Debating Hall to hear that the Vikings have decided to embark upon a Quest to seek Mimir's Well. Mimir lives in a cavern in the desolate mountains. Anyone who looks into the water from his Well will obtain the wisest answer to any question. Only then can they find a way to defeat Maledict. But Mimir's Cavern is guarded by the ferocious Frost Giants and it is a dangerous journey from York. The Princess volunteers to go, and Peter and Dunstable reluctantly agree to go with her.

That night, Peter learns about some of the incredible things that the sap from Yggdrasil has allowed the Vikings to do. The Princess teaches him how to fly, and together they race over the city at night, absorbed in the thrill of flying. The following morning the Queen gives them three magical gifts to help them in their journey: a transformation mask that turns its wearer into any living creature, a phial of speed potion and some ordinary looking chocolate that contains pure essence of joy.

Peter, the Princess and Dunstable leave York, just managing to avoid the troll army outside the Walls. With Dunstable proving an unreliable guide, they get lost in Ironwood and are attacked by Wolves. As Peter is attacked by the enormous Wolf Chieftain, Sigurd's talisman burns in his pocket and he feels magic flow through him. Without thinking, he whispers magic words and the Wolf Chieftain is flung from him.

After escaping from the Frost Giants, they finally reach Mimir's Cavern, but Mimir is nowhere to be seen. As the Princess and Dunstable are distracted by the shining diamonds in the cavern walls, Peter lowers a wooden pan into the Well and gazes into the water. He sees three visions: Maledict watching over his enormous army in York with the Viking Stone shining from the centre of his crown; dragons circling in a blood red sky above a stormy sea; and a strange figure betraying the Vikings to Maledict. Confused by the second and third visions, Peter finally realises the meaning of the first vision: the only way to defeat Maledict is to steal the Viking Stone from his crown!

Despite the seeming impossibility of this task, the Princess is undeterred and they race back to York, terrified that it may already be over-run by Maledict's army. As they approach the city, his vast army lies between them and the City Walls. The Princess boldly steals troll uniforms and leads them through the army disguised as trolls, but soon they are discovered. As they race for the safety of the Walls, they are over-taken by trolls. Fighting for their lives, Peter is struck down and descends into darkness....

Chapter 1

The Second Great Viking Council

Peter woke suddenly. He was lying in a wonderfully comfortable bed in a well-lit room, dressed in strange yellow pyjamas. Then the pain in his head hit him, knocking him back into the soft pillow.

'Where am I?' he asked to no one in particular, massaging his forehead with his fingers.

'You are safe in the Viking Halls. You're lucky to be here! We thought you had been crushed! It took four Vikings to heave that troll off you!'

Peter turned around in surprise. The Queen was sitting on a wooden chair beside his bed gazing down at him, concern clearly showing on her face.

'Damn lucky if you ask me boy!' said a gruff voice from somewhere at the back of the room. 'Crazy idea to *walk* through the troll army! Good job we were there, that's all I can say!'

Raising his head, Peter was surprised to see the Prince dressed in silver chain mail with a long sword sheathed at his side as he leant against the far wall of the room. Suddenly their mad sprint across the racecourse came back to Peter.

'The Princess? Dunstable? What happened?'

'They are safe. You needn't worry about them,' continued the Queen, casting a quick disapproving glance at her son. 'Our scouts spotted you from the Walls. You did stand out a little. Either you were the shortest trolls we had ever seen or you were in disguise. We had been waiting for your return and hoped it would be you. When you were discovered, we sent a rescue party…'

'Led by myself of course,' interrupted the Prince. He strolled casually towards Peter with his chest puffed out and leaned over the bedstead. 'We got to you just after the trolls did. The stupid creatures were so busy gloating over you they didn't see us coming! Damned fools! We made short work of them of course.'

The Queen shot him another warning glance then returned her attention to Peter.

'Suffice to say, we got to you just in time. We carried you through a secret entrance in the Walls before the rest of the troll army could catch us. That was yesterday morning – over a day ago. Since then you have been sleeping. We have given you some of our medicine and your injuries are almost healed, though your head will remain sore for several days I'm afraid.'

Peter touched the large lump on his forehead again and winced in pain.

'A troll's helmet struck you there, I believe. You will have a scar for the rest of your life, though it will be small. In a few hours there will be another Viking Council to discuss what you have discovered in your travels. You will be asked to speak, along with the Princess. From what I have heard, you have a great tale to tell. Until then, you must rest and regain your strength.'

Whatever medicine the Queen had given Peter was clearly making him sleepy as he could barely stay awake, despite the throbbing pain in his head. He forced himself to concentrate a moment longer.

'Just one more question. How is the battle with Maledict going? We saw hundreds of trolls. Have they broken through the Walls yet?'

The Prince spoke, his voice unusually low and subdued.

'No boy, they haven't broken through, not yet. They have made a few sorties, nothing more. We have easily repelled them. Maybe Maledict is waiting. More trolls are arriving every hour, damn them! But we will be ready for him when he comes! We will make him pay for his arrogance!'

The Queen rose to her feet and leant over Peter. Her eyes lingered for a moment on the bruise on his forehead.

'We will call you later. For now you must rest.'

Reaching down, she placed her white hand on his forehead over his scar. For a second Peter froze, expecting there to be pain, but instead he felt a comforting warmth spreading out from her fingers. Almost immediately he felt irresistibly tired and his eyes began to close. As he fought to stay awake, her wide blue eyes held his for a moment and he saw concern and anxiety written there, despite her comforting smile. Then he felt himself slipping into peaceful sleep.

*

Peter woke with a start, pulled out of the dream he was having of a stormy coastline with dragons circling overhead. Then he heard her again.

'Wake up Peter! Wake up!'

A tall girl with a serious face and long blonde pleated hair was shaking him, forcing him back into the present.

'Get dressed quickly! The Viking Council has started! We're waiting for you!'

Before he could answer she left the room, leaving him dazed and confused.

Wearily he pushed back the blankets and rose unsteadily to his feet. He touched his forehead gingerly. Though it was still sore, the pain was a lot less than it had been.

Feeling slightly dazed, he glanced around the small room, looking for his clothes. They were lying neatly folded on the chair where the Queen had previously sat. Suddenly he had a horrible thought and dived for his trousers. He breathed a sigh of relief. Sigurd's talisman was still safely hidden in the right pocket. Placing it back inside, he dressed quickly then splashed some cold water on his face from a stone basin at the far end of the room. Finally ready, he walked through the solid stone archway at the end of the room without even thinking and appeared in a wide brightly lit corridor.

The girl who had woken him had disappeared and there was no one about. Perhaps they were all in the Debating Hall? Just ahead an archway was built into the wall. He knew that a room must lie beyond it. For a moment he hesitated. The Queen and Prince and hundreds of Vikings would be waiting for him. But there was no time for delay – he was already late. Pushing his apprehension aside, he stepped boldly through the solid stone.

As he had guessed, he immediately found himself in the Debating Hall. Clearly the debate was heated as hundreds of Vikings were shouting at the top of their voices, waving their arms as they argued with one another in the balconies above him. To his horror, the instant he stepped into view they were hushed into silence. In a moment all he could hear was the excited whisperings of some of the Vikings in the front row nearest to him: *'There he is!'; 'About time too! Fancy turning up late to a Council meeting! Does he have no manners?'; 'He took a bit of a bash on the head I believe!'; 'Fell over a troll I heard!'*

Feeling distinctly uncomfortable, he took a step forward onto the long smooth marble floor then froze. All around him, the tiered balconies rose to the lofty ceiling. Once again, each of them was lined with inquisitive faces, blinking as they peered down at him.

'Come on! Hurry up! We haven't got all day you know!' barked the Prince irritably.

As before, the Prince was sitting on a golden throne beside the Queen in the centre of the hall. Both were dressed in the same clothes they had worn at the first Council – the Prince in a long elegant robe that changed colour when he moved and the Queen dressed simply in white. This time the Princess was sitting between them on a third slightly smaller throne. She was dressed in the same blue shimmering dress she had worn when Peter had first met her, though her long blonde hair, which normally flowed down her back, was pinned on her head, making her look like an Egyptian queen. She nodded to him regally, looking extremely pleased with herself. There was no sign of Dunstable.

Feeling like he had been summoned before the Headmaster in front of the whole school, Peter made his way towards the centre of the forum and stood awkwardly in front of the three thrones, wondering what he should do next. With a slight smile, the Queen nodded towards an empty seat in the lowest tier. Once he sat down, she rose to her feet to address the assembly.

'We have gathered together once more to discuss how best to defend ourselves against Maledict and his troll army. Since we last met and declared the Quest, the trolls have been gathering outside the city. So far, the magic in the Walls has prevented them from attacking us but we cannot rely on their protection forever. Maledict is strong. Soon he will attack us in great force and bring all his magic craft to bear. When that happens, the Walls will surely fail.'

A gloomy silence fell as each Viking peered nervously over the golden railings above her.

'But now we have been given a chance. The Quest to find Mimir's Cavern and obtain his counsel has been successful and the three travellers have returned to us safely. We praise them for their bravery!'

'*Here! Here!*' shouted a dozen voices close to Peter. At the same time several Vikings struck the floor with their feet in typical Viking fashion as they clapped with their boots. '*Jolly good effort I say!*'; '*Knew they had it in them!*'; '*That Princess, she'll certainly go far! Takes after her mother of course!*'

The Queen waited for the clamour to subside. Beside her, the Prince shuffled impatiently on his throne and glared at anyone he saw talking.

'Now we will hear them speak,' continued the Queen when silence was finally restored. 'The Princess will recount their journey, though no doubt Peter will need to speak also.'

The Queen sat down and the Princess rose to her feet. For a moment she surveyed her audience to ensure she had their full attention, then she began to tell the tale of their journey.

As Peter listened he couldn't help admire her. The Princess was a born storyteller and immediately had her audience hanging on her every word. At several points, however, he noticed that she embellished upon the truth. In particular, she expanded upon her role, going into great detail about how she had saved them all on numerous occasions whilst scarcely mentioning anything Peter or Dunstable had done.

The Queen listened silently, but the same could not be said for the Prince and the other Vikings, who cheered and stamped their feet in appreciation when she detailed her numerous heroics. When she described how she had defeated the Wolf Chieftain for instance, the Prince leapt to his feet in excitement. '*Well done Princess! That'll show him what happens when you mess with a Viking!*' And he positively spun on his throne when she recounted at great length how she had single-handedly defended Peter and Dunstable against the attack of the Frost Giants, neglecting to mention that it was Peter who had saved her when she had fallen. '*Good job she was there, eh?*' the Prince barked at Peter, prodding his forefinger towards him. '*What would you have done without her, boy? Be buried under a pile of rocks that's what!*' Peter gritted his teeth and tried to remain calm.

After what seemed like hours, she finally got to the point in her story where they reached Mimir's Cavern. Here she deliberately didn't go into details, quickly glossing over what had happened and stating only that Mimir had mistakenly spoken to Peter instead of her (which, had he known she was a Princess, he obviously would have done). She concluded her long tale with their disastrous flight back to York (in which she described Peter's panic in expansive detail), their encounter with Betty the Witch (she completely missed the part where Peter had freed her), and their precarious dash across the racecourse (which the Prince now thought a very good idea indeed).

When she finished, the Queen and Prince questioned her at length. The Prince was chiefly concerned with their battles with Frost Giants and wolves, and their encounters with the trolls. But the Queen questioned her keenly on Mimir and Betty. Both of them asked her to describe the strange figure they had seen after they had escaped from her cellars, each nodding darkly to the other.

Finally they seemed content and the Princess sat down with an extravagant bow to the wildly applauding Vikings in the balconies above her. *'Fine show!'; 'That girl's a hero – an absolute hero!'; 'First class bravery, I say! A credit to the Queen!'* When they finally subsided, the Queen rose to her feet again.

'It has been a long time since any of us except Dunstable have ventured beyond the Walls and the world is still a dangerous place it seems. We already knew much about the Frost Giants. They are fearsome foes and you did well to escape them. We have also heard of evil witches luring unsuspecting Vikings into their dens, though I have never heard of one in league with trolls before. Clearly this witch has made a deal with Maledict which has now turned sour upon her. But though the Princess's account is a good one, I wish to hear Peter speak also.'

'Is that *really* necessary?' bellowed the Prince irritably, twisting on his throne to frown at Peter. 'Haven't we heard enough already? If the boy can just tell us what he saw in the water from the Well and what Mimir said to him then that will be enough surely? Quite why Mimir would choose to speak to a City Dweller when a Viking Princess was present, I have no idea! I am beginning to think that perhaps he isn't quite what he is cracked up to be!'

'Here! Here!' cried several voices from above.

The Queen raised a hand to silence them.

'Mimir has lived for hundreds of years. He is wise beyond our understanding. He did not speak to Peter in error, I think.' She turned to Peter as she sat down again. 'Now Peter, tell us what you know. In particular, speak of Mimir's Cavern and what you learned there. Do not fear! The information you bring is vital to our cause.'

Suddenly everyone's attention focused on Peter. Immediately his heart began racing as he cringed under the weight of hundreds of pairs of eyes peering down at him. The Queen smiled encouragingly, but the Prince glared at him in obvious irritation, slouching on his throne as if already bored. But by far the worst was the Princess. He could feel her eyes boring into him as if warning him not to contradict her version of what had happened.

Rising to his feet nervously, he began to speak. At first he was cautious, saying as little as he could get away with. But the Queen listened carefully to his every word and encouraged him when he stuttered, and soon he was speaking more freely. When he spoke of what had happened at Mimir's Cavern she continually interrupted him, making him describe every detail he could remember. Mindful of Mimir's warning not to reveal the secret of the Well, he carefully skipped around the detail of how he had found the Cavern. But soon he was faced with an even greater dilemma. The Princess had said nothing of the diamonds embedded in the Cavern walls or of Mimir himself, only that Mimir had mistakenly spoken to him and not her. Though he deliberately avoided mentioning the Princess's obsession with the diamonds, he couldn't entirely hide it either. Meanwhile, he could feel the Princess's eyes staring daggers at him. The fact that she was the daughter of the Queen only increased his agitation.

Choosing his words carefully and avoiding the Queen's direct questions as best he could, Peter skipped diplomatically to the first vision he had seen in the water he'd drawn from the Well, though he deliberately didn't explain how he had interpreted it. He also didn't mention the second and third visions, partly because he didn't yet understand them and partly because he was wary of being mocked again. When he finally finished, the Queen studied his face thoughtfully for a moment.

'You have spoken well and truthfully, I see it in your eyes, though you have not told us everything. But one thing you must tell us. What do you conclude the meaning of this vision to be?'

Peter hesitated for a second before he spoke, realising the effect his words would have.

'That we must steal the Viking Stone from Maledict's crown. Only then can we defeat him.'

There was a brief moment of stunned silence before everyone in the hall except the Queen leapt to their feet, the sound of chair legs screeching across the balcony floors almost as loud as their furious voices.

'Preposterous! There must be another way!'; 'It would be suicide! No one would dare it!'; 'This Mimir is a mad man! Does he not know how powerful Maledict is?'

The Prince, as usual, was the loudest of all as he swung on the armrests of his throne in outrage.

'We must forget this nonsense! Let's not waste any more time on foolish quests! We must attack I say! *Attack!* Drive Maledict from our door! *That* is the only way to defeat him!'

Beside the Prince, the Princess was looking uneasy, as if unsure whether to approve or disapprove. Only the Queen remained calm. When Peter met her eyes he could sense a terrible sadness as if she was resigned to a desperate fate. With a wave of her hand, silence fell instantly.

'It seems your destiny, Peter, is entwined with ours, as I thought it would be when you first came to us. A grave task has been set, one that would seem beyond our abilities. But its seeming impossibility may yet be our only chance of success, for not even Maledict could anticipate such a bold move. If we are brave enough, we may even catch him unawares. What we cannot achieve by force, we may yet achieve by stealth.' She paused for a moment and bowed her head as if the decision she was about to take was almost too much for her to bear. When she spoke again her voice was barely a whisper. 'We must heed the wisdom of Mimir. It now remains for us to decide how best to attempt this task.'

The Prince, whose face had been slowly turning from flustered pink to livid red, suddenly jumped up from his throne as if he was on a spring.

'But this is *madness!* Madness I say! We cannot expect to simply creep up behind Maledict and take the crown off his head! Anyone foolish enough to try it would die instantly! Maledict would destroy him!' There was loud foot stamping from the Vikings above. *'Here! Here!'; 'Madness I say!'; 'Listen to the Prince, he knows what he is talking about!'* Encouraged by the response, the

Prince continued. 'It is quite simple what we must do! We must *attack!* Attack him when he least expects it! If we must have the Viking Stone, I say we cut it from his head!'

Hundreds of Vikings roared their approval then took up the Prince's chant. *'We must attack!'; 'We must attack!'; 'Cut the Viking Stone from his head!!'*

Again, the Queen silenced them so she could speak.

'No. We cannot attack. His army is too great. We would surely be defeated. Peter is right. The key is Maledict. Time runs short. We must act now before it is too late.' She rose to her feet again. There was complete silence as everyone in the hall watched her, waiting for her judgement.

'We must listen to the counsel of Mimir. His advice cannot be ignored, no matter how desperate it may seem. We must attempt the impossible. We must steal the Viking Stone from the crown of Maledict.'

There was complete silence as everyone took in the horror of what the Queen had declared. Finally the Prince spoke, his voice hesitant with reluctant acceptance.

'Who will volunteer for this task?'

Hundreds of nervous faces slowly slid below the golden railings of the balconies. If it had been quiet before, you could have heard a pin drop now.

'Come on! Are we not Vikings?' bellowed the Prince, jumping to his feet and glaring at the disappearing faces. 'We must have volunteers! Is no one brave enough to attempt this deed and reap the glory? Surely there is at least one?'

Again there was complete silence. Then a clear voice spoke from the centre of the hall.

'I am brave enough! I will attempt this task!'

Immediately hundreds of faces re-appeared over the railings, blinking in relief.

'I will do it! *I* am brave enough!' repeated the Princess firmly as she rose to her feet, staring back at them with her head raised high.

The Queen regarded her, a sad smile on her face and the same resignation in her eyes that Peter had noticed before.

'I believe this task is fated to you my daughter, though it burns my heart to say it. But you should not go alone. One other should go with you.'

Instantly everyone ducked back down again. Though she didn't say anything or even look in his direction, Peter felt the Queen's attention fall upon him. He hesitated for a moment, wondering whether he would be brave enough, but then the Princess's eyes met his. Gone was her usual arrogance. Now she was just a girl, probably even younger than himself, who had been given a dangerous task to do. Her eyes gave her away. She was asking for his help.

Suddenly Peter realised that it was not only the Princess who was staring at him - hundreds of pairs of eyes were peering down at him over the railings, waiting for him to decide. Even the Prince was staring at him as he fidgeted impatiently on his throne. The silent expectation slowly grew until Peter couldn't stand it any longer. Finally he spoke, hardly realising what he was saying.

'I – I will go too. I will go with the Princess.'

There was a collective sigh of relief as hundreds of Vikings breathed again. *'Good show!'; 'He's not a bad fellow after all – considering he's not a Viking of course!'; 'Knew we could rely on him! I always said so!'*

The Queen searched his face briefly then inclined her head in gratitude.

'I hoped it would be so! Once more the two of you will embark upon a Quest. This time you will go alone. Dunstable has done well but this second Quest will be beyond him. I hoped his nerve would return but it has not been so. He will stay with us here where, for the time being at least, he will be safe.'

Peter sighed. Though he couldn't deny that even the thought of stealing the Viking Stone from Maledict's crown would turn Dunstable into a quivering wreck, still he regretted he wasn't going with them. He had found an ally in Dunstable and wasn't looking forward to having to cope with the Princess's temper alone.

'The new Quest has been declared!' announced the Queen. 'Darkness has fallen in the city. The Princess and Peter must set out immediately. Before this night is over, our fate will be decided!'

*

As everyone rose to leave, the Queen called out to Peter to wait. He stood in awkward silence in front of her as everyone else shuffled slowly out of the hall through hidden exits in the walls. When they were finally alone, she indicated that he should sit on the Princess's empty throne beside her. Feeling extremely uncomfortable, he sat on the golden seat. Once again, he felt the weight of the Queen's penetrating gaze as she leaned toward him, her eyes searching his.

'We owe you an enormous debt already, a debt that will not be forgotten. No matter what happens in the night to come, you have earned our eternal gratitude.'

Peter nodded self-consciously, words failing him. He longed to jump off the throne before anyone noticed him, but clearly the Queen had something important to say. She continued to stare deeply into his eyes.

'You have agreed to accompany the Princess on this new Quest. It was a brave decision. So far you have faced danger and seen things no one has witnessed since the time of Sigurd, things that would terrify most City Dwellers. And yet you have come through them all and have met every challenge. But now you will face still greater danger and it may be that you will not survive this Quest. I am telling you this so you know that you have a choice. Now, when we are alone, I ask you again. Do you wish to accept this Quest? Think carefully before you answer.'

Peter stared into her clear eyes, determined to meet her gaze.

'I accept the Quest,' he replied simply.

The Queen smiled and her face softened.

'Good! We will speak no more of it!'

Feeling as if he had just passed an exhausting test, Peter was about to slide off the throne when the Queen laid her hand on his.

'Before you go, there is something further I would discuss with you. I listened to your account of what happened in Mimir's Cavern carefully. It is clear that Mimir favours you, and that alone proves your worthiness. But you have not told us everything. Do you wish to discuss what you saw in the water with me now?'

Her eyes searched his again and Peter squirmed uneasily on the throne. Should he tell her everything? But what would he say? He wasn't even sure himself what he'd seen!

'The choice is yours Peter,' continued the Queen, still watching him closely. 'It is for you to decide whether you wish to speak of what you saw and I trust in your judgement. But should you feel the need to discuss these matters then I may be able to help you.'

Peter gazed into her eyes and slowly relaxed. He thought about the second and third visions. They had been nagging at the back of his mind and he still didn't fully understand their significance. If anyone could explain them, it would surely be the Queen. He breathed a sigh of relief and decided to tell her everything.

'I saw three visions at Mimir's Well,' he began cautiously. 'The first was Maledict and the Viking Stone. But the second and third were…confusing.' He paused, finding the words difficult to come by.

'Go on,' urged the Queen.

'The second vision was…*strange*. I'm not sure what I saw. The sky was bright red, but it was night. There was a storm and I was looking out to sea. Then…'

But he did not finish the sentence. At that moment the Prince burst into the hall, his face livid with rage. For a second Peter feared he was angry with him for sitting on the Princess's throne, but the Prince completely ignored him as he raced to the Queen, his right hand clutching a gleaming sword.

'He has come! Maledict has come! We are under attack! *We are under attack!*'

Chapter 2

Assault on the
Walls of York

As the Minster bells rang out the midnight hour, all was still on the frozen streets of York. It was then, just as the final toll struck and silence fell once more, that the troll army appeared out of the gloom. With their long spears held upright in front of them, they marched through the streets and pavements of the outskirts of York until they were less than fifty yards from the City Walls. There they waited silently, a vast mass of muscle and steel, several lines deep.

The attack came at a section of the Walls close to the Castle Tower. Strategically positioned at the apex of the River Ouse and River Foss, the Tower rose menacingly above the eastern side of York, guarding the city that lay behind. The original Tower had been built by William the Conqueror after the Vikings had been defeated almost a thousand years ago. Later, it had been expanded and strengthened, and a strong castle had been built around it, big enough to hold an army. But those who built it centuries ago could not have imagined the terrible purpose it would later serve.

Standing as still as statues in the cold night, the trolls faced the Walls silently, the rain bouncing off their dull grey armour. Then their lines parted. Sitting slightly stooped on his huge black horse, Maledict rode between them. He was dressed in a long brown waxed coat. His face was hidden behind a black hood, though his shining eyes could be seen from behind its folds. As he rode slowly forward, a light shone from his forehead, creating an eerie glow around his hooded profile. There, embedded in his crown, the Viking Stone was gleaming in the darkness.

Halting his great horse thirty yards from the Walls, he paused, turning his head from side to side as if expecting a challenge. But all remained quiet except for the constant patter of rain striking the ground around him. Calmly, he urged his horse forward until he halted in the middle of the empty road, ten yards from the base of the Walls.

Bowing his head slightly, he sat perfectly still as if concentrating. The air around him seemed to shimmer and flicker. He raised his right hand and faint words could be heard, carried on the wind. Suddenly a ball of red energy appeared, as large as a football and blindingly bright. It hovered impatiently in front of him. Then, with a wave of his hand, it raced forward and struck the Walls with a deafening *boom!* that shook the ground with its force.

For a moment, nothing appeared to happen and the trolls behind him groaned in disappointment. Then the Walls started to shudder and the ground trembled. But it only lasted a second. Somehow, the Walls had held.

The trolls groaned again and Maledict's horse pawed the ground in impatience, but he remained unmoved. Well he knew the strength of the magic that coursed through every stone in the Walls, binding them together. They formed a magic girdle around the city, admitting none who harboured evil intentions. Since they had been built long ago, no enemy had broken through. But now he had come.

Once again, he bowed his head and whispered the spell. A second energy ball appeared, as bright as the first. With a dismissive shake of his hand, it sped towards the Walls, striking them in the same place as the last with a terrible *boom!* The Walls shuddered in pain. A shimmering light appeared where the ball had struck, first shining brightly, then gradually waning. At the same time, a cloud of dust rose and formed a grey mist. It drifted towards Maledict and hung like a curtain in front of him, obscuring what lay behind. Finally, the ground steadied and the dust was brushed aside by the cold wind. Still the Walls remained intact.

Once more, Maledict bowed his head in concentration. For several seconds nothing appeared to happen. The trolls waiting behind him became restless, some even daring to question their master's ability to break through the Vikings' magical barrier. Then a third energy ball appeared, larger and even brighter than the others. It spat black sparks as it bobbed in the air in front of him. Maledict swayed in his saddle, as if the effort to create it had almost been too much for him, and the Viking Stone in his crown dimmed for a moment before shining brightly again. Then, with a tired wave of his hand, the ball streaked towards the Walls, exploding into them at precisely the same place as the previous two.

Once again, the ground shook with the impact, but this time the reaction was much more violent, causing several of the trolls closest to the Walls to stagger. But Maledict remained perfectly still in his saddle as he stared ahead expectantly. Again, a strange light appeared around the Walls. It blinked on and off like an exhausted light-bulb. At the same time, several bright holes began to appear, as if the fabric of the air around the Walls was being torn apart. Suddenly there was a blinding flash of light and a thunderous explosion. A vast cloud of brown-grey dust rose, blinding the trolls on the other side of the road. Then, from behind the veil of dust, there was a sharp cracking noise followed by the sound of something heavy falling.

It seemed to take forever for the dust to clear. The trolls held their breath, straining to see what had happened. But Maledict didn't wait. Spurring his horse, he rode forward. For perhaps ten seconds there was an expectant silence as the trolls waited, then they screamed with delight. The Walls had been breached! Clearly visible through the retreating dust they could see it: a hole ten feet high and eight feet wide!

Still screaming, their voices almost two thousand strong, they raised their arms aloft and shook their spears in awe of their master's power. Now they knew it for certain. The time had come at last – the time to take the ancient city and destroy the Vikings forever!

Quickly forming into lines two abreast, they marched across the road behind Maledict as he guided his horse through the broken Walls and into the centre of the city of York.

Meanwhile, barely a mile away, a frantic call to arms was echoing through the Viking Halls beneath the Minster. Vikings were racing back and forth, gathering their swords and shields for the battle ahead.

Within minutes of the Walls falling, an emergency council was announced and hundreds of Vikings poured into the forum at the back of the Debating Hall. The Queen was already there. Seemingly unmoved by the commotion, she was sitting on her throne watching everyone arrive.

Peter followed the Princess as she raced to the lowest balcony. They sat just behind the Queen. Feeling rather awkward, Peter shuffled aside as a dozen tall Vikings sat beside him and talked anxiously with the Princess, barely noticing he was there. Suddenly the Prince stormed into the hall. His sword was drawn and he was clutching the hilt as if he longed to wield it. Without a word, he marched to his throne. But he didn't sit down. Instead he leapt onto the seat and addressed the assembled Vikings, silencing them instantly.

'The Walls have been breached! Maledict has entered the city!'

There was a second of stunned silence before hundreds of voices cried out in disbelief. But they were instantly hushed when the Prince spoke again.

'I have dispatched scouts to see where the trolls are now! We are waiting for their return. Then we will make them *pay* for daring to enter our city!'

A handful of muffled half-hearted voices murmured apprehensively, clearly dreading what the scouts would find. The Prince had barely spoken when three Vikings appeared through the golden gates at the far end of the hall. They sprinted across the marble floor towards the thrones with incredible speed, covering the hundred or so yards in a few seconds, then whispered urgently to the Queen and Prince. By the time they had finished, the Prince's face was a mask of horror.

Looking grave, the Queen addressed the assembly. For once, her voice was faltering.

'The troll army has entered the city. More than a thousand have already marched through the Walls and still they come. Maledict has…' She paused as if she could hardly believe what she was about to say. Hundreds of pairs of eyes stared at her with terrified intensity. 'Maledict has taken the Castle!'

There was a sharp intake of breath as everyone gasped. But the Queen hadn't finished.

'He has changed the course of the river the City Dwellers call the Ouse. The ground around the Castle is flooded. It can only be accessed from the east. The trolls have been seen carrying boats. They no longer fear the water!'

There was complete silence. Every Viking understood the significance of the Queen's words. The Castle with its imposing Tower was now almost completely surrounded by water. Only the higher ground to the east remained above the flood level, but that was where the busy road lay, and anyone approaching the Castle would be seen before they got within a hundred yards of its walls. It would make it almost impossible to assault Maledict, even if they dared. But what was worse was that he had cured the trolls of their fear of water. No longer could the Vikings rely on the protection provided by the city's two rivers, between which lay the Minster with the Viking Halls beneath. Now they could be attacked from all sides.

'We must fly over the Castle walls and attack them from the air!' urged the Prince, red-faced with fury as he glared down at the Queen, still standing on the seat of his throne.

'No. We cannot,' replied the Queen sadly. 'The Tower is raised high above the city. We would be spotted immediately. We cannot hope to win such a battle from the air. The troll archers would repel any assault and our losses would be great. In any case, our laws forbid us from flying where we can be seen by City Dweller children.'

'But we cannot stand idle whilst he makes his plans!' protested the Prince. 'This is no time for wavering! We must put aside our laws before it is too late!'

The Queen turned to face him, fixing him with her eyes.

'We cannot win such a battle. We must find another way.'

But the Prince was consumed by a fury greater than any Peter had ever seen in him before. He leapt down and stood resolutely in front of the Queen. Leaning forward, he gripped both sides of her throne, his face inches from hers.

'There *is* no other way! We must attack *now* before it is too late!'

For a moment they faced each other, the Prince's face livid with rage and the Queen's calm, though her eyes bore into her son's. The Debating Hall fell deathly silent. No one, not even the Prince, had ever dared challenge the word of the Queen before. Then, just when the silence was becoming unbearable, a small timid voice spoke out from the back of the hall.

'I say! I think I err…I think I might know another way!'

As one, everyone's head spun around to stare up at the person who had spoken. There, almost hidden in the middle of the top-most balcony, Dunstable was peeping over the golden railings, his eyes darting from the Queen to the Prince, looking as if he wished with all his heart that he'd kept his mouth shut.

'What is this!' yelled the Prince, leaping onto his throne again to peer over the heads of the Vikings in the lower balconies. 'Who is that? *Dunstable?* What are you doing here? This is no time for weaklings! Come on, speak up!'

But after his initial bold outburst, Dunstable was struck dumb with fear. He pulled on his jumper with both hands, stretching it mercilessly, whilst his eyes flitted from face to face. Finally he spoke again.

'I know I'm not supposed to be here. I, err, just wanted to see what was happening, you know! I couldn't help hearing your, err… problem, and I just…*thought* that you might not have considered the, err, *secret passageways?*'

'Secret passageways?' roared the Prince, standing on the tips of his toes. 'What is this fool talking about? Who let him in? We have no time for jokes!'

But the Queen's face was deadly serious.

'I heard of these passageways when I was young. It was said they were built long ago when we were searching for the root of Yggdrasil. How do you know about them, Dunstable?'

Dunstable wrung his hands on his jumper, looking like a trapped animal. Everyone in the hall was staring at him intently.

'I, err, stumbled across them, you know! I was lost. I thought they might take me to the Magic Snickelways. They're hidden, you see. I was going to mention it, but…'

'Can we use these passageways to get into the Castle?' interrupted the Prince, suddenly interested in what Dunstable was saying.

'Oh yes! One of them goes from an old church straight to the Castle. It goes underground – deep underground. You would be able to go that way, you know!'

There was silence whilst everyone digested what Dunstable had said. The Prince rubbed his chin thoughtfully.

'These passageways – how wide are they? Could we fit an army through?'

Several of the Vikings murmured in excitement as they considered the possibility of a surprise attack. But Dunstable shook his head.

'No…no! They are only narrow! Even I could only just squeeze through! They are very dark! Very wet!'

'Blast!' swore the Prince in disappointment.

Again there was silence for several long seconds. Finally the Queen spoke.

'Dunstable. Could you find these passageways again?'

'Err, I think so! At least I could show you where they are. As long as I don't have to go down them myself of course!'

The Queen nodded.

'Then our hope is renewed.'

All eyes turned towards her, waiting for an explanation. She turned to the Prince.

'We need to create a distraction. We need to keep Maledict and his trolls busy.'

The Prince nodded, happy that his help was needed, though he clearly had no idea what the Queen had in mind.

'We'll circle the Castle with archers! We won't let them rest! And if any trolls try to get out, they'll have us to deal with!'

'Good. Then the plan is this. The Prince will lead our army. Its purpose will *not* be to defeat Maledict. We cannot hope to achieve such an aim through force of arms alone.' She held the Prince's eye until he nodded in reluctant agreement. 'Its purpose will be to distract Maledict and the trolls long enough to allow a greater goal to be achieved. For whilst their attention is focused on our army, the Quest will begin.'

She paused for a moment, her eyes surveying the assembly.

'As soon as the Prince has surrounded the Castle, the Princess and Peter will follow Dunstable into the city. He will show them the secret passageways of which he has spoken, though he need go no further himself,' (she added the last words quickly after noting the distress on Dunstable's face). 'It will be with the Princess and Peter that our hopes will lie, for they will seek to fulfil the Quest: to steal the Viking Stone from the crown of Maledict. With luck, they may find him distracted and his guard may be down.

'In stealth, good fortune and brave hearts our hopes now lie. We stand on a knife-edge, and all that we love is in the balance. This is the challenge we have been set. Let us hope we have the strength to meet it!'

Chapter 3

The Battle of York Commences

The Viking army was ready. Four hundred male Vikings with long swords and shields plus two hundred lightly clad female archers to face almost two thousand trolls. They crowded into the centre of the Debating Hall around the crystal trees awaiting the return of the Prince, who was with the Queen in her private chamber.

As Peter watched them from the lowest balcony, he felt hopeful. They looked so proud and strong, so supremely confident. Perhaps Maledict had underestimated them and they would yet be victorious, despite being faced by such a vastly superior army.

Beside him, the Princess was also watching them, her expression twisted by mixed emotion. Her natural instinct was to go with them - to march to battle and glory against the trolls - and her eyes lit up when she saw them gathered together looking so bright and splendid! All her life she had dreamed of leading the Vikings to victory against Maledict and the acclaim she would receive as a result. But fate had dealt her a different hand. Instead of the open confrontation across the battlefield she yearned for, she would soon be creeping through underground tunnels in a dangerous attempt to steal the Viking Stone. Though she was well aware of the importance of her task, she couldn't help feeling like a thief in the night. She consoled herself by imagining the expression on everyone's face when she returned triumphantly with the Viking Stone in her hand, and began to feel a little better.

After about half an hour, Dunstable joined them, looking slightly sheepish as he sat down beside Peter. By then several of the Vikings were muttering impatiently.

'Where is the Prince?'; 'What is he waiting for?'; 'The trolls will have overrun the whole city by the time we leave!'

Just when their restless mutterings were rising ominously in volume, the Prince returned. Looking extremely irritated as if he'd been forced to agree to something, he stormed across the hall towards his waiting army and barked the command to leave.

Immediately the Vikings formed into neat lines behind him. In moments the Prince had reached the far end of the hall. Without breaking stride, he stomped through the golden gates whilst the Vikings jogged to keep up with him. A few minutes later, the last of them disappeared into the snickelway beyond the gates and the Debating Hall fell silent.

The Prince was in a hurry, anxious to make up for the time he'd lost in his frustrating argument with the Queen. There had been too much pointless debating and not nearly enough action for his liking. Racing along the *MINSTER GATES* snickelway, he quickly reached the tall lamp-post at the first junction. Two passageways were illuminated. To the right was *STONEGATE*; to the left *QUEEN'S PATH*. Without hesitating, he turned to the right then turned left into *LITTLE STONEGATE*.

At the end of *NETHER HORNPOT LANE* at the junction with *ST SAMPSON'S SQUARE* he was faced with a choice. One option would be to go into *SILVER STREET*, pass through *LITTLE SHAMBLES* then *SHAMBLES*, before turning into *LADY PECKETT'S YARD*, emerging behind the Merchant Adventurers' Hall. This would allow them to creep up behind the troll army at the Castle. But the exit from the snickelway was almost four hundred yards from the Castle walls, and there was little cover to conceal them in their final approach.

The alternative was to head down *FEASEGATE* through *PETER LANE* into *LE KYRK LANE*, then turn into *ALL SAINTS' PASSAGE*. The advantage would be that they would emerge into the city two hundred yards from the Castle at St Mary's Square. They would also have the benefit of reasonable cover provided by the buildings and shops on their final approach. But there was a risk. They would exit the snickelways so close to the Castle that they could easily emerge right into the middle of the troll army.

The Prince considered the pros and cons of both options before making up his mind. The risk of being spotted before they were within reach of the Castle was too great. He chose the second option.

He issued his orders quickly, and within seconds the Viking army moved again, entering *FEASEGATE* in single file behind him. Eager to discover if his plan would succeed, the Prince led them quickly through the snickelways. After turning into *ALL SAINTS' PASSAGE*, he slowed. Though the magic in the snickelway concealed them from prying eyes (of both children and trolls), it couldn't disguise any sound they made, and trolls had exceptional hearing. Immediately he whispered the command for quiet, his order passed almost silently from one Viking to the next down the line behind him.

The tension grew as they approached the Castle and drew closer to the moment they would step out into the city and discover whether they were surrounded by trolls. Even the Prince felt it, bold though he was. He gripped the hilt of his sword tighter. The trolls had dared to enter his city. Now he would make them pay!

Without making a sound, he stopped in front of the white painted outline of a door on the snickelway wall that would take them into St Mary's Square. He could see nothing beyond the brick walls of the snickelway and the featureless night sky above them, but he knew he was little more than a stone's throw from the Castle walls. Behind him, the Vikings prepared themselves for battle, clutching their swords and stringing arrows to bow strings. Not a word was spoken, not a sound made. The defining moment had almost come. They would either find themselves in the middle of the troll army or they would emerge unseen, gaining a crucial advantage. They were trusting entirely to fate.

The Prince made a gesture to the Vikings crowded behind him, ordering them to wait in the safety of the snickelway for his signal, then stepped through the snickelway wall into St Mary's Square.

He had prepared himself for anything. If he emerged into the middle of the troll army, he was ready to fight for his life. If the Square was clear, he was ready to take cover behind the nearest buildings and ensure it was safe before returning to the snickelway to signal to his waiting army. He was prepared for anything - but totally unprepared for nothing. Absolutely nothing. All around him, impenetrable grey fog hung over the Square like a thick grey blanket. It was so dense he could barely see the sword in his hand.

For a moment, he didn't know what to do. The whole troll army could be hiding silently just a few yards away from him and he wouldn't be able to see them. In sudden panic, he spun around with his sword outstretched, half expecting to strike leering trolls reaching out to grab him. But he simply made a narrow cut through the grey fog before it rolled in again, smothering him with its damp clinging touch.

Furious at himself for his momentary panic, he clenched his sword a little tighter. Standing perfectly still, he listened intently. If there were any trolls close by, they wouldn't be able to see him any better than he could see them, but he would surely hear them first. After ten long seconds he calmed down a little. The only sound he could hear was the soft fall of rain on the pavement around him.

Denied sight, he tried to picture the scene around him, recalling the last time he had been in this part of the city. He was standing at the corner of the Square, which was ringed by shops. Just in front of him, if only he could see it, was a Viking church, which the City Dwellers had turned into a museum. In the centre of the Square was a ring of benches arranged around a tall tree, whilst less than a hundred yards away opposite him was a narrow passage that led to a large car-park. There, rising high upon an enormous earthen mound in the Castle, was the Tower.

Suddenly he froze. He was almost sure he'd heard voices behind him, but the fog was so thick it even muffled sounds. Tensing, he held out his sword ready to fight as he stared into the foggy darkness. All he could see was grey wisps of mist swirling around him. Then he heard the voices again and relaxed. They were City Dwellers' voices. The fog must have fallen suddenly as some of them sounded frightened. Eventually, they faded into the distance. Once again he was alone.

For perhaps another minute, he stood perfectly still. But he didn't hear anything that sounded remotely like a troll. Finally he began to think more clearly. Perhaps the fog wasn't such a bad thing after all. Not even trolls, whose eyesight was keen at night, could see through fog this thick. Suddenly he became excited at the possibilities. If they were careful, his army could use the fog to launch a surprise attack. In fact, it could be just what they needed to gain the advantage! But where were the trolls? Were they still in the Castle, or had they emerged onto the streets outside? Maledict's whole army could be waiting for them at the edge of the Square and they wouldn't realise until they stumbled into their path! How could he make plans when he knew so little?

Then something else occurred to him: the nature of the fog itself. Was it natural, or had Maledict had a hand in it? He was a powerful sorcerer, and he could certainly create fog should he wish to. And if he had, what was his purpose? Could they be walking into a trap? He cursed as he thought through his options. Strategy wasn't his strong point. He much preferred a straightforward fight!

Swearing under his breath again, he forced himself to concentrate. There was still a chance, a good chance, that the fog was natural. They were close to the river after all, and fog wasn't unusual in winter. He could still use it to his advantage. Slowly he became excited again. He would be a fool to miss such a golden opportunity!

Suddenly he heard a slight sound directly behind him and felt, rather than saw, two Vikings appear from the snickelway exit. In their impatience they hadn't waited for his signal, thinking he'd met resistance. Immediately he spun around and grabbed them, furious that his command to wait had been ignored. Unable to speak in case trolls were lurking nearby, he made frantic gestures with his hands in front of their noses. The Vikings blinked in bemusement as they took in the peculiar experience of being able to see nothing but thick grey fog and the Prince's wildly gesticulating fingers two inches from their noses. It took the Prince several minutes before he finally got his message across, by which time he was practically slapping them across their faces. His instructions were simple. The Vikings hidden in the snickelway were to emerge into the Square one by one and spread around its perimeter with their backs to the shops. If they saw the enemy, they should withdraw before they were seen and await his instructions. Above all, he emphasised the need for absolute silence.

The two Vikings disappeared back into the snickelway. Then, one by one, the Viking army began to appear. As they emerged, each stared in surprise at the thick fog for a moment before disappearing behind its grey swirling folds. Following the Prince's instructions, they slowly spread out around the Square, their swords drawn, avoiding the dull light of the shop windows as best they could. To ensure they didn't get lost in the fog, each grasped the scabbard of the Viking in front of him.

The atmosphere grew tenser as each Viking emerged. The

Prince waited by the snickelway exit, half hoping and half fearing to hear the unmistakable sound of battle commencing. But, other than the constant patter of rain, not a single sound came back through the fog, and the line slowly formed around the Square.

It took almost half an hour for all the Vikings to move silently into position. When the Prince received the signal that the line around the Square was in place, he immediately felt more confident. They had not encountered any trolls and his army was now safely hidden in the fog. Most importantly, they still had the advantage of surprise. His initial suspicions about the nature of the fog were receding. So far, everything was going to plan.

Now it was time to move onto the next stage of his plan. First, the line would sweep across the Square towards the narrow passageway that led to the Castle. Assured that no trolls were behind them, they would quickly spread out again across the car-park until they ringed the Castle walls. When they were ready, they would edge forwards, closing in on the Castle until they reached the edge of the flood water. If they succeeded, they would have penned Maledict's army within the Castle walls. But if they came across any trolls, battle would inevitably commence.

Once more, the Prince's orders were passed silently along the line. But due to the poor visibility and the need for silence, each Viking could only pass the message onto the person next to him. It therefore took a painfully long time for the word to spread. Finally, the Viking line began to edge forwards.

Within a minute they had successfully crossed the Square without encountering any trolls. One by one, they silently passed through the narrow passageway that led to the Castle. But it was immediately apparent that the Prince's plan was going to be more difficult to execute than he thought. In order to surround the Castle, the Vikings at the front of the line had to make their way through the fog to the back of the car park, two hundred yards from the Square. Only being able to creep forward step by fearful step in case they encountered trolls, it took them far longer than the Prince had anticipated. He become increasingly impatient as he waited for news of their progress. But still no signal came. Finally, just when his patience was wearing dangerously thin, the message was passed back to him that the Castle was surrounded. Relieved, he passed the order for a slow march forward, and the Viking line began to advance towards the Castle walls.

The fog was even denser now, hanging stubbornly in the air and totally obscuring everything more than a few feet ahead of them. With every step, they inched nervously into the unknown, half expecting to suddenly find themselves facing an army of trolls vastly superior to their own. To make matters worse, each of them knew that the Viking line was now spread so thinly to surround the Castle that they couldn't hope for immediate help if they were attacked. They would each have to defend themselves for long enough to allow other Vikings to come to their aid, assuming they could even find them in the fog.

Several minutes passed without incident as they crept across the car-park, still clutching each other's scabbards to ensure they didn't get separated. The Prince calculated that they should now be no more than thirty yards from the Castle walls. The flood water around the Tower couldn't be much further ahead, yet they still hadn't encountered any trolls. Cursing the fog, he slowed still further until they were advancing less than a foot at a time. It was now over an hour since he had emerged from the snickelway and he still had no clear perception of where the trolls were. How he hated this creeping around! An honest fight was more to his liking, where he could see his enemy and stare into his eyes! Not this endless suspense, not knowing where the trolls lay!

Angrily, he took another step forward. Immediately his foot sank ankle deep into slimy mud. Pulling it back rapidly, he bent down so his face was just a few inches above the ground. He could just see the faint glimmer of water through the fog. He breathed a sigh of relief. They had finally reached the edge of the flood water around the Castle. Immediately he gave the command to halt. But the Vikings didn't need to be told. They had each stepped into the mud at precisely the same time he had and were wondering what to do next.

The Prince was pondering the same question. Could they wade through the water? How deep was it? He took a tentative step forward then rapidly withdrew as his foot sank several inches into the mud. Should they go forward? What if they were caught, stuck in thick mud and hardly able to move as the trolls rained arrows down upon them? The thought was too horrifying to contemplate.

The obvious alternative was to fly. His whole army could fly across the water almost soundlessly. But what if they were seen? There was nothing that gave them away as Vikings as quickly as being spotted in flight. Then again, the fog was thick. Surely no troll could possibly see them until they were diving out of the sky to attack?

Still he hesitated. Maledict was no fool. He knew how to fight Vikings better than any. He would surely have insured against an airborne attack. In any case, how could they attack the trolls in fog so dense? What would his archers aim at? They would risk shooting each other in the confusion! No, Maledict could not be so easily surprised. There must be a better way.

He thought through his options. The Queen had insisted that he shouldn't attack the trolls, but the last thing he wanted to do was sit around in the freezing cold, waiting for the trolls to find them. She had asked him to provide a distraction so the Princess and Peter could steal the Viking Stone, but it would be impossible to distract the trolls if they couldn't even see them! No, the fog had given him an advantage the Queen hadn't foreseen, and now he had the means to defeat Maledict within his grasp! He might never get such an opportunity again!

He made his decision. The time had come. The time to defeat Maledict once and for all.

He made his final plans quickly, anticipating (he hoped) every eventuality. They were now positioned, he guessed, about twenty-five yards from the Castle. Twenty-five yards of water lay between them and its stone walls. Amongst his army were two hundred deadly female archers. Some of them were girls younger than the Princess, but their eyes were keen and their hands steady, and they never missed what they were aiming at. Though the fog hid their targets, they could still create a hail of arrows upon the trolls inside the Castle. Blinded by the fog, the trolls would have no way of knowing they were coming and no time to take cover. The result would be panic in the enemy ranks.

Whilst the archers caused havoc, the rest of his army would cross the water. They wouldn't risk the mud but would fly silently above the water. Once on the opposite side, the Vikings who were most skilled in magic would create a hole in the Castle walls large enough for his army to pass through. If they were careful, they would be able to enter the Castle without being seen or heard.

Then, when the trolls' confusion was at its highest, he would give the signal for his archers to cease firing and the battle would finally begin!

His excitement rising, he issued his orders quickly and silently. Now that his mind was made up, he was eager to begin the great battle in which he would make his name at last. But just as it had before, it took an infuriatingly long time for his orders to be passed along the line. Long minutes passed and still he waited, his temper gradually rising. Surely there had been enough time for his orders to have reached everyone in his army by now? But still no confirmation came back that everyone was ready. What could possibly be taking so long? He was strongly tempted to make his way down the line and bash some heads together! Then they would understand the importance of prompt action on the battlefield!

Suddenly a noise came out of the fog. A woman was calling for her dog somewhere nearby. The dog was barking furiously, but still the woman called its name. The Prince cursed. Could she not hear the dratted animal? Was she deaf? Then, just when the dog's barking and the woman's high-pitched voice were at their loudest and most irritating, they abruptly stopped. Once again, there was complete silence.

But not for long. At that moment he heard another sound. At first he wasn't sure what it was, then his heart started pounding. Though the fog dulled it, there was no mistaking the sound. Something was moving on the water.

He stared into the darkness, cursing the impenetrable fog. The sound was gradually becoming louder. Whatever was in the water was getting closer. But still he couldn't see it! Sweat dripped off his hand as he gripped his sword tighter. Then he heard another noise, a dull thudding noise. Was it an oar striking a laden boat?

Suddenly a dark shadow loomed through the grey veil of fog in front of him. At first it had no shape, but in a heartbeat he recognised it as the prow of a rowing boat. But the desperate command he was about to scream died on his lips. At that moment, there was a loud splashing noise. Something – no, judging by the thunderous racket, it must surely be some*things* - had just jumped into the water no more than a few yards in front of him, still hidden in the fog! Then he saw them. The Viking closest to him cried out in alarm, followed by another further away then countless more as the whole Viking line recoiled in panic. An army of gigantic trolls was racing through the shallow water towards them, their spears held aloft. When they saw the Vikings, they paused just long enough to scream their deep-throated battle cries. Then, with all the ferocity and cruelty of their wicked kind, they attacked.

Chapter 4

The Haunted Graveyard

Shortly after the Prince and his army left the Viking Halls, Peter, the Princess and Dunstable set out on the Quest. They made their way across the empty Debating Hall then passed through the golden gates into the snickelway.

Despite the seriousness of their task and nagging doubts whether the Queen was right to place such trust in him, Peter felt his spirits rise the moment he stepped into the snickelways. He was embarking upon an incredible adventure! The time when he would have to face Maledict seemed far away. For the moment, he could distract himself in the magical world of the Vikings. Walking a few steps behind the others, he ran his hands along the snickelway's brick walls, then tapped on the tall lamp-post at the junction with *STONEGATE* as if to say *'I am here!'*

The Princess's mood also improved as she skipped along the narrow snickelway ahead of him. She had used the time it had taken for the Prince's army to assemble to dress herself, and for over an hour she had tried on an endless selection of brightly coloured clothes before finally settling on a blue coat and matching trousers. She carefully brushed and styled her hair, and selected her favourite strapped shoes. Happy with her appearance at last, she looked forward to the time when she would return triumphantly to the Viking Halls with the Viking Stone held aloft and the acclaim she would receive.

Only Dunstable looked troubled. He was muttering under his breath and nervously cleaning his glasses with his handkerchief, as if even the thought of their journey was too dreadful for him to contemplate.

At the junction with *LITTLE STONEGATE*, they paused for a moment. Since leaving the Viking Halls, the Princess had been thinking about the best route to the secret passageways Dunstable had described. The problem was that the snickelways formed a complex maze across the city, and there were several routes that would take them to the church from which the secret passageways led. Determined to plan to the very last detail, she had been pondering for several minutes and still couldn't make up her mind.

'Well, we could go through *GRAPE LANE* of course,' she mused, tapping her chin with her forefinger thoughtfully. 'Or perhaps it would be better to go back up *STONEGATE* and then turn down *COFFEE YARD* into *MUCKY PEG LANE*? No, that would take us out of our way...'

Realising that her deliberations were likely to take some time, Peter leant against the *LITTLE STONEGATE* junction lamp-post. With nothing better to do, he studied the snickelway in which they were waiting. Other than the elegant lamps that marked each junction, they all looked so ordinary! Simple brick-walled passageways that twisted and turned as if whoever had built them was unsure which direction they should take. Leaning forward, he examined the bricks more closely, running his fingers over the dull red stone. They weren't even particularly well made! At several points the mortar had dripped to leave an ugly brown smear, and he was sure the walls weren't straight! Yet, ordinary though they looked, they still contained an incredible secret that kept them hidden from the City Dwellers. What magic concealed them? Who had built them and how had they done it? How old were they?

There was something else that was puzzling him. When he had flown over York with the Princess he hadn't seen the snickelways, yet above the wall opposite him he could clearly see grey clouds drifting across the night sky. Obviously there was even more magic at work than he'd first thought. He studied the wall and made a calculation. It was maybe four times his height – that made it about twenty feet high. Suddenly he had an overwhelming desire to fly to the top of it to see what lay beyond. Then he would surely unlock the snickelways' secret!

He was about to leap into the air when suddenly a sharp finger poked him in the ribs.

'*Excuse me!*'

The Princess was glaring at him, her arms crossed in obvious irritation. He grinned back weakly.

'What did you say? I wasn't listening.'

'*Really?* I would never have guessed! Whilst you were day-dreaming, *I* was working out the best way to get us to the secret passageways! So, if you have *quite* finished, do you think we could go now? *Thank* you!'

Turning abruptly on her heels, she immediately marched off down *LITTLE STONEGATE.*

The Princess, like the Prince before her, was in a hurry. Now that she had decided which route to take, she was eager to get to the church as quickly as possible. It wasn't long before they came to another junction. Illuminated by the iron lamp-post, the sign-post revealed two choices: *NETHER HORNPOT LANE* to the right or *SWINEGATE* to the left. Without hesitating or even looking back to ensure they were following her, she darted down *SWINEGATE*, then turned left at the next junction into the curiously named *MAD ALICE LANE.*

They were now nearing their destination. At the end of the snickelway, the Princess skidded to a stop and spun around. Frowning, she crossed her arms in frustration at their tardiness.

'Come on! Come *on!* We *do* have a rather important Quest to fulfil you know!'

As Peter ambled behind Dunstable, deliberately slowing to annoy her still further, he noticed the pale white outline of the exit door beside her. Above it, the junction sign was written in elegant letters:

'HOLY TRINITY CHURCHYARD THIS WAY →

B-E-W-A-R-E! DO NOT ENTER AFTER DARK!'

Dunstable had spotted the sign also. Suddenly he looked terrified as he stared up at it, his eyes enormous behind his glasses.

'Oh dear! I had forgotten about that!'

'Why does it say *'DO NOT ENTER AFTER DARK'*?' asked Peter, beginning to feel a little uneasy as he peered over Dunstable's shoulder.

'Oh it is just a silly old ghost story, that is all!' said the Princess dismissively as she turned to the exit to leave. 'Nothing to worry about!'

But Dunstable didn't look at all keen on leaving the safety of the snickelway.

'It's *not* just a silly ghost story, you know! The graveyard *is* haunted! That's why the City Dwellers shut the gates and don't go in after dark!'

'Oh come on!' said the Princess firmly as she turned around to glare at him, angry at the unnecessary distraction. 'Surely you do not believe in those old children's stories, do you? Anyway, all you have to do is show us where the entrance to the secret passageways is. Then you can go back to the safety of the Viking Halls and leave the rest to us.'

But Dunstable was now looking even more uncomfortable.

'But...But...' he whimpered, pulling so hard on his tie his face was turning bright red. 'There's something else – something I haven't told you!'

The Princess turned to face him again, furious at yet another delay.

'Well? Precisely *what* have you not told us Dunstable?'

'The passageways. They're err...a little *smelly*, you know.'

'A little *smelly*? What *are* you talking about?'

'Well, actually, they're quite a lot smelly in fact. They are, I do believe, sewers you see. Very, *very* smelly sewers.'

'*Sewers!*' exclaimed Peter and the Princess in horror.

'Why didn't you tell us this in the Debating Hall?' demanded Peter.

'Well...it was just that...well, everyone was *looking* at me! The Queen and the Prince – they seemed so pleased when I told them how to get into the Castle. It seemed such a shame to ruin it, you know!'

'*RUIN IT?!*'

The Princess looked absolutely livid. After carefully selecting her favourite clothes, the last thing she wanted to do was immediately ruin them.

'What *exactly* are these sewers like, Dunstable?' she whispered, turning pale.

Dunstable bowed his head to avoid her eyes and hopped from one foot to the other uneasily, as if dreading giving an answer.

'Well, there's lots of water of course. Yes, quite a lot of water! And they're err...a little dirty I recall.'

'A *little* dirty?' asked Peter tentatively, his heart sinking even lower.

Dunstable nodded vigorously, still unwilling to meet their eyes.

'Well, actually, the water is a bit on the murky side, you know. In fact, it's practically black if you want to know the truth. Very foul! Very smelly! Don't drink it!'

'Really? Thank you *so* much for the advice!' snapped the Princess. Somehow she managed to suppress her revulsion long enough to speak again, her voice barely a whisper. 'And where do the passageways go? One *does* go to the Castle I hope? I assume you got that part right at least?'

'Oh yes! The deepest, wettest, smelliest one does!' replied Dunstable. Peter and the Princess groaned in unison. 'It runs far underground beneath the walls of the Castle! Trolls don't know anything about it! Or maybe they think no one could stand the smell…' He paused and twitched his nose, as if even the thought of the tunnel was enough to make him feel ill. 'It really is *very* smelly… very smelly indeed! Wouldn't like to think what's in it!'

'Is there no other way?' asked Peter hopefully, cringing at the thought of wading through filthy water.

'No! No! No other way if you want to get inside the Castle!' replied Dunstable with irritating brightness, as if he had just comforted himself with the thought that they would be making the journey and not him. 'Unless you want to knock on the Castle walls of course! If you got that far without being squashed, that is.'

The Princess sighed, resigning herself to her fate. She would rather face a hundred trolls than suffer a single hair out of place, and the thought of wading through sewage was enough to freeze her heart. But her sense of duty and hunger for fame was even stronger than her considerable vanity. She would put up with anything for her moment of glory. Even wading through a sewer.

'Come on then. Let us get it over with, shall we?'

Reluctantly, they walked towards the white outline of a door on the snickelway wall. Immediately the bright snickelway disappeared and they found themselves standing in a dark deserted city street. In front of them was a tall iron gate, beyond which was a small church set behind a dark graveyard.

It was immediately apparent why the church had such a sinister reputation. As they gazed through the iron gate, it appeared darker than the surrounding night, as if the faint street light had no power to illuminate it. Only a hazy outline of its low sunken roof and arched windows could be seen. Its creepy air was enhanced still further by the mist that suddenly enveloped them. But unlike the impenetrable fog around the Castle, here it floated past them in grey wispy waves.

Undeterred, the Princess pushed the iron gate, which opened with a shrill metallic whine, and stepped into the graveyard. Peter and Dunstable followed hesitantly, both feeling a sudden chill that felt like ghostly breath upon their skin. They had only gone a few steps when several grey shapes suddenly loomed out of the mist in front of them. They were surrounded by gravestones! Previously hidden by the mist, they rose out of the muddy ground around them.

'Oh dear! I had forgotten how scary this place was!' whimpered Dunstable, his eyes darting from side to side as if expecting to be attacked by ghosts at any moment.

Pushing past the Princess, he scampered across the damp grass, almost immediately disappearing into the hanging mist. Peter and the Princess jogged after him, squeezing between two large gravestones that were blocking their path. Suddenly a tall grey wall rose up in front of them. Dunstable was crouching beneath it, urgently beckoning them forward.

'We can follow this wall to the back of the graveyard. That's where the entrance to the passageways is! If we keep our backs against it, we can avoid the gravestones and nothing scary can creep up behind us!'

The Princess tutted, clearly thinking Dunstable was being ridiculous. But Peter immediately felt safer as he pressed his back against the wall, though his heart was still pounding in his chest.

Slowly they shuffled along the edge of the graveyard, hugging the wall behind them. Peter and Dunstable tried to move as quietly as possible, taking tiny sideways steps and hardly daring to breathe for fear of what they might disturb. All remained silent and still except for the wisps of mist that drifted like restless souls in front of them.

They hadn't gone far when an eerie creaking noise arose from somewhere hidden in the mist nearby. It sounded like an old tree swaying in the wind. A door swung open on rusty joints behind them then slammed shut again as if caught by a sudden gust. But there was no wind in the graveyard, not even a breath of it.

'I don't like this place!' whined Dunstable. 'I don't like it at all!

Funny noises in the night! So very dark! So very scary!'

The Princess, who alone appeared unconcerned, turned towards him and whispered in his ear.

'I have heard some of the City Dwellers' stories about this place. They say it is haunted by the ghost of the Earl of Northumberland. Long ago, they beheaded him and placed his head on a spike on Mickelgate Bar. One of the City Dwellers took it and hid it in the church. They say his headless ghost wanders through this graveyard at night, searching for his head!'

Peter suspected the Princess was mischievously trying to scare Dunstable and had made the whole thing up, probably to gain revenge for him neglecting to mention that the secret passageways were, in fact, sewers. If so, it certainly worked. Dunstable's face filled with terror as he stared across the graveyard as if expecting the headless Earl to emerge from the mist at any moment and stumble blindly towards them. Though he couldn't see the Princess clearly, Peter was sure a wicked grin had spread across her face.

Though he was careful not to show it, Peter was almost as nervous as Dunstable.

'Where is the entrance to the secret passageways, Dunstable?' he whispered urgently. But Dunstable was standing absolutely still as if paralysed with fear, his eyes fixed on something hidden in the mist in the middle of the graveyard. 'Dunstable?'

Suddenly Dunstable jumped in shock as if someone had shaken him.

'I think we should leave! I think we should leave now!'

Peter stared in the direction Dunstable was looking. It might have been his imagination playing tricks on him, but he was almost sure he could see a human-like shape in the drifting mist. Ominously, the figure appeared to be without a head.

'Where's the entrance to the passageways, Dunstable?' Peter asked again, his voice suddenly acquiring a higher, more anxious pitch.

'Entrance? I almost forgot! It's at the back of the graveyard. A big tomb then steps leading down. Deep down.'

Peter stared at him, his disbelief momentarily overcoming his fear.

'A *tomb!* The entrance is inside a *tomb?*'

Dunstable nodded, his eyes darting anxiously from Peter's face to the graveyard. Peter was incredulous.

'How did you find it? Did you just *happen* to look at what was inside?'

Dunstable opened his mouth to speak but no words came out. He suddenly looked confused.

'Come on you two!' interrupted the Princess, saving him. She was already strolling across the graveyard ahead of them, seemingly unimpressed by the possible presence of ghosts. 'Is that it over there Dunstable?'

They stared in the direction the Princess was indicating. Looming out of the mist beside the church a few yards away from them was the dark outline of an enormous rectangular tomb. Peter jumped in surprise. He'd been so busy looking for ghosts, he hadn't even noticed it! As they crept closer, the mist slowly thinned to reveal it in more detail. Over ten feet long and six feet wide, it was big enough to accommodate a giant. It was crowned by a thick slab of stone about six inches deep that extended a few inches beyond its grey rim.

'Who's buried here?' asked Peter, gazing at the tomb in amazement.

'I have no idea!' said Dunstable, his eyes peering over the top of it. 'Someone very important I think. Someone very big too! But not anymore. No one is buried here now.'

'What's that?' Peter pointed to a strange carving cut into the stone slab on top of the tomb. He brushed aside the layer of dirt that was covering it. 'It looks like some kind of…*animal?*'

Suddenly Dunstable turned paler than the mist.

'I don't think it's just an animal. I think it's a…'

'It is a *Serpent*, of course! A very large Serpent,' said the Princess, glancing at it matter-of-factly. 'Can you not tell? It is perfectly obvious to me.'

There was no doubt that the Princess was right. The creature had a long body that curled around itself in thick muscular layers, giving the impression of great size and strength. But it was the head that really gave it away. Rising from its body, the large callous eyes seemed to gaze at them scornfully through the stone. No other creature had the same evil intensity in its stare.

'It is probably the Midgard Serpent, I imagine,' continued the Princess in the same bored tone. 'Maybe there was a Viking settlement here once.'

'The *Midgard Serpent?*' whispered Peter, a cold shiver running down his spine.

'*Jormungand? The Great Serpent? Ragnarok? The end of the world?*' the Princess droned despairingly, as if she could scarcely believe his ignorance. 'Do they not teach Viking prophecies in schools anymore?' Noting his blank expression, she glanced exaggeratedly skywards and crossed her arms. 'Long ago, Fenrir - the *Great Wolf?* - was chained by Odin. According to the prophecy, when he finally breaks free it will trigger the end of the world. The Vikings call it 'Ragnarok'. The Fire Giants will set the world on fire and the Midgard Serpent will rise from the bottom of the sea. At least that is what the old Vikings think. Complete rubbish of course!'

Dunstable's face was now as white as snow. Covering his eyes with his hands, he recoiled from the tomb in horror. But Peter found himself hypnotically held by the serpent's malevolent stare. It looked ominously real to him, as if it could come to life at any moment and slide out of the stone into the world. He recalled the morning he had met Sigurd. Sigurd had mentioned something about Ragnarok, though at the time he'd been so shocked by meeting the ghost of someone who'd been dead for a thousand years, he hadn't realised what he was saying.

'Let us get a move on then, shall we?' snapped the Princess impatiently, bringing Peter quickly back to the present. She paced around the tomb, examining it from every angle. 'Is the entrance to the secret passageways inside, Dunstable? How do we get in?'

But the combination of the misty graveyard and the infamous Midgard Serpent was too much for Dunstable to cope with at the same time. He looked absolutely petrified as he stood with his hands covering his eyes, which strangely also rendered him deaf to the Princess's question.

The Princess glared at him.

'*Dunstable!* Is the entrance inside or not? A simple yes or no will do!'

Still Dunstable didn't answer. Standing as still as stone, he looked like he desperately wanted to flee but was terrified of what he might run into if he did.

What little patience the Princess possessed was rapidly exhausted.

'*DUNSTABLE!* IS THE ENTRANCE INSIDE OR NOT?'

Slowly a gap appeared between Dunstable's fingers and his eyes flickered behind his glasses. Barely moving his head, he nodded, his features seemingly set in the same terrified expression.

'*Thank* you! Peter – get hold of the other side.'

Peter walked reluctantly to the other side of the enormous tomb, his heart suddenly beating faster at the thought of what they might discover inside. Placing his hands underneath the rim of the stone slab, he glanced at the Princess to indicate he was ready. At the count of three, they heaved upwards.

He expected the slab to be heavy, but much to his surprise they lifted it as easily as if it weighed no more than a few kilograms. Gently, they eased it down and leant it against the side of the tomb. Peter was about to peer inside when a sudden noise caused all three of them to jump in alarm. Somewhere hidden by the mist in the graveyard behind them, something - or someone - was definitely moving. They could clearly hear a strange shuffling sound like something staggering blindly back and forth. Then, just as suddenly as it began, it stopped. It might have been nothing more than a bird burrowing for worms or a cat prowling through the undergrowth, but in the icy cold graveyard in the misty night, it was impossible even for the Princess to not believe that something far more sinister was creeping toward them.

'Come on!' said the Princess to Peter urgently, forcing his attention back to the tomb. 'Let us see what is inside!'

Together they leaned over the side of the tomb and peered inside. Peter was half expecting to see a horrifying skeleton suddenly spring to life in fury that its rest had been disturbed. He was relieved, therefore, when he looked down and saw - absolutely nothing! The tomb was completely empty. Then, just as he was about to turn away, a stone staircase was slowly revealed in the gloom, its grey steps leading down into the ground before disappearing into darkness.

At that moment, the strange noise returned, but this time it was far louder than before. Both Peter and the Princess jumped in alarm. Dunstable recoiled against the church wall, his hands still covering his face. Something was definitely shuffling through the graveyard towards them, hidden in the mist.

'Come on then! Shall we go in?' said the Princess, trying to sound unconcerned, though there was an undeniable tremor in her voice. She jumped lightly over the side of the tomb and ran down the first few steps until her head disappeared below the tomb walls. 'It is okay!' she called out, her voice echoing up the staircase. 'There are lots of steps leading down, that is all. Nothing to worry about!'

The moment she started speaking, the strange shuffling noise in the graveyard stopped, as if the ghostly creature had paused to listen. But when she finished, it began again, even louder than before. Dunstable shrieked in terror. Pressing himself against the church wall behind the tomb, he began to whimper.

Peter decided it was time to leave. Vaulting the tomb wall, he landed squarely on the step behind the Princess. Turning around, he gestured urgently to Dunstable.

'Come on! *Jump!*'

The mist was now so thick that Peter could only see his dim outline and his terrified wide eyes staring across the graveyard. For a second they darted to Peter's face as if he couldn't decide which scared him most: staying alone in the haunted graveyard or following Peter into the dark tomb. Blinking in wide-eyed bewilderment, he sank lower to the ground beside the church wall, unable to make up his mind what he should do.

Then he froze. There was another noise in the graveyard. At first, neither he nor Peter could tell what it was. Then they heard it again - a low melancholy moaning noise made by some evil tormented creature.

That was enough for Dunstable. With one final terrified glance across the graveyard, he broke into a frantic sprint towards the tomb. Leaping over its side with surprising agility, he landed on the step behind Peter.

'*Come on! Come on!* What are you waiting for?' he whispered urgently as he pushed past them down the narrow steps. 'There's no time to waste, you know! I've decided I'm coming with you after all! Let's get down into the sewer where it's nice and safe, shall we?'

Chapter 5

An Unpleasant Journey in the Dark

They descended into the secret passageway. Soon it was almost pitch black, the only light coming from the stone steps that shone faintly to show them the way down. The stairway was narrow and low, as Peter discovered painfully when his head struck the ceiling shortly after Dunstable had pushed past him, and the steps were uneven, forcing them to tread carefully for fear of tumbling forward into the darkness below.

For several minutes they descended behind Dunstable. It was the longest staircase Peter had ever known! Soon he lost count of how many steps they had walked down. They were clearly deep underground, far beneath the city. Glancing over his shoulder, he could just see a speck of grey light high above him marking the open tomb in the graveyard.

'How much further down is it Dunstable?' whispered the Princess, clearly having the same thoughts as Peter.

'Not too far! Not too far at all!' replied Dunstable, seemingly recovered from his ordeal in the graveyard. 'Only a few more minutes, I think!'

Finally they heard the sound of rushing water coming from the darkness below. At the same time a pungent smell wafted up the stairway, rapidly becoming more and more nauseous.

'We've almost reached the tunnel that leads to the Castle!' Dunstable whispered, sounding strangely nasal as if he was holding his nose. 'Oh dear! I had forgotten how smelly it was!'

Almost as soon as he spoke, a faint light appeared below them, revealing the walls of the passageway for the first time. As they crept down the last few steps, the source of the light became clear. Just beneath them, glistening water was racing along a narrow tunnel. As they approached it, the smell intensified revoltingly. It was easily the most disgusting stench Peter had ever smelt, despite living on a farm most of his life! If a hundred dirty toilets had been combined with a hundred rotting cabbages and a hundred sweaty socks, it still wouldn't have come close. He began to feel sick.

'Is there no other way, Dunstable?' he whispered as he stared at the murky water in disgust. 'Surely we don't have to wade through…through *that?*'

Dunstable gazed at him forlornly. Peter could clearly see him now in the pale light, holding his nose so tightly his eyes were watering.

'No other way I'm afraid! I did warn you, you know! I did tell you that it was a little smelly!'

Peter glanced at the Princess, wondering whether she would dare go any further. Judging by the revolted expression on her face, she was relishing the prospect of wading through the tunnel even less than he was. Feeling his eyes upon her, she tried to sound positive.

'So…Dunstable…this is the tunnel that leads to the Castle, is it?' Her voice sounded strangely muffled, as if she was trying to speak without opening her mouth. 'Do we head upstream or downstream?'

'Mmmm? Oh, er, upstream I'm afraid.'

'Right! Ok then.' She put on a brave face, pretending to be unconcerned by the prospect of entering the water. 'I will, err, jump in then, shall I? How far is it to the Castle?'

'Quite far I'm afraid!' Dunstable whimpered. 'It's right across the city almost!'

'Right. We had best get on with, err, it then, should we?'

Gingerly, she shuffled forward on the last step. The tunnel below her was lighter than the stairway they had emerged from and, as they crowded reluctantly behind her, they could see the 'water' quite clearly. A muddy brown colour, it oozed rather than flowed, making revolting slopping noises against the tunnel walls. The smell was worse than ever.

Despite her bravado, the Princess was in no hurry to jump in. For a moment, she tottered on the edge of the step, staring down in disgust. Then, summoning all her considerable courage, she closed her eyes and leapt into the oozing sewage. On her scale of achievements, she had never done a braver thing in her life.

For several seconds she froze in absolute disgust as she stood, waist deep in water. When she finally spoke, her voice was barely audible.

'It … is … not … actually … that … bad. Not … that … bad … at … all! Come … on … you … two!'

Peter and Dunstable exchanged resigned glances. Then, with their noses clamped firmly between their fingers like a couple of reluctant swimmers entering a swimming pool, they dropped into the water beside her.

For a moment, all three of them stared at one another in shock as they stood bolt upright in the disgusting water, words not enough to convey the utter wretchedness they were feeling.

'Lovely!' exclaimed Peter finally, holding his nose so tightly his fingernails dug into his skin, though no matter how hard he squeezed, he still couldn't block out the smell.

As fast as they dared, they began to wade against the fast oozing water, determined to get this part of their journey over with as soon as possible. Any hopes they might have had of avoiding the worst of the stinking sludge were soon forgotten as they felt the unpleasant sensation of slime soaking through their clothes onto their bare skin. To make matters worse, the tunnel was low, and Peter and the Princess had to duck their heads and walk with their shoulders bent, which soon gave them painful backache. To compound their agony, the 'water' was full of unseen objects. Several times Peter felt his feet strike something large and heavy beneath the surface.

'Do I want to know what's at the bottom?'

'Probably not I'd imagine,' replied Dunstable miserably, his high-pitched voice echoing in the low tunnel.

Poor Dunstable was in fact suffering more than Peter or the Princess. Being the smallest of the three, the water level rose almost to his neck, meaning that his nose was perilously close to the water. All that could be seen above the surface was his bright red face, his expression so sour it would have terrified him had he seen his reflection. The Princess showed no sympathy when she occasionally glanced over her shoulder to make sure he was still behind her and hadn't been swept away. She clearly thought he deserved his plight for not telling them about the sewage earlier.

Step by step, they waded through the tunnel. It was heavy going. Not only were they fighting the current but also the sludge-like water itself, which was so thick it resisted their passage through it. Despite their fatigue though, none of them wanted to rest. They just wanted to get out of the tunnel as quickly as possible.

They had been wading for about half an hour when they were faced by their worst nightmare. Just ahead of them, the roof of the tunnel suddenly dipped, leaving a gap of about eight inches above the water level. The horrible truth struck them all at the same time. Whereas they had previously been wading with their heads well above the sewage (except for Dunstable that is), to continue their journey they would have to crouch in the water and twist their heads sideways so their mouths and noses remained above the surface. The consequences were almost too vile to contemplate. Half their faces would be submerged beneath the disgusting water whilst the other half would be pressed against the equally revolting tunnel roof.

But there was no going back now. Once again, the Princess demonstrated incredible bravery. Approaching the low roof, she crouched down and edged forward one step at a time, her long hair floating on the surface behind her. As she passed beneath the roof, she twisted her head sideways. The half of her face that was visible above the surface winced in disgust as the sewage lapped onto it, leaving a horrible brown smear on her skin. Walking sideways like a crab, she slowly disappeared into the low tunnel.

Dunstable and Peter glanced at each other, their expressions mirrored in torment. Forcing their heavy legs forward, they reluctantly followed.

It was even worse than they thought. They could no longer hold their noses without risking falling over. With their unprotected nostrils now barely an inch above the water, the stench was unbearable! Wading was also difficult. Their legs were bent awkwardly in order to duck beneath the low roof, and the strain on their knees and backs soon became excruciating. To make matters worse, what little light there was faded the further they crawled beneath the low tunnel. Within a minute, it was pitch black.

'Ugh! How long is this horrible tunnel?' moaned the Princess through clenched teeth, her voice coming abruptly out of the darkness and echoing off the unseen tunnel walls. It had a croaky tone to it as if she had just been sick.

'A...few...hundred...yards...I...think!' mumbled Dunstable,

blurting out the words one by one to ensure his mouth was open for as short a time as possible.

'We could be wading into anything!' groaned Peter. 'I can't see a thing!'

'Wait a minute,' choked the Princess. 'I will see what I can do…'

There was a wet clapping noise then a faint ball of light appeared a few inches above the water ahead of them, providing just enough light for them to see each other's tortured faces beneath the low tunnel roof.

'That is the best I can manage I am afraid. I am feeling a little off colour at the moment.'

For the next twenty minutes they crept forward, crouching low in the water with their heads bent painfully to one side, as the Princess's light ball drifted ahead of them. No one spoke again for fear of swallowing a mouthful of foul water. Eventually, to their enormous relief, the roof began to rise and there was enough room for them to stand upright once more. It also became slightly brighter, and the Princess extinguished her magic light.

'Are we almost there, Dunstable?' whispered the Princess, looking pale and tired as she stretched her back painfully. The left side of her face was covered in slime and her long hair, which she had spent several minutes combing luxuriously in the Viking Halls before they left, was matted and dripping rancid water down her back.

'Not far!' replied Dunstable, who was the only one not to have acute backache. 'We've done the nasty part! We're almost there now!'

Encouraged by the prospect of finally leaving the sewer, they waded wearily on until a dull orange glow appeared in the tunnel ahead. They raced forward then breathed a sigh of relief. There, just a few yards ahead, the narrow tunnel widened into a large bright cavern.

Desperate to get out of the sewer, they stumbled into the cavern, then suddenly stopped and stared around them in astonishment. The cavern was absolutely enormous - as high as an office block and as wide as a football pitch! The sewage ran straight through its centre. Its source was halfway up the rocky wall at the back of the cavern, where putrid water was gushing out of a large black hole to form a waterfall. Green-brown in colour, it splattered its way down to a rock pool, from which the sewage oozed its way toward them.

Strangely, despite the horrible slime running through its centre and the overpowering stench, the cavern was far from ugly. It was, in fact, alive with light as multi-coloured spotlights darted around it, leaping from wall to wall, spinning and dancing like sparkling ballerinas. It was difficult to tell what caused such a display. Perhaps it was the reflection from the water, or perhaps there was some magic at play. Whatever it was, the effect was spellbinding.

For the moment though, all they could think about was getting out of the sewer and resting their aching limbs. Staggering the last few steps, they hauled themselves out of the water and collapsed onto the smooth sandstone bank.

The effort it had taken to wade through the thick slime had taken its toll. For several minutes they lay perfectly still. Finally, Peter and the Princess rose shakily to their feet.

'Where are we?' asked the Princess moodily, wiping the slime from her previously immaculate clothes as best she could.

'Directly beneath the Castle!' replied Dunstable, still lying flat on his back with his arms outstretched and his eyes firmly shut. 'We've waded all the way across the city, you know! No wonder I'm so exhausted!'

Peter couldn't take his eyes off the mesmerising lights that were flitting across the cavern walls around them.

'You know, if we weren't deep underground covered in stinking sewage with a Castle full of trolls above us, I might actually quite like this place!'

Beside him, the Princess had long since stopped marvelling at the sparkling light display. Now she was looking for a way out.

'Dunstable. How far down are we?'

'Oh, not far! Not too far to climb back up again!'

'And how do we do that? How *exactly* do we get up to the Castle from here?'

'The staircase of course,' Dunstable mumbled, his eyes still shut as he sprawled on his back beside the water, looking like a sunbathing seal.

'Staircase? What staircase?'

'On the wall where the water comes out!' replied Dunstable irritably, annoyed that he was wasting energy answering unnecessary questions. 'Are you blind? It leads to the door!'

The Princess and Peter stared at the wall behind the waterfall. There was no sign of a staircase or a door.

'The *door?*'

'The door to the passageway that goes underneath the Dungeons! You can get up to the Castle from there! Now, if you'll kindly let me rest for a moment and stop asking stupid questions, I might be able to get my breath back!'

'Dunstable, where *exactly* is this staircase?' asked the Princess crossing her arms, her voice dripping with sarcasm. 'Would you mind pointing it out to us?'

Dunstable grudgingly forced himself into a sitting position and squinted up at the wall. Immediately his eyes bulged in disbelief.

'Goodness gracious! It was *there!*' He pointed to the far wall in bewilderment. 'It was *there* I tell you! It's gone! I don't understand! Where is it?'

'Gone?' queried the Princess sceptically.

Dunstable scratched his head, still staring at the far wall of the cavern as if expecting the staircase to reappear at any moment. He took off his glasses and stared at them accusingly as if they were somehow to blame for the staircase's mysterious disappearance, then put them back on and squinted at the wall again.

'I don't understand! I just *don't understand!* Look! The door's still there!'

They stared at the cavern wall again to where Dunstable was indicating. Sure enough, there was a small circular black hole near the topmost corner of the cavern.

'That's a *door?*' asked Peter incredulously.

'You can crawl through it if you duck down low enough! I've done it! Long ago, when I was lost, you know.'

'*Hmmm...*' said the Princess and Peter dubiously.

There was a minute's silence whilst Dunstable, now on his feet at last, continued to study the wall in wide-eyed confusion. Meanwhile, the Princess took hold of Peter's arm and pulled him to one side.

'There is only one way we are going to get up to the Castle from here,' she whispered, her mouth close to his ear so Dunstable couldn't hear. 'We are going to have to fly up!'

'But what will we do with Dunstable?' asked Peter. 'We can't leave him here!'

'We will carry him between us. We might still need him to show us the way once we are up there.'

'He won't like that very much! Remember what happened last time? What if he panics and we drop him?'

'Have you got a better suggestion? I thought not. Dunstable?'

Dunstable turned towards her. He interpreted the look in her eye immediately.

'What have you two been talking about? This isn't going to involve magic, is it? You know I don't like magic!'

'Of course not!' insisted the Princess, not very convincingly. 'It is just that we think we know where the staircase is hidden, but it is not very wide and some of the steps are broken. We know how much you hate heights, so if you close your eyes and let us guide you, you will not need to look down until we reach the top!'

Peter thought this sounded a little lame, but after a few seconds of puzzled contemplation, Dunstable seemed almost prepared to accept it.

'Umm, well – if you think that's best I suppose, but why…?'

'Good! It is agreed then!'

With a final, slightly bemused glance at Peter, Dunstable closed his eyes. Guessing that he might not like what he saw if he opened them prematurely, he took the added precaution of covering them with his hands. Peter and the Princess stood either side of him and looped their arms under his. They were about to leap into the air when Dunstable turned blindly towards the Princess, his hands still clamped over his eyes.

'Excuse me. You *will* watch the steps won't you? I wouldn't want to trip or anything.'

'Do not worry, Dunstable,' assured the Princess with false patience. 'We will take good care of you. We will not drop you.'

'*Drop* me? What do you mean *drop* me?'

But before he had even finished speaking, they had lifted off the ground and were rising into the air. Peter felt his body tingle with excitement as he experienced the joy of flight once more. Dunstable, though, was clearly not sharing his enthusiasm.

'Excuse me! Why are my feet no longer on the ground?'

'We are lifting you over the broken steps,' explained the Princess curtly. 'Do not ask stupid questions!'

They slowly rose higher, holding Dunstable firmly between them. Below them the cavern looked vast and empty. The sound of falling water echoed off the cavern walls around them. As they got closer to the door Dunstable had indicated, they began to see it more clearly. It was the entrance to a dark narrow passageway about four feet high and wide.

As soon as they reached it, the Princess stretched out a leg and stepped into the passageway. Peter edged in behind her, pushing Dunstable forward whilst treading air.

'Can I open my eyes?' squeaked Dunstable when he felt his feet touch solid ground. Both of his hands were still clamped over his eyes.

'We are there now. You can open your eyes,' said the Princess as she shuffled forward to give Peter enough room to squeeze behind them.

Dunstable dropped his hands and sighed in relief.

'I *told* you there was a staircase! I'm glad you found it at last!'

Peter pushed him gently forward before he had the chance to see that there wasn't actually any steps at all, then glanced around. The passageway was even smaller than he'd thought and narrowed still further a few yards ahead of them. Its rock walls were damp to the touch, probably due to the vapour rising from the cavern below, and as black as coal. Still, at least there wasn't any sewage running through it. Even so, there was a lingering smell of something unpleasant that hung stubbornly in the air.

They were about to duck into the passageway when suddenly they stared at one another in alarm. Coming from somewhere above them, a deep thudding noise had suddenly started. It sounded like some great engine at work.

'Straight on?' suggested the Princess, pretending to be unconcerned about the ominous noise.

Dunstable stared at her, his large terrified eyes shining behind his silver glasses.

'We're just below the Dungeons now! There are strange machines there! That must be what is making all the noise! I don't know what the trolls use them for! I don't think I want to know!'

An image of a vast torture device being operated by enormous grinning trolls flashed through Peter's mind. Dunstable took several deep breaths before continuing.

'The way out is just around the corner. There's a hatch in the roof! On the other side is a circular corridor with lots of doors where all the prisoners are kept. There was no one there last time I was here, but now *He* has returned, who knows? It might be full of trolls now! Big nasty trolls that would squash you as soon as blink! I don't think I want to go there! I think I'll stay here where it's safe!'

Peering through the darkness ahead, they could just make out what looked like a bend in the passageway. The Princess and Peter squeezed past Dunstable as he shrank against the wall then shuffled ahead, their backs bent painfully beneath the low roof. A moment later they reached a junction. They could either continue in the same direction, or take passageways to the left or right. Peering timidly over their shoulders, Dunstable whispered '*Left!*' and they cautiously turned the corner. They hadn't gone more than a few steps when they saw something shining ahead of them. There, embedded in the roof of the passageway, was a large metal grille.

'That's the way in!' whispered Dunstable, creeping forward and peering at the grille before quickly retreating again. He was now shaking from head to toe. 'Yes, that's definitely it! The Dungeons are just the other side! You go ahead. I think I'll stay here, thank you very much!'

'Why don't you come with us? Surely it's better than staying here?' asked Peter, unwilling to leave him behind in the dark passageway. But Dunstable recoiled from him, shaking his head vehemently.

'No thank you! I don't want to go there! No, no, no, *NO!* You don't need me anymore anyway! I'll stay here and wait for you to come back and get me, if that's quite all right with you!'

The Princess ignored him. Her expression determined, she ducked underneath the grille to examine it more closely. It was about two feet square and covered in dirt and damp moss. Though faint light was filtering through the bars, they were so thick with muck it was impossible to see what was on the other side. Experimentally, she pushed up at it with the palms of her hands, wincing slightly as the dirt smeared over her fingers. It didn't budge. She tried again, grasping it with both hands and pushing up with all her strength, but it was wedged into the roof. Clicking her tongue in frustration, she turned to Peter.

'It is going to take two of us to move this! Let us try together!'

Peter squashed up beside her, ignoring the stabbing pain in his back from continually crouching down. On the Princess's count, they pushed against the grille as hard as they could with their arms and shoulders. At first it didn't move, but as they strained it suddenly popped out the other side like a cork from a bottle. Instantly, bright light flooded into the passageway. The Princess grinned at Peter.

'I never thought we would move that! You must be stronger than I thought!'

Peter frowned at her and was about to respond when she pushed the grille out of the way and pulled herself up through the hole in the roof. She quickly peered into the dungeon above them.

'Nobody there!' she whispered. 'Quick! Whilst no one is around!'

Agile as a cat, she leapt up and disappeared through the hole. With a quick glance at Dunstable, Peter pulled himself reluctantly behind her.

They found themselves in a long circular corridor that looked like it had been carved out of solid rock. On the inner wall were several black doors at intervals of about ten feet, whilst on the outer wall were numerous torches held in steel brackets, their flames gently flickering.

Peter paused for a moment as he crouched over the hole they had come through and stared down at Dunstable, who was still cowering in the passageway, peering up at him with wide terrified eyes.

'Stay there Dunstable! We'll be back as soon as we can! I promise!'

Heaving the grille back, Peter placed it carefully over the hole. As he turned away, the last thing he saw was Dunstable's plaintive eyes blinking up at him from the darkness below. Trying to ignore the horrible feeling of guilt rising within him, he jogged after the Princess, who was already striding purposefully ahead.

In contrast to the tunnels they had just crawled through, the corridor was wide and high, its ceiling several feet above their heads. As it was circular, they couldn't see more than twenty yards ahead or behind before it curved away from sight. Fortunately, there was no sign of any trolls. If it hadn't been for the burning torches, Peter would have thought that no one had been there for decades.

As they made their way cautiously along it, Peter glanced at the black doors, half expecting an enormous troll to suddenly leap out from inside. Dunstable had said something about a dungeon, so presumably they opened into prison cells, though judging by how quiet it was he doubted if any of them were occupied. He was almost tempted to open one and peer inside, but the Princess was jogging ahead in her eagerness to find the way up to the Castle.

For several minutes they followed the corridor. But they saw nothing except the endlessly curving rock walls, the low-burning torches and the black cell doors. After about ten minutes, Peter began to get worried. The corridor seemed to go on forever! Surely they must have travelled a full circle by now? The Princess shared his anxiety.

'Does this corridor never end? I wish we had forced Dunstable to come with us now! I do not like being stuck in the open like this! If any trolls come down, we will be trapped!'

'I don't think we need worry about that,' said Peter. 'I don't think any trolls have been here for a while. It's so quiet!'

But, as if in some cruel jest, the moment he'd finished speaking the silence was ripped apart by the thunder of heavy marching feet. It seemed to have come out of nowhere! One moment there was silence – the next ear-shattering noise!

For a moment they froze, unsure which direction it was coming from. Frantically they spun around in confusion. The only thing stopping them from being seen was the curve in the corridor!

The Princess's fears had been realised. They were trapped!

Chapter 6

The Troll Patrol

The sound of heavy feet was now so loud the whole corridor was shaking. The trolls were heading straight for them! Suddenly a deep voice called out, echoing in the narrow corridor.

'LEYYYYFT-RIGHT! LEYYYYFT-RIGHT! COME ON YOU 'ORRIBLE LITTLE TROLLS! I'LL EAT YOUR FLESH AND FEED WOT'S LEFT TO THE SNIVELLIN' RATS IF YOU DON'T GET A BLEEDIN' MOVE ON!'

Peter stared urgently at the Princess, who was strangely hesitant, as if unsure whether to run or fight.

'Come on!' he urged, his heart pounding. 'We must run!'

Still the Princess wavered. The sound of marching feet was now horribly close.

'Princess! *We must run!*' he repeated frantically, unable to understand her hesitancy.

But the Princess's delay had at least enabled Peter to establish which direction the trolls were coming from. Deciding they couldn't wait any longer, he grabbed her arm and pulled her after him as he raced down the corridor, back in the direction they had come.

The trolls were right behind them, still hidden by the bend in the corridor. The sound of their marching feet drowned out all other noise. Peter and the Princess were running just fast enough to keep ahead of them, but not fast enough to pull away. Within a few minutes, they passed the grille they had crawled in through. Peter would have liked to have checked whether Dunstable was still there, but there was no time.

Suddenly they skidded to an abrupt stop. Up ahead, the corridor came to a dead-end. There was nowhere left for them to run!

The marching feet were right behind them.

'*LEYYYYFT-RIGHT! LEYYYYFT-RIGHT! YOU CALL YOURSELVES SOLDIERS? I SHOULD BUY YOU ALL FRILLY SKIRTS AND NECKLACES! IF YOU WEREN'T SO BLEEDIN' SOFT YOU'D 'AVE BEEN IN THE ARMY SQUASHIN' VIKINGS LIKE RESPECTABLE TROLLS INSTEAD OF MESSIN' AROUND DOWN 'ERE WASTIN' MY BLEEDIN' TIME!*'

At any moment the trolls were going to appear around the bend and they would be caught! Peter searched desperately for somewhere to hide. Then he saw it. Right in front of them was the last prison cell. It was their only hope! The Princess immediately realised what he was thinking, and together they raced forward. Pushing the heavy black door open, they tumbled into the small room beyond. Spinning around, they closed the door behind them as quietly as they could.

Just in time! The door had barely clicked shut when the trolls marched around the bend.

'*HALT!*' cried the gruff leader.

Hidden behind the door, all Peter and the Princess could hear was the exhausted breathing of the trolls. Then heavy footsteps walked slowly towards them.

'*Sergeant!*' called out the leader. 'I thought I 'eard summut! Did you 'ear anything?'

'*Sir! No! Captain Sir!*' replied the Sergeant, clearly afraid of his superior.

'Sergeant. I don't think you 'eard me correctly. I said, *I* 'eard summut. Are you callin' me a liar?'

'*Sir! No! Captain Sir!* Err, actually Sir, I think I did hear summut after all!'

'Thought so. Knew you'd cum round to my way of thinkin'. Now, what's this?'

There was the sound of exaggerated sniffing from the other side of the door.

'*Hmmm.* I can smell summut! I know that smell! That's Viking that is – horrible stinkin' Viking! Can you smell 'orrible stinkin' Viking too, Sergeant?'

'Err? *Yes Sir! Most definitely, Captain Sir!*'

'Thought so. Where do you reckon it's cumin' from then, eh Sergeant?'

There was a moment's silence whilst the Sergeant's slow brain stuttered into turbo boost.

'*Sir!* I , er, urmmm, not sure Sir...?'

'Thought so! That's why I'm a Captain and you're only a Sergeant! No bleedin' brains in your 'ead! Do you want to take a look around and tell me what you see, Sergeant?'

There was another pause. Clearly the Sergeant was struggling.

'Errrr. I, err, see some walls and some torches and errr...'

'Do you see anything *unusual* about the floor, Sergeant?' The Captain's voice was oozing sarcasm.

'*Sir!* I see...Oh! *Yes, Captain Sir!* I, err, see what you mean, Sir!'

'Footprints, Sergeant! Muddy footprints! Two pairs of 'em an' all! Tell me. Are you *blind* Sergeant? Did I eat your eyes one day and forget about it?'

'*No Sir!* You didn't Sir! I would have, errr, noticed Sir!'

'Hmmm.'

Behind the cell door, Peter and the Princess stared at each other in horror. Both of them were still covered in slime from the tunnel! It had been so long since they had been clean, they had completely forgotten about it!

'Let me see now...' pondered the Captain.

There was the sound of more sniffing, this time much closer to the door. A shadow suddenly fell across the narrow gap at the bottom. Peter and the Princess held their breath as they stood as still as stone in the centre of the tiny cell.

'They're in 'ere I reckon!' bawled the Captain confidently. Judging by the closeness of his voice, he was now standing right outside the door. 'They smell funny an' all! In fact, they smell so bleedin' bad I can hardly smell you any more Sergeant!'

The Sergeant sounded confused.

'*Yes Sir!* But how did they get in, Sir? We'd 'ave seen 'em if they'd cum down from the Tower?'

'Well you obviously *missed* 'em, didn't you? Good job I was 'ere to check up on you! Otherwise we'd have a couple of Vikings wandering about the place, wouldn't we? Now Sergeant, let's see what we've got. Open this door!'

Peter's heart was pumping like an engine. They were coming in! There was nowhere left for them to hide! But the Princess was undeterred. Her eyes blazing, she stepped forward, ready to meet head-on any troll who dared enter.

There was a sound of keys clinking together, then the cell door swung open to reveal a Wood Troll clutching two pairs of handcuffs in one hand and a spear in the other. Standing behind him was a gigantic Mountain Troll. Dressed in full battle armour, a long whip was dangling from his right hand.

The trolls in turn studied them, the Wood Troll looking rather confused. Finally, the Mountain Troll cuffed the Wood Troll's head with the back of his hand, propelling him into the cell.

'What did I tell you Sergeant? *Vikings!* Well, one Viking and one City Dweller! Very suspicious! I smell summut 'ere Sergeant and it ain't pleasant! Spies I reckon! Dirty, smelly spies!'

Peter prepared to fight or run. Beside him, he could sense the Princess bristling with anger. At any moment she was going to leap forward and attack the trolls. The Sergeant knew it too. He was slowly backing away as far as he dared and looking distinctly uncomfortable, as if unsure who frightened him the most: the enormous Captain or the furious Princess. Then, to Peter's immense surprise, the Princess stepped forward and meekly offered her wrists to be cuffed.

The Sergeant stared at her for a moment as if fearing a trick. Then, as quick as a flash, he darted forward. Before Peter recovered from his own surprise, he had handcuffed them both. He breathed a huge sigh of relief.

Now that they were safely cuffed, the Captain ducked beneath the door and entered the cell, filling the whole doorway with his enormous bulk.

'So, Sergeant. Do you want to explain to me what these two maggots are doin' 'ere? You were meant to check these dungeons were clear, weren't you? Have you got summut you want to tell me, Sergeant?'

The Sergeant paled.

'*Sir!* I dunno how they got 'ere! Honest Sir! Me and the lads were down 'ere an hour ago. We didn't see a thing! Honest Sir!' He glanced at the Princess suspiciously. 'Some kind of Viking magic, I reckon!'

The Captain leaned forward until his sweaty bulbous face was less than an inch away from the squirming Sergeant's.

'You missed 'em, didn't you Sergeant? You forgot to check the cells and let 'em wander around my nice clean dungeon, didn't you Sergeant? You made a *big* mistake, didn't you Sergeant? Fortunately for you, I decided to check meeself to make sure you'd done your job properly. Good job for you I was 'ere, *isn't it Sergeant?'*

There was a terrifying pause. The Captain's face was now so close to the wincing Sergeant's that Peter thought he was going to bite him.

'Do you know what I'm going to do to you when we get back top-side Sergeant?'

'*N-N-No Sir…?'*

'I'm going to take your arm, roll up the sleeve, dip it in Worcester sauce and eat it up to the elbow!'

'*Sir! Thank you, Sir!'*

Turning away from the quivering Sergeant, the Captain stepped towards the captives. An evil grin spread across his chubby, malevolent face as he caressed his whip lovingly.

'Thought we'd missed you, did you my little maggots? Thought you could creep around down 'ere and mess up my nice clean dungeon?' His grin spread even wider, revealing two sharp teeth over either lip. 'But you didn't reckon on me, did you? Bet you thought you'd just 'ave these idiots to deal with?' Without even looking, he cuffed the Sergeant's face with the back of his hand. 'Sergeant!'

'*Sir! Yes Sir!'* said the Sergeant, stepping forward tentatively, poised to duck more quickly next time.

'Take 'em to the pit!'

They were marched back down the corridor, surrounded by a dozen trolls. The Captain led them at a brisk pace, constantly barking orders and snapping his whip against the legs of the hapless trolls behind him. As Peter jogged alongside them, he couldn't help noticing how miserable the trolls looked. With their heads bowed and their expressions sullen, they looked like they simply wanted to escape the whip and get to wherever it was they were going as quickly as possible. Clearly they would far rather have been in their distant homes, jumping out on unsuspecting passers-by like trolls do best.

As if to confirm their misery, the Sergeant, who was at the head of the line and therefore taking most of the Captain's abuse, began to sing a dreary marching song, his deep voice echoing off the walls of the narrow corridor. It was immediately taken up by the other trolls, repeating the song over and over again in time to the pounding of their marching feet:

Tum, tum, toil and trouble,
We hate work but we get double!
Squishing, squashing, choking, fighting
Scratching, crushing, bashing, biting!
From dusk till dawn we have no fun
A soldier's work is ne-ver done!

Whilst they continued their doleful marching song, Peter was able to whisper to the Princess without risk of being overheard. Immediately he asked the question that had been weighing on his mind since they had been captured.

'What were you doing? I thought we were going to fight or make a run for it, not just let ourselves be captured!'

The Princess threw him a withering look.

'Think about it, dummy! We do not know the way up - they do! We could have been here for hours! Anyway, where would we have run *to* exactly? Hiding in a prison cell did not work, did it?'

'But now we've been captured! How are we going to escape?' protested Peter, refusing to give in to her logic.

The Princess fixed him with an arrogant stare and tossed her head loftily.

'I do not think we need worry about that! We will wait until they take us up to the Castle and put us in the 'pit' the Captain mentioned, then we will escape. Easy!'

Peter was silent. Despite his considerable respect for the Princess and her magical abilities, he didn't quite share her confidence that escaping would be so easy. And waiting until they were thrown into a pit was definitely *not* what he had in mind! Still, for the moment at least, they had no choice but to go wherever the trolls led them.

For the next few minutes they trudged silently between the trolls, who sang their gloomy song over and over again. Surprisingly, the Captain seemed to enjoy the song and even stopped shouting and whipping them for a while. Before long though, he got bored and decided it would be more fun to sneer at his captives. Almost skipping down the line in his eagerness, he barged past the trolls and grinned down at them.

'I wouldn't like to be in your shoes my little maggots! We don't take kindly to spies, you know. There might be a bit of torture in the offerin', I shouldn't wonder! What do you think of that, eh?'

They both tried to ignore him, which was extremely difficult as his gigantic flabby face was almost touching theirs as he bent over to deliver his insults. He stank of stale sweat and his breath was so bad that Peter almost wished they were back in the sewers.

'I've got a lot of hungry lads 'ere who could just do with an arm or leg to chew on!' continued the Captain, clearly enjoying himself immensely. 'These little trolls, they've got terrible appetites, you know! Food, food, food – that's all they ever think about! An arm or two would go down a treat, I reckon! Keep 'em goin' till breakfast that would! Or maybe I'll just let 'em take a bite out of you both, eh? Just a little bite to see how juicy you are?'

As he said the word 'juicy' he reached out an enormous hand and pinched the Princess's arm, causing her to jump in surprise. Peter rolled his eyes and prepared to run, expecting the Princess to strike out at any moment. Slowly, her face red with fury, she turned and glared at the Captain, her fingers twitching ominously in her handcuffs. The Captain lost his smug grin and looked momentarily unsure of himself. Then, just when Peter was expecting her to exact her terrible revenge, she somehow managed to restrain herself. Turning her head away, she stared ahead determinedly, her expression like thunder.

The Captain quickly recovered his sneering expression, though he was clearly shaken.

'You Vikings! You're nothin' but trouble you are!' he whined, sounding like a bully who had just been frightened by someone he thought was a weaker opponent. 'Over-rated too, I reckon! We should 'ave squashed you all ages ago! And we will too! You'll be sorry you ever lived, you will! Every single one of you!'

Trying to act as if nothing had happened, he quickly returned to the front of the line, thumping several trolls along the way to make him feel better.

Peter glanced enquiringly at the Princess. She was still staring rigidly ahead, her face set in a furious grimace.

'Once this is over, that troll is going to *really* regret pinching me! If it is the last thing I do, I swear I will...'

She left the rest of the sentence unsaid. Peter was glad he wasn't in the Captain's shoes. He dared not imagine what unspeakable things she had in mind.

With the Captain leading at an even faster pace, they raced along the circular corridor. They had passed the point where Peter and the Princess had first heard the trolls and still they were following the seemingly never-ending bend. Peter was beginning to wonder whether the corridor would go on forever when the Captain suddenly held up his hand.

'*HAAALT!*'

Instantly the trolls ground to a stop – so instantly in fact that Peter crashed into the back of the troll in front of him, who grunted in protest though he didn't dare turn around.

Much to his relief, the corridor came to an abrupt dead-end just ahead of them. Peering through the gaps between the massive trolls, Peter tried to spot a door or anything that could possibly be a way out, but there appeared to be nothing there. No door, no window, no hatch – just a featureless rock wall spanning the end of the corridor. But as he looked more closely, there *was* something slightly different. The last burning torch was positioned higher up the wall than the others. The Captain stood directly beneath it, flicking his whip threateningly.

Satisfied that he had everyone's attention, he smirked at the Princess, his sharp incisor teeth shining in the torch-light as they protruded over his thick lips.

'Almost home lads! Soon be time for dinner, I reckon! We might 'ave a special treat planned for tonight, eh?'

The trolls stared at the Princess hungrily, a spark of excitement suddenly lit behind their tiny dull eyes.

Making sure the Princess was watching, the Captain reached up and pulled on the base of the strange torch. Instantly there was a dull rumbling noise as if something very heavy was turning above them. Then, as Peter and the Princess watched in nervous fascination, the whole back wall rose like a stone theatre curtain, revealing a grey staircase behind it.

'Up we go lads,' bellowed the Captain, who seemed to have recovered his former bullishness. 'Let's take our guests to their accommodations, shall we? I'm sure they're eager to make 'emselves *un*comfortable!'

As soon as the wall had risen high enough, the trolls marched up the staircase behind the Captain, who seemed particularly keen to show the Princess and Peter whatever terrible place he was taking them to. They had not climbed far when Peter caught a glimpse of a large red door at the end of a narrow corridor that led off from the staircase to the left. But they didn't pause. Climbing higher, the staircase gradually became brighter and the air colder. They were close to the surface at last. Suddenly a door opened ahead of them and they were struck by a blast of freezing air, heavy with the acrid smell of burning. Then, as they were pushed up the final few steps by the trolls behind him, a terrifying scene was slowly revealed.

They had entered the Castle. At first, all Peter could see was the grey Castle walls rising thirty feet on either side of a wide courtyard. Then, as they stumbled up the last steps and passed through a wide door, his heart missed a beat. Swarming across the courtyard in front of them was a vast army of trolls. Each was armed with a fearsome club or spear and had a short stabbing sword at his side. Crowded together in tight battalions, they were waiting silently for the command to march against the Vikings. Peter felt a cold shiver run down his body. It was exactly the same as his vision in Mimir's Cavern, but all the more terrifying for being real.

But it wasn't just the trolls that had startled him. Rising high into the foggy night directly above them was the dark forbidding Tower. They had entered the Castle at the base of the mound beneath it. As Peter stared up at its gloomy heights he shivered again, feeling something more sinister than the freezing night air. There was something about the Tower that had changed. Perhaps it was simply the combination of the darkness and the fog, but somehow it appeared more menacing than it had before. Peter had no doubt that Maledict was there, gazing out of the highest window, surveying his mighty army. Tearing his eyes away from it, he glanced at the Princess. The time had almost come when they would attempt the impossible. There, directly above them, was the end of their Quest. Within the Tower they would face the dreaded Necromancer at last.

The Captain noted their reaction and grinned evilly, his hot breath forming vapour clouds in the cold night air.

'Welcome to York Castle my little maggots! Do you like the alterations we've made since we arrived? No? Don't worry. I think you'll find your stay will be very short and *very* unpleasant!'

Peter took advantage of the Captain's gloating to study the courtyard in more detail. At the far side were two enormous wooden gates, both of which were wide open. Beyond them was the high ground to the east – the only place that the Castle walls were raised above the flood level. In the distance was a road. A solitary car was making its way into the city, its headlamps like sparkling eyes in the night. Escaping now would be easy. All they would have to do is leap into the air and fly faster than the trolls could react. He knew how quickly they could fly – surely faster than any troll could throw a spear or loose an arrow. In seconds, they would be out in the open air, speeding across the city, away from the Castle and the terrible danger they were in.

He was brought painfully back to the task in hand by the Princess who, guessing his thoughts, dug her elbow into his ribs. Nodding towards the Tower, she cast him a meaningful glance as if to remind him of their Quest and the reason they were here.

Just as his hopes of a daring escape were extinguished, there was a warning cry. All eyes turned towards the gates where an army of trolls suddenly marched into view from the city. At first there were only Mountain Trolls like the Captain, their enormous frames lumbering out of the fog. But then came dozens of Wood Trolls, lagging wearily behind. Clearly they had been in a battle. Many were wounded and they all looked tired.

As soon as they were inside the Castle walls, another even larger army of trolls marched out through the gates to replace them in the battle that was taking place in the streets of York. Barely a minute later they had disappeared into the darkness outside. As the gates slammed ominously shut, Peter's heart sank. How could the Vikings hope to defend themselves against such a relentless attack?

He was brought abruptly back to the reality of their own predicament when he felt a sharp point dig into his side.

'No time to waste gawkin'!' growled the Captain, his face grinning hideously. 'I wouldn't be worried about the battle if I was you, little maggot. Your Viking friends will be fillin' the dungeons soon enough, I reckon!' He turned to the trolls who were waiting anxiously for instructions. 'Let's get a move on then, lads! Now them trolls have moved, we can get these scum to their accommodations! Sure they're *dyin'* to see 'em!'

Immediately the trolls marched across the busy courtyard with Peter and the Princess still penned in the middle. Unfortunately, as they moved forward, the troll battalion that had just returned from fighting the Vikings was marching in the opposite direction. To make matters worse, another group of Mountain Trolls also chose that moment to make their way across the crowded courtyard. The result was chaos. In true troll fashion, each group tried to barge their way past the others. The trolls returning from the battle decided they had right of way. Suddenly speeding up, they barged through the Captain's trolls just in front of Peter and the Princess. At the same time, the second group of trolls crashed through behind them from the opposite direction, taking obvious satisfaction in beating the smaller trolls out of the way.

Clearly some violent game was being played, and the Captain's trolls were losing badly. With much swearing and grumbling, they were forced to retreat, much to the fury of the Captain who raced up and down the line, lashing his whip at the beleaguered trolls' legs. Finally, after more shoving and cursing, the Captain's trolls managed to race to the far side of the courtyard, where they finally came to a weary halt.

As the Captain screamed at the unfortunate Sergeant, who he seemed to think was solely responsible for their humiliating defeat, Peter glanced around the courtyard, searching for the 'pit' the Captain had promised. At first he couldn't see it. Then he spotted two enormous wooden doors lying flat on the ground side by side a few yards in front of them. Each had a heavy black metal ring at its centre. A sudden dread rose from the bottom of his stomach as realisation struck him. The 'pit' was underground in a courtyard full of trolls! Escaping would be practically impossible! He glanced at the Princess in alarm, but she simply nodded and stared back at him nonchalantly, clearly confident in her ability to break out of any troll hole.

Finally, the Captain stopped yelling at the red-faced Sergeant and barked a command. Two trolls raced forward and looped a rope through each of the metal rings at the centre of the wooden doors. Stepping back and facing each other, they heaved on the ropes, straining with all their considerable strength. The doors screeched in protest at being disturbed. Then, as the trolls slowly backed away in opposite directions, the two doors rose in the centre to reveal a dark pit dug into the ground.

Immediately, Peter and the Princess felt the sharp prod of spears in their backs, urging them forwards.

'There you go my little maggots!' sniggered the Captain. He was now standing just behind them, looking immensely pleased with himself. 'I think you'll find these accommodations to your likin', as long as you don't mind dark places full of worms, that is! Help 'em in boys! Let 'em make 'emselves at home!'

Strong arms grasped them, roughly unlocking their handcuffs before pushing them forwards. Tottering on the edge of the pit, Peter gazed anxiously down. It was so dark he couldn't see the bottom. Suddenly fear overcame him. He glanced at the Princess and saw fear in her eyes too. He was about to leap into the air and flee, despite the spears behind him and the urgency of their Quest, when he was violently shoved from behind. Before he could react, he was tumbling into the darkness.

He landed at the bottom of the pit twenty feet below, his head striking the ground painfully. The Princess landed heavily behind him, crying out briefly in pain and anger before falling ominously silent.

Peering over the edge of the pit above them, the Captain was perfectly framed against the night sky. As the wooden doors began to close, he grinned down at them smugly.

'Bye bye my little maggots! Don't worry! We'll be seein' you at dinner-time!'

Then, with an ominous crash, the doors slammed shut and they were left in total darkness.

*

Peter rose slowly to his feet and tenderly touched the large bump on his forehead where his head had struck the ground. Darkness surrounded him. He could see nothing, not even his hand as he waved it in front of his face. Fighting to suppress the wave of panic building in his stomach, he forced himself to think. Where was the Princess? Was she all right? He had seen her fall close by just before the pit door had closed, but the darkness and the blow to his head had disoriented him. He took a step in, what he hoped, was the direction he'd last seen her and immediately kicked something heavy lying on the ground.

'Ummph!' moaned the Princess.

Peter was so overjoyed to hear her voice that he reached down too quickly and stuck a finger in her ear by mistake.

'*Ouch!* What are you trying to do? Poke me to death?'

Peter sighed in relief. She sounded just like her usual self: arrogant, insulting and extremely irritated. For once, though, she didn't annoy him in the slightest. In fact, in the cold darkness of the pit, her arrogance was a positive comfort.

'Those trolls! They pinched me, they stabbed me with their spears and then they *threw* me into this horrible hole!' she exclaimed, her outraged voice echoing around the pit.

There was a shuffling noise as she rose to her feet.

'What happens now then?' asked Peter, who was still not used to hearing her but not seeing her in the darkness.

'We escape of course! I am certainly not hanging around here any longer than is absolutely necessary! Then we steal the Viking Stone from Maledict's crown and get back to the Viking Halls as quickly as possible! Did you see the trolls that came through the gate? There is a battle being fought and the Prince needs me to win it!'

Peter couldn't help grinning in appreciation of the Princess's unflappable confidence. She made their seemingly impossible task sound so easy he almost felt they had succeeded already.

'How are we going to get out then? Are you going to do a…' Peter waved his arms vaguely in the darkness, '…spell to get us out? What about the trolls in the courtyard?'

'One thing at a time! First we break out of this pit. Those wooden doors should not be a problem. The trolls will not be a problem either. We will be out before they can catch us! Then we will find Maledict. He will be right at the top of the Tower I bet, watching his wonderful army.'

'Are you sure you can break the doors?' asked Peter doubtfully. 'They looked pretty strong to me.'

'Do not be silly! You forget who I am and how good I am at magic! I can break through any troll hatch! Now, let us have a quick look first.'

There was the sound of a single clap. Immediately the darkness fled and the pit was revealed around them. The Princess was standing just in front of him, frowning at her filthy clothes and trying to re-arrange her hair. A bright light ball was hovering beside her. For some reason, the sight of the Princess at the bottom of a troll pit trying to make herself look more presentable as if that was her only care in the world struck Peter as funny, and he couldn't help grinning. Despite her best efforts, she still looked decidedly shabby. Her face was dirty and her hair was covered in dust. Worst of all, the clothes she'd spent so much time fussing over in the Viking Halls were torn beyond repair and absolutely covered in dried green slime.

'You think I look funny, do you?' said the Princess, spotting his smirk before he had the chance to hide it behind his hand. 'You should take a look at yourself if you think I look bad! You look terrible!'

Suddenly feeling self-conscious, Peter glanced down at himself. His coat and jeans were absolutely caked in muck, and in numerous places the fabric had been cut, exposing sore looking skin underneath. In fact, he was absolutely covered in cuts and bruises! He winced as the pain suddenly hit him. How hadn't he felt it before? Worst of all, he could smell himself, and he smelt absolutely revolting!

Feeling the Princess's eyes upon him, he ran his hands through his hair in an attempt to straighten it, but it was so covered in slime his fingers immediately became stuck. He consoled himself by flattening it down as best he could with the palm of his hand and stepped away from her, hoping she hadn't smelt him.

Turning away from him with an arrogant toss of her head, the Princess studied the roof, now perfectly illuminated by her hovering light ball. Then she glanced around the pit, muttering under her breath as if making calculations.

Peter followed her eyes. The pit was about the size of a small house, with black muddy walls rising to the wooden doors. The ground beneath their feet was rock solid, as he had discovered painfully when his head struck it. There were no doors and no exits. The only way out was the way they had come in.

Her calculations done, the Princess rose into the air to inspect the doors more closely. As there was nothing else to do, Peter flew up with her until they were hovering just beneath the roof, twenty feet above the bottom of the pit.

'Hmm,' she pondered, prodding the wood with her forefinger. 'These doors look pretty thick to me. Let us see how strong they are! Help me test them!'

Bracing themselves against the walls as best they could, they pushed on the doors with their hands and shoulders. But they barely moved.

'This is going to take an especially powerful spell, I think!' declared the Princess, tapping her chin with her forefinger in contemplation. 'Right! We had better get back down and out of the way!'

They dropped to the ground and pressed themselves into the corner of the pit.

'Brace yourself against the wall and cover your head,' the Princess warned. 'When the roof breaks, it will probably fall on top of us!'

Standing just in front of him, she began an incantation, her voice quiet but commanding. Peter could feel the air around her crackling with energy, slowly building in intensity. Then, with her arms raised above her head, she released it! A blinding bolt of light raced towards the wooden doors of the roof and struck them dead centre, exploding with incredible force. Ducking down, Peter covered his head with his hands to protect himself from the falling timber. There was a distant rumble as the ground shook and the air filled with dust. Then there was complete silence.

Cautiously, Peter rose to his feet. He stared up towards the roof, trying to peer through the cloud of dust. For a few seconds he could see nothing, then it slowly began to clear. Suddenly the Princess gasped in astonishment. The doors were still there, completely intact! There was barely a mark on them!

'I do not believe it! *I…just…do…not…believe…it!*'

Peter was almost as shocked as the Princess.

'But…what happened?'

'The roof! It must have some magic built into it! Maledict must have cast a protecting spell!'

Peter felt the same horrible sinking feeling he'd felt when he'd first seen the pit.

'How are we going to get out then?'

There was a pause of several seconds before the Princess replied, her voice barely a whisper.

'We cannot. I...I cannot break the spell! We are stuck here until the trolls let us out.'

'But they'll only do that when they want to kill or torture us!'

The Princess turned to face him. He saw the horrible truth in her eyes. They were trapped in the pit with no possible means of escape.

'Oh dear,' he whispered.

Chapter 7

The Captives

Outside the Castle walls, the battle was not going well for the Vikings. Overwhelmed by the trolls' surprise attack, they were slowly being pushed back, unable to counter the sheer number and ferocity of their attackers. But it wasn't just the trolls that were defeating them, the strange weather was also taking its toll. The fog made it almost impossible for the Prince to organise an effective resistance or send reinforcements to places where the attack was the strongest. And still their attackers kept coming. Led by Mountain Trolls, they poured across the car-park, wielding their huge battle clubs and spears, whilst behind them the Wood Trolls kept a continuous hail of arrows whistling over the Vikings' heads to stop them from taking to the air.

After half an hour's furious fighting, the Prince had no choice but to give the command to retreat into St Mary's Square where, he hoped, they would be able to re-group. His orders were shouted from Viking to Viking and slowly the withdrawal began. But, yet again, the dense fog caused confusion. Unable to see, the Prince couldn't co-ordinate the retreat effectively. Some Vikings began to withdraw before others had received the command. The result was catastrophic as the trolls, who seemed somehow able to see through the fog, concentrated their attack on the Vikings who lingered.

But all was not yet lost. Faced by overwhelming odds, the Vikings were brave and strong. When those who hadn't received the Prince's command to retreat were surrounded, still they were uncowered. Forming a defensive triangle, they fell back one step at a time until the Prince finally realised the danger and came to their rescue.

An hour after the Prince had given the command to retreat, the whole of the Viking army finally made it back into St Mary's Square.

Here, the occasional lamps on the pedestrian walkways provided some relief from the fog. But the Prince knew they couldn't linger. As he watched the trolls flood out of the car-park after them, he realised the terrible danger they were in. There were only two exits from the Square. If the trolls managed to block them they would be trapped and utterly defeated. He didn't hesitate. He ordered an immediate withdrawal.

Backing away step by step, the Vikings retreated into Parliament Street, York's widest street. For the time being, there was a lull in the fighting as the trolls swarming out of St Mary's Square in pursuit held back, though they kept firing arrows over the Vikings' heads. Perhaps they were revising their tactics now they were in a much wider street, or perhaps they were teasing their prey, like a cat playing with a mouse, letting them rest for a moment before attacking again with even greater ferocity.

The Prince used the unexpected break in the fighting to review his position. Now they were further away from the river, the fog wasn't as thick and he could finally see the size of the army they faced. The seriousness of their plight was immediately apparent. Their situation was hopeless. They were outnumbered at least three to one and his army was already close to collapse through fatigue. The time for desperate measures had come.

On his command, the Vikings retreated to the far end of Parliament Street and gathered in St. Sampson's Square, forty yards from the troll army. Then he gave his final orders. He and the strongest Vikings would form a defensive wall across the corner of the Square in front of a narrow street that led to the nearest snickelway entrance in *NETHER HORNPOT LANE*. The bulk of his army would then quickly retreat behind them into the snickelway. Once safely inside, the magic in the snickelway would stop the trolls from following, and most of the Vikings would escape to fight another day.

But for those who remained to secure their passage, the situation would be desperate. Faced by an army more than twenty times their number, they would somehow have to hold out until the fleeing Vikings had escaped. As soon as the last of them had safely passed into the snickelway, they would take to the air, risking the arrows of the troll bowmen, and seek to escape back to the Vikings Halls by any route possible. It was a risky plan but a brave one. Everything depended on the remaining Vikings being able to hold out for long enough. If they couldn't, the whole Viking army would be trapped in the narrow street before they had the chance to escape into the snickelway, and devastating defeat would swiftly follow.

The Prince was well aware of the risks as he gave the orders. But the Vikings were brave and not one hesitated. In an instant, those who the Prince had chosen to remain formed two defensive lines, one behind the other, across the corner of St Sampson's Square in front of the narrow street where the snickelway entrance lay. Those two lines would have to withstand the onslaught of the entire troll army. Meanwhile, the rest of the Vikings raced behind them towards the snickelway entrance thirty yards away.

Suddenly the trolls realised what was happening. They charged across Parliament Street, seeking to crash through the Viking lines and cut off their escape. As they ran they screamed in fury, their deep voices rebounding off the buildings and shops lining the street. No longer were they content to play with their enemy to prolong the pleasure of the kill. Now they sought to crush them once and for all.

With the Mountain Trolls spearheading the attack, they hit the Prince's protective lines like a battering ram, using their enormous strength to maximum effect. The Vikings barely had room to use their swords as the trolls forced them backwards. But just when it seemed the trolls would break through and cut off the fleeing Vikings' escape, the Prince shouted an order. With uncanny speed and precision, the hard-pressed front line gave way as the Vikings leapt into the air. At the same time, the second line stepped forward to counter the troll thrust head-on, whilst the air-borne Vikings landed just behind them, immediately forming a second defensive line once more. The whole manoeuvre took barely a second and they had retreated only a few feet. More importantly, the confusion it caused allowed many more Vikings to escape through the snickelway entrance behind them.

But the trolls were better led than the Prince had anticipated. Maledict had hand-picked the commanders to lead the assault. They were more intelligent than other trolls and possessed a cruel cunning in battle. Their confusion lasted only a few seconds, then they attacked again with even greater ferocity than before. This time they concentrated their attack in one place. Using their greater numbers and strength, they hit the centre of the Viking line, seeking to break through before the Vikings could re-group.

Bravely though the Vikings fought, the power of that attack was too great. There were simply not enough Vikings to repel it. The protective lines broke almost immediately.

Weary and bloodied, the Prince screamed the command to retreat. The two lines had now merged into one disorderly mass, each Viking desperately defending himself against countless enemies whilst blocking the entrance to the narrow street behind them. But their main purpose hadn't yet been achieved. As the Prince twisted away from a troll's spear thrust and hacked at another with his sword, he glanced over his shoulder and saw the remaining Vikings queuing up outside the snickelway entrance. A hundred or more were still there. They needed to hold the trolls back for another minute at least to allow them all to escape to safety.

But the battle was turning into a rout. The defending Vikings were beginning to panic as the trolls surged forwards, using their massive strength to push them back against the shops at the edge of the Square where there would be no escape. In desperation, the Prince stood his ground and shrieked the command to form a line, grabbing those closest to him and forcing them to make a final stand by his side.

Somehow, perhaps through pride or respect for the Prince and his bravery, the Vikings rallied. Though many were so weary they could barely walk, they formed a protective semi-circle at the very edge of St Sampson's Square in front of the snickelway entrance. Eighty exhausted Vikings with the Prince screaming commands at the centre faced the entire might of the troll army.

Using sheer brute strength, the trolls slowly pushed them back into the narrow street they were protecting. But the Vikings' last effort had been enough. Just as the trolls were about to break through for the final time, the last of the fleeing Vikings stepped through the snickelway entrance behind them and vanished.

The Prince didn't wait a moment longer. Cut and dazed from a troll club that had grazed his forehead, he immediately gave the command to take to the air and flee. But it was already too late. The last effort had been too much. The remaining Vikings could barely stand, let alone fly. In seconds they were surrounded by trolls, cutting off all hope of escape. Spear points were thrust forward and bowstrings armed.

Too weary to fight any longer, the Prince staggered and dropped his sword as the giant troll commander stepped forward. He towered over even the largest Mountain Trolls, his cruel face contorted into a furious grimace. In one final desperate attempt, the Prince tried to leap into the air. But he only rose a few feet above the ground before the enormous troll swatted him out of the air as if he was nothing more than an irritating fly. Behind him, the massed trolls laughed and sneered. The giant commander threw the Prince towards them like a rag doll, then nodded towards the rest of the defeated Vikings, most of whom were so weary they had collapsed onto the pavement.

'Bind 'em! Bind 'em all!'

*

The Princess's magic light ball zigzagged across the top of the pit as if mirroring her mood as she paced up and down, her face like thunder.

'We *must* get out! We *must* get out!' she repeated over and over again.

Sitting on the hard ground, Peter ignored her. He didn't care about her frustration. After all, if she'd listened to him for once they wouldn't be in such a mess! Feeling utterly miserable, he huddled up tightly against the cold, his hands clenched into fists beneath the sleeves of his long coat.

'We *must* get out! We *must* get out!' repeated the Princess furiously.

Eventually she flopped down in the corner of the pit beside him and held her head in her hands.

'We cannot fail now! Not when the trolls have begun their attack!'

Side by side they sat in silence, wondering what was going on in the Castle and city streets outside, and feeling completely helpless. The Princess's magic light slowly faded until it provided barely enough illumination for them to see each other.

Just when their mood was ebbing to a dangerous low, the silence was shattered by the thunder of heavy feet above them. A moment later, the wooden doors of the roof began to open at the centre and faint night light flooded into the pit. As the doors were slowed pulled back, the dark outline of the troll Captain appeared as he peered over the edge of the pit, a whip dangling from his right hand.

'Hello again my little maggots! You didn't think I'd forgotten about my special guests, did you?'

The Sergeant and the other trolls crowded around the edge of the pit beside him, looking confused about what was going on but relieved that someone else was the subject of the Captain's scorn for a change. Meanwhile, the Captain glared at the Princess, completely ignoring Peter.

'How you feelin' down there little girlie? Cold? Wet? Well don't you worry! I've got an extra-special treat planned for you that'll warm you up good and proper!'

Whilst he was speaking, two of the trolls behind him heaved a large steel barred cage over the side of the pit and began to lower it using a thick knotted rope. The Captain watched their horrified expressions as they gazed up at it, clearly enjoying their reaction. He turned his attention to Peter.

'Say goodbye to your friend, little City Dweller! You may not see her for a long time – a *very* long time indeed! But don't you worry! You'll soon get the chance to try out our facilities too, you know! Tis only polite to ask the lady first though! That's proper eticket that is!'

As he spoke, the cage swung menacingly in the air above the Princess's head as it was lowered slowly towards her.

'Now, if you'd kindly step inside, there's someone I'd like you to meet!' continued the Captain to the Princess, sounding immensely pleased with himself. 'Someone very special indeed! He has a rare talent, which you're goin' to see first hand, so to speak! Oh yes! *Very* first-hand!'

The trolls crowded around the edge of the pit started laughing knowingly as if the Captain had just made an extremely funny private joke. The two trolls who were lowering the cage laughed so much that the rope slipped between their fingers and the cage crashed to the bottom of the pit, narrowly missing the Princess as she leapt aside.

'Careful lads! We don't want to damage her do we? Plenty of time for that later!' said the Captain with a malicious grin. 'Now little Viking – if you'd be so kind as to step into your chariot.'

To Peter's horror, the Princess took a step towards the cage. Darting forward, he grabbed her arm and pulled her back.

'What are you doing? You can't be thinking of actually going with them? They've obviously got something terrible planned! I don't know who they are talking about, but I'm sure I wouldn't want to meet him!'

The Princess stared back at him, her expression determined.

'I have to! What other choice do we have? Stay in here until we starve to death or Maledict takes the city? Did you not see the trolls at the gates? The battle has already begun!'

'But they've got something terrible planned – you know they have!'

The Princess leaned towards him and whispered in his ear.

'Do not worry about me! I can handle trolls! I will come back for you once I have escaped! Then we will finish the Quest together!'

Before he could answer, she shook her arm free and stepped boldly into the cage. Turning around, she shut the steel door behind her and glanced up at the Captain.

'What if you *can't* come back?' insisted Peter, grasping the cage and pulling on the bars in frustration. 'What if…!' Running out of words in his panic, he desperately tried to prise the cage door open.

But the cage was already rising into the air as the trolls heaved on the rope.

'Do not worry!' whispered the Princess, kneeling down so her face was level with his through the steel bars as the cage rose higher. 'I will be back! I promise!'

'*Princess!*'

It was too late. The cage was now level with the top of the pit. Immediately several trolls grasped it and locked the cage door to secure the Princess inside, chuckling to themselves in their horrible throaty voices in anticipation of whatever terrible scheme they had in mind. The Captain looked particularly pleased. As the pit doors began to lower again, he grinned down at Peter.

'Don't you worry little City Dweller! We'll take *good* care of her, won't we lads? She'll get five-star treatment she will! She's going to have all sorts of nice toys to play with before we're through with her!' The trolls around him were now almost hysterical with laughter. 'Now, don't get too lonely down there in the dark! We'll be back for you soon enough! Wouldn't want you to miss out on all the fun, would we?'

As Peter watched in desperation, the wooden doors came crashing down again. Once more, he found himself in complete darkness. But this time he was alone. And he had a horrible feeling he might never see the Princess again.

*

Alone in the pit, Peter waited for the Princess to return. He could see nothing but impenetrable blackness. All he could hear was his own agitated breathing, seemingly magnified a thousand times. With an ever-growing feeling of fear and hopelessness, he sat on the cold hard ground at the bottom of the pit and tried to calm his growing fear.

Time crept slowly on. In the pit there was only darkness and silence. He closed his eyes and tried to reassure himself that everything was going to be fine, but when he opened them again there was no change. He could still see nothing. He could still hear nothing.

Suddenly he leapt up and began to jog on the spot. For some reason, he felt that he had to move – that if he stayed still a moment longer he would go crazy. He raised his knees as high as he could to stamp out his fear and swung his arms like a deranged keep-fit instructor. Soon though, his sudden burst of energy was exhausted and he collapsed onto the ground.

As he stared across the pit, a light appeared. It was shining just in front of him. What could it be? It was a strange shape. It looked like a snake, or was it a dragon? Then he recognised it. It was Sigurd's talisman, its two red dragon eyes shining in the darkness. It must have fallen out of his pocket whilst he was running!

He remembered the morning in the church graveyard when he had met Sigurd and he had told him of the Vikings and their plight. Suddenly he felt a strange assurance. It didn't matter that he was alone in the darkness. He simply had to stay calm and wait.

Picking up the talisman, he placed it back into his pocket. Once again there was total darkness. But it no longer held any fear for him. Completely calm, he rolled onto his back on the ground and closed his eyes. Immediately he fell into a deep untroubled sleep.

*

Peter woke suddenly. At first he couldn't understand what had startled him. Then he heard it again. In an instant he was on his feet. He could hear it clearly now - a faint scraping noise coming from somewhere above him!

His heart began to race. It was the first noise he'd heard since the Princess had left. What could it be? Could it be some sort of signal? But from whom?

The strange noise suddenly stopped. Devastated, he stood perfectly still and listened intently. Within a few seconds it returned, this time louder and more urgent.

'Who *is* that?' said Peter out-loud, and was startled to hear his voice coming out of the darkness.

But he'd already decided who it was – who it must be. The Princess must have escaped and was trying to free him!

Almost without thinking, he rose into the air and drifted towards the roof.

By the time he'd risen to the top of the pit, the scraping noise had stopped again. For a moment he hung in the air, straining his ears to catch the slightest sound. Then, to his immense relief, the noise returned, as loud as it was before. It sounded like someone was scratching the outside of the doors with their fingernails. It *had* to be the Princess!

Hesitating for a moment, he reached up and knocked three times on the wood. Immediately the scratching noise stopped. Then, after an agonising silence, someone on the other side knocked in response, precisely mirroring the sound he had made.

Peter almost screamed in relief! For a second he wondered whether it could be a troll trying to torture him, but then he forced the thought from his mind. It was the Princess – it *had* to be the Princess!

Barely able to control his mounting excitement, he knocked again - three quick knocks followed by a brief pause, then two more. There was silence for a few seconds before the knocks were repeated in precisely the same order, including the pause in the middle. Then, as he pressed his ear against the wood, he heard a faint voice from the other side.

'*Hello? Hello?*'

Peter dropped several feet in the air in surprise. He recognised the voice immediately. But it wasn't the Princess. Rising back up, he pressed his ear against the door once more, desperate to hear it again.

'Hello? Is any...er...*thing* down there?' said the voice. 'I hope you're not a troll! I really hope you're not a troll!'

'*Dunstable!*' cried Peter, so overjoyed to hear his familiar timid voice that he banged his head on the wooden roof. On the other side of the door, Dunstable sounded equally pleased to hear Peter.

'Peter? Is that *really* you? You're not a troll pretending to be him are you?'

'Dunstable! It's me! Let me out!' said Peter, as loud as he dared.

'Peter! It *is* you! I'm so glad I found you! I thought they'd squashed you! It's a good job I...'

'Dunstable! Stop chattering! Get me out!'

Peter was in no mood for idle banter. Now Dunstable had found him, he suddenly began to wonder what might have happened to the Princess. He had to get out and find her!

'Oh, right! Errr...How do I do that then?'

There was silence for several long seconds as Peter tried to think of a way to escape.

'He's never going to be able to open the doors,' he muttered to himself. 'It took two trolls with ropes to do that. But how else can we do it? There *must* be a way!'

'Err, hello? Are you still there?' squeaked Dunstable. 'Only, I'd like to get this over with as soon as possible before I get squashed by a big ugly troll!'

'Wait a minute Dunstable – I'm thinking!'

'Right. Ok. But could you think a *little faster?*'

Peter bobbed in mid-air beneath the wooden doors as he tried to think of a way out. Then he had a brain wave. If they were strong enough, it might just work! They *had* to be strong enough!

'Dunstable – there should be two ropes lying on the ground nearby. Can you see either of them?'

'*Errr...* yes! There's one just behind me. I almost fell over it, you know!'

'And can you see two big rings in the centre of the doors?'

'Err, *yes…?*'

'Good! Now, listen carefully!' Peter closed his eyes to recall exactly how the trolls had opened the doors. 'Tie the end of one of the ropes to the ring at the centre of the door on the Tower side.'

'The Tower side? Oh! Right!'

Peter waited about ten seconds.

'Done it?'

'It's tied. Very tight. Hope I don't have to undo it again!'

'Good. Now, take hold of the rope and be ready to pull on it as hard as you can. But not before I say! If you pull at the same time as I push up, we might be able to open one door wide enough for me to get through!'

'Err, ok…?' said Dunstable, not sounding at all convinced that Peter's plan would work.

'Good! When I say go, pull on the rope as hard as you can!'

Peter hesitated for a moment. It had taken a troll's strength to open each door. But they only needed to open one wide enough for him to squeeze through – a foot or two at the most. Would they really be strong enough? It *had* to work! It just had to!

'Ready then?' He braced himself against the centre of the pit wall and pressed his shoulders against the edge of the door.

'Ok then! I'm ready…I think!' replied Dunstable hesitantly.

'*PULL!!!*'

Dunstable dug his heels into the ground and heaved on the rope with all his strength. At the same time, Peter pushed up against the door with his shoulders, his feet finally finding purchase on the pit wall.

At first nothing happened. Then a thin beam of light streamed into the pit as the door rose an inch above the ground.

'*All…most…there!*' gasped Peter, suppressing his elation at being able to see again as he strained against the door's weight. '*All…most…there!*'

Again they heaved and pulled, their shoulders and arms stretching in agony. Slowly the gap widened to half a foot and then a whole foot. Peter could hardly believe it!

'*Just…a…little…bit…more!*' he screeched through gritted teeth.

But Dunstable was struggling.

'I…can't…hold…on…much…long…ger!!' he squealed, suddenly sounding incredibly close. 'My…arms…are…go…ing…to…fall…off!'

The gap between the door and the ground was now almost two feet. It was enough, barely, for Peter to escape through. But he would have to stop pushing to do it. If he could just get through the gap before the door slammed shut again!

'Read…dy…Dun…stab…ble? Hold…on…tight! I'm… com…ing… through!'

With a final heave up at the door, Peter pushed off from the pit wall and sped towards the gap as fast as a lightning bolt. It had been some time since he'd flown flat out and he was surprised by the speed he flew, his desperation to escape giving him added impetus. His head was through the gap in the wink of an eye. Then, as his freedom hung in the balance, time seemed to suddenly slow. As he felt the glorious night air against his face, he watched in horror as the door began to fall, knowing that if he didn't get through it in time he would be crushed. He was travelling so fast that the Castle and everything else but the door was a blur, though he just managed to see Dunstable out of the corner of his eye, still pulling on the rope. Then his body shot through the gap, leaving only his legs inside. More by instinct than design, he whipped them up to his stomach as the door came crashing down.

It was close! As the door slammed shut, it caught his ankle. Fortunately his momentum was enough to propel him through, but the impact sent him spinning through the air before he crashed painfully onto the ground behind Dunstable. Rolling on the hard stone of the courtyard, he instinctively clutched his foot. But he didn't care about the pain. He was outside in the open air again! Somehow he had escaped!

Chapter 8

Crusher's Torture Chamber

Peter's relief was overwhelming! For several seconds he simply sat on the ground, overcome by the wave of elation he felt from escaping such a terrible place. Breathing in the night air, he raised his head to the sky, luxuriating in the biting coldness of the wind and rain against his face.

Slowly he began to take in the scene around him. It was still night-time. The fog had cleared, though a thin veil of damp mist still hung in the air. Despite the murkiness, he felt as if he'd stepped into a bright room after the complete darkness of the pit. He felt like a blind man whose sight had been miraculously restored.

Reluctantly, he forced himself back down to earth. He was, after all, still in incredible danger. Suddenly he realised how horribly exposed he was. He threw himself onto the ground and scoured the courtyard around him. It appeared to be deserted, but he knew the trolls couldn't be far away.

Leaping to his feet, he jogged over to Dunstable, who was still pulling on the rope with his eyes tightly shut.

'It's ok Dunstable! I'm here! You can let go now!'

Dunstable opened one startled eye then dropped the rope and leapt with joy.

'It *is* you! It really is! I wasn't sure, you know! I really wasn't! I thought you might be a nasty troll! Goodness gracious! We did it! We *actually did it!*'

Still overcome with relief at his escape, Peter shook Dunstable's hand awkwardly, feeling that he should express his gratitude but unsure quite what was required.

'Yes…thank you very much Dunstable. It was…very kind of you to…to come and…help me.'

Dunstable grinned back meekly and began cleaning his

glasses with his tie, looking as embarrassed as Peter. Their clumsy celebrations, though, were short lived as the reality of their situation came quickly back to them. Immediately they glanced around the courtyard again. Though it appeared to be deserted, they were still in full view of any troll who happened to be looking in their direction. Wasting no more time, they raced to the back of the courtyard and wedged themselves against the Castle wall, crouching as low as they could.

'How did you find me, Dunstable?' whispered Peter, his eyes shooting from side to side. 'I thought you were waiting for us in the passageways!'

Dunstable's face lit up with pride.

'Well, I suddenly remembered that I hadn't told you how to get out of the circular corridor!' he replied excitedly (and a little too loudly for Peter's liking). 'So, once I was sure the trolls had gone, I followed you! I was very scared, but it wasn't nearly as bad as I thought it would be – not nearly as bad! I don't know what is happening. I've hardly seen any trolls! Perhaps they've all gone to the big battle?'

'*Shhh!* Speak quietly! How did you get out of the circular corridor? That torch lever must have been ten feet up the wall!'

Dunstable grinned at Peter, looking very smug indeed. He tapped the side of his nose knowingly.

'I was hoping you were going to ask me that! I went the *other* way – the *secret* way!'

'The secret way? But why didn't you...' Realising he was speaking too loudly, Peter glanced nervously across the courtyard again. Seeing it was still deserted, he decided to let Dunstable have his moment of glory. 'Ok then. Tell me about the *secret* way.'

Dunstable beamed indulgently.

'Well, at the back of each of the prison cells there is a flap to let the air in, otherwise all the prisoners would suffocate, and the trolls wouldn't want that, not before they could squash them anyway! The flaps are small, very small – a troll would think them tiny! But I can squeeze through, you know, just about! They lead up – up to the Castle. When I got to the dungeons, I couldn't find you anywhere so I assumed you must have been caught. It wasn't hard then, of course. As you weren't in the dungeons, I knew they must have taken you to the pit...'

'I see!' said Peter, quickly losing interest in the story. He was beginning to feel vulnerable out in the open and wanted to get under cover as soon as possible. 'Have you seen the Princess?'

Dunstable's face dropped.

'We'll, err, yes, in a manner of speaking…'

Peter stared at him in alarm.

'What do you mean? Tell me!'

'She's been taken by the trolls, you see…'

'Yes I know. But *where* was she taken?'

'To the, err…' He blanched and began pulling on his tie, bowing his head in misery. 'She's been taken to the Torture Chamber!'

Peter leapt up in horror.

'*The Torture Chamber!* But…why didn't you say? We must save her!'

Dunstable winced at Peter's noisy outburst and pulled even harder on his tie, looking as if he was the one being tortured.

'It's probably too late now anyway! She was taken *hours* ago! And the troll torturers…you really don't …they're so…'

Peter had heard enough.

'Where is she? *Show me!!*'

Dunstable shrank back against the Castle wall and pointed a shaky finger across the courtyard towards the misty outline of the grassy mound at the base of the Tower.

'*There!*' he whispered. 'The Torture Chamber is down there! But we can't follow her! The troll torturers, they'll…'

Peter wasn't listening. He was staring in the direction Dunstable was indicating, oblivious to everything except the plight of the Princess. Across the dark courtyard, the Tower loomed high above them through the thin mist. Dunstable appeared to be pointing to the same door he and the Princess had come through after the trolls had captured them, though his arm was shaking so much it was difficult to be sure. The Torture Chamber must be behind the red door he'd seen on the staircase leading up from the dungeons!

'Are you sure?' queried Peter, the door had looked so unimportant.

Dunstable nodded solemnly and pointed again, though his eyes were now firmly shut.

Peter considered the best way to get across the wide courtyard. From where they were crouching beneath the Castle wall, the distance to the door was approximately a hundred yards. There were no trolls in sight, but it was dark and he couldn't see around the Tower. Surely the Castle couldn't be completely deserted? There was only one way to be sure.

'Right!' said Peter decisively. 'Dunstable, cling onto my back!'

Dunstable's eyes flicked open in alarm.

'*What?* Oh no! We're not going to fly are we?'

But Peter was in too much of a hurry to enter into a debate.

'There's no time to argue! Just get on my back! *Now!*'

Moved by Peter's urgency, Dunstable wrapped his arms reluctantly around Peter's neck.

'I really don't know why we can't just *walk*. Or perhaps I could stay here? I am rather afraid of heights you kn...*ooooooooh noooooooooo!*'

Peter had decided that he couldn't wait any longer. The moment he felt Dunstable's arms link around his neck, he shot vertically up into the air like a rocket. Dunstable squealed in terror.

'*Stop!!! Take me down! Take me down!!! Pleeeeaseeeeee take me down!!*'

Peter wasn't listening. In just a few seconds they were high above the courtyard, despite Dunstable's terrified thrashing. Once they were high enough to survey the whole Castle, Peter slowed and hovered in mid air to survey the scene below. Beyond the Castle walls, the city lay sleeping. It was clearly deep into the night as there were no cars or pedestrians and no lights in the houses. Only the street lamps were twinkling in the darkness, illuminating the misty puddle-strewn roads beneath them. He turned his attention to the Castle. He couldn't see any trolls in the courtyard, but several were standing on the battlements gazing across the silent city, completely unaware that he was hovering above them. They appeared to be the only trolls outside, though he suspected that many more could be hidden in underground barracks. On the far side of the courtyard at the bottom of the Tower mound was the door that led down to the Torture Chamber. If he was quick, he might be able to get to it unseen!

He dived back down to earth as fast as he dared. Levelling up when he was thirty feet above the Castle walls, he shot across the courtyard towards the Tower like a bullet, speeding over the heads of the troll sentries on the battlements. If one of them looked up, he would surely be seen, but their attention was focused solely on the city. Meanwhile, Dunstable was clinging onto his back with his eyes firmly shut, too frightened to make a sound.

With less finesse than he intended, Peter landed on the top-most step outside the grey door that led down to the Torture Chamber. Dunstable immediately let go of him and rolled onto the next step down, clinging onto it with both arms as if he'd never been so relieved in his life.

Peter didn't wait. Leaping up, he raced to the door. He was about to dash inside when he realised that Dunstable wasn't following him. Furious, he span around.

'Come on Dunstable! The Princess is in there!'

But Dunstable didn't seem to hear him. He was staring at the door in terror, his face contorted in pain as he relived some dreadful memory.

'No! I won't go in! Not the Torture Chamber! I won't do that again! No, no, *NO!!*'

Under any other circumstances Peter might have felt sorry for him, but now he was in too much of a hurry. The only thing he could think about was the Princess being tortured.

He was just considering whether to leave Dunstable behind and find the Princess on his own, when a shrill noise rang out across the courtyard. It sounded like the resonant high-pitch clash of metal striking metal. It was coming from inside the Tower mound below them. Then, rising above its ringing echo, came the unmistakable sound of deep-throated troll laughter.

Dunstable went white and froze in terror.

'Something horrible is happening in there! Torture and unspeakable things!'

As Dunstable shrank against the step, the piercing sound rang out again. It was so sharp that Peter cringed in pain, stuffing his fingers into his ears in a desperate attempt to block it out. At the same time, several deep-throated troll voices broke into a coarse song, singing in time to the pounding metallic beat:

We crunch!
We crunch!
And when we crunch we have our lunch
And this is what we munch!

One Viking! Two Vikings!
Who ate all the fat Vikings?
C-R-U-S-H-A – CRUSHER!!

Dunstable had never looked more terrified in his life! He pointed to the door that led to the Torture Chamber then clamped his hands over his ears to block out the terrible beat.

'It's *Crusher!! Crusher the Viking Squasher!!!!*'

'Who's Crusher?' shouted Peter, hardly able to hear his own voice the beat was so loud. Receiving no response, he staggered across the step to Dunstable and pulled his hands away from his ears. *'WHO IS CRUSHER?'*

'Crusher? He's the *Chief Torturer* of course! He's the worst troll of all!' shouted Dunstable, quickly blocking his ears again. His eyes were fixed on the ground, his expression absolutely petrified. 'He is very big and very mean, and he loves to torture people before eating them! No one who ever met him has lived! Not one!'

Peter forced Dunstable's hands away from his ears again, his sense of urgency only intensified by what Dunstable had just said.

'The Princess is in there! We must save her!'

'But it's *Crusher!* Don't you understand?' Freeing his hands from Peter's grip, he clamped them back over his ears again and stared at the ground determinedly, refusing to meet Peter's searching eyes. 'He'll squash us flat! He'll stick horrible things in us! He'll eat us limb by limb!'

'I don't care who he is! We must save her!' Peter glanced towards the door. 'Is this the only way in?'

Reluctantly, Dunstable stared at the door and nodded, grimacing in horror of what lay beyond it. Caught between his fear and his concern for the Princess, he couldn't have looked more tortured if Crusher himself had been squashing him.

'But it's *Crusher!*' he pleaded, as if nothing more needed to be said. *'It's Crusher!'*

Furious, Peter spun away and strode towards the door. He was not about to leave the Princess at the mercy of the trolls, Crusher or no Crusher!

Catching the determined look in his eye, Dunstable rocked back and forth on the step, tormented by the dilemma he faced. Suddenly he leapt to his feet and stood bolt upright. Shaking his head, he banged his ears with the palms of his hands as if trying to drown out the ominous metallic beat. Then, after a moment's pause, he leapt up and sprinted past Peter. Determined to outrun his fears, he burst through the door and leapt down the steps on the other side.

Hardly believing his eyes, Peter sprinted through the door after him, struggling to catch up despite leaping three steps at a time. At the bottom of the staircase was the wall that had mysteriously risen when the trolls had captured them. But Dunstable didn't follow the steps all the way down. Instead, he darted through the narrow passageway that led off from the stairway. At the far end was the red door. Without slowing, he bolted through it with Peter hot on his heels. But his miraculous courage evaporated the moment he saw what lay on the other side. His fear had caught up with him at last. Stopping dead in his tracks, he stared at the horrifying sight before him, paralysed by complete and utter terror.

But it was too late for Peter. Unable to stop in time, he ran straight into Dunstable's back, sending them both flying forwards. Tumbling over each other, they fell head over heels down the staircase that led down to the large chamber below and landed in a painful heap on the bottom step. Embarrassed and furious, Peter shoved Dunstable off him and leapt to his feet in a desperate attempt to regain some dignity. Ready for anything, he surveyed the chamber in one swift glance.

It was only in that moment that Peter fully understood what had so terrified Dunstable. The chamber was full of the most gruesome torture devices he could ever have imagined. Directly in front of him was an enormous torture table, complete with binding straps and various knobs that released sharp points into the most sensitive parts of its victim's anatomy. An array of knives and bladed instruments lay on a table beside it. In fact, all manner of torture devices were hanging from the blood stained walls or strewn across the floor: thumb screws, nose probes, bone-breaking pliers, various odd looking blunt instruments similar to hammers whose horrific purpose was unclear, and countless other multi-pronged instruments. At the back of the chamber was a large open fireplace. Several pokers were warming there, no doubt in preparation for some grisly use later. Hanging from the ceiling above the fire by a thick metal chain was a vast cauldron of bubbling green liquid that smelled like linseed.

Peter's eyes finally rested on the fireplace. Crouching over an anvil in front of it were six of the largest, most muscle-bound trolls he had ever seen, their hulking shapes horribly outlined against the fire's flickering red flames. Armed to the teeth with countless dreadful looking torture implements, they dropped the enormous metal hammers they were holding. Then, with all the menace of stalking tigers, they strolled towards him, the expression on their ugly faces like that of a greedy child who had just been handed his favourite bag of sweets.

Peter froze. The trolls were just a few yards away from him now, grinning ominously. They seemed to be in no hurry to lay hands on him. They were happy to give him time to take in the full horror of what he was facing. Then, just as panic threatened to overwhelm him, Peter felt something warm against his leg. Without thinking he reached into his pocket. There, temporarily forgotten, was Sigurd's talisman. Instinctively he grasped it. Immediately a wave of calm surged through his body, but this time there was something else; something far stronger. His fear was replaced by a powerful assurance. He felt as if he could do anything - as if he was in total harmony with the world around him.

Calmly and confidently, Peter took his eye off the trolls and glanced behind him. Dunstable was cringing half way up the steps they had fallen down, rolled into a tight ball. One eye was blinking through a gap between his arms whilst the other was tightly shut in terror. Behind him, the door they had fallen through was wide open.

The trolls stopped a few yards in front of Peter, surprised (and disappointed) that he wasn't attempting to run away. Snarling like bull terriers, they towered above him, their shoulders like boulders and their bulging arms as thick as his waist. As Peter readied himself for the fight, two of them stepped aside and in-between walked the largest, fattest, ugliest troll he had ever seen.

As soon as he appeared, Dunstable let out a terrified shriek.

'Oh no! Save us! It's *Crusher! Crusher the Viking Squasher!*'

Crusher grinned proudly, revealing a mouth full of broken black teeth. He liked to be recognised. After all, he had a reputation to protect.

'So glad you could join us!' he boomed. His enormous mouth curled into an evil grin as he casually sharpened the long straight knife he held in one hand against the shorter curved one he held in the other. 'We're about to 'ave a party, and you're the entertainment!'

Peter stepped forward. Still completely calm, he clutched Sigurd's talisman tightly in his right hand.

'The Princess. Where is she?'

Crusher smiled girlishly and pretended to brush his few greasy stands of hair with his gigantic hand, somehow managing to look even uglier than before.

'*Princess?* You want the Princess? *Oooh* look at me, *I'm* the Princess!'

The other trolls roared with laughter at their leader's rather pathetic imitation. Encouraged by their reaction, Crusher started to bat his eyes-lids and purse his lips in truly revolting fashion.

At that moment, something inside Peter became very clear. He felt it deep inside him. He was connected to a mysterious source of power, a power that gave him incredible abilities. And now he could control it. Somehow, he knew exactly what to do. With his eyes fixed on Crusher as he danced hideously in front of him pretending to be a Princess, he calmly reached out his right hand with the talisman clutched inside and turned it over, as if giving a thumbs' down sign. A strange tingling sensation shot through his body as the magic built inside him. Then he let it go.

Immediately Crusher was flung forward as if he had been shoved in the back and spun around until he was suspended upside-down in the air just a few inches above the ground. As Peter lowered his hand, Crusher's bald head began to bounce painfully on the blood-stained floor. His smug expression instantly changed to one of pure terror.

'*Oww! Me 'ead!!*' he screeched, screaming in fear and pain. He tried to turn towards the perplexed trolls standing behind him. 'Don't just stand there! *Squash 'im!* Squash 'im *NOW!!*'

It took a moment for the trolls to get over the shock of seeing their renowned leader bouncing on his head upside-down in front of them with no visible means of support - then they charged. Dunstable, who was momentarily peeking out from behind his arms to stare at the strange scene, let out a horrified squeal before ducking his head behind his arms and legs again. But the trolls only advanced a couple of feet before they too suddenly swung into the air as if they had slipped on soap, and hung upside-down behind their leader, their heads bobbing up and down above the floor and their eyes wide with terrified incomprehension.

Peter alone remained composed. He walked calmly towards Crusher and bent down so he was level with his enormous upside-down head.

'Are you going to tell me where the Princess is, or am I going to have to get *really* angry with you?'

Crusher licked his lips anxiously.

'Err, right. The *Princess* you say? I, er, don't recall any Princesses! I'm sure I'd remember one of those! Honest I would!'

Without taking his eyes off Crusher, Peter waved his hand up and down. Instantly, all the trolls started to bounce from a greater height, making painful cracking noises as their skulls thumped the stone floor.

'This is your last chance before I start bouncing you from the ceiling. Where is she?'

All the trolls were now looking very ill indeed. Crusher was suffering even more than the others, partly because the momentum he built up when he hit the ground was greater due to his enormous weight, and partly because Peter ensured he bounced the highest.

Receiving no response, Peter lost his patience. With a wave of his hand, he began to bounce Crusher more quickly, making his few remaining teeth rattle.

'*Aww me-ee h-head!!!* Oh-h-ho? Y-you m-m-mean the lit-tle Vi-king g-girl-lie? I th-th-think I-I a-ate h-her! I w-was a b-bit peck-peck-ish you s-see! *P-Pleeee-eese-s-stop!!!!*'

'Ooo-ops!' groaned the other trolls in unison, cursing their leader.

For a moment, there was complete silence as Peter stared at Crusher in horror. On the steps behind him, Dunstable re-appeared from behind his arms, his face white with shock. Forgotten for the moment, the other trolls hung suspended in mid-air, their beady eyes staring at one-another anxiously. Then Peter's previously calm expression changed to one of absolute fury. He raised his hands. Crusher and Dunstable both winced, then...

'*Excuse me!!*' cried one of the upside-down trolls. 'You didn't eat her. She's still in the pot! You ate *Grafter* chief. He fell in!'

'Grafter?' exclaimed Crusher, looking even more ill than before. 'Ugh! That's disgustin' that is! I thought she were a-bit tough!'

But Peter wasn't listening. Ignoring the trolls, he was staring at the enormous cauldron above the fire at the back of the chamber, his eyes wide with renewed hope. With his attention diverted, the trolls suddenly dropped heavily onto the ground. But Peter didn't notice. He raced to the cauldron and pulled on the chain from which it was hanging, desperately trying to drag it away from the fire.

'Dunstable! *Help me!*'

Warily dodging the prostrate trolls, Dunstable raced over to him, and together they hauled on the thick chain. The cauldron was heavy, but eventually they managed to swing it far enough so that it slipped off the metal hook at the end of the chain and crashed onto the ground. It tottered for a second on its side then tipped over, spilling several gallons of water, numerous carrots, potatoes and other unknown vegetables, and then, finally, the Princess! She was sealed upside-down in a transparent pouch like a cook-in-a-bag fish. Her face was pale, and even when she skidded across the wet floor, her body remained worryingly still.

Fearing the worst, Peter raced over to her and ripped the pouch open. But her eyes remained shut and her face lifeless. He lifted her head frantically, wondering whether she had suffocated. Then he remembered something he'd seen in films. Kneeling in front of her, he lowered his mouth to hers to give her the kiss of life. He had barely touched her lips when, to his immense relief, she suddenly gasped for air.

'What are you doing? Get off me!' she spluttered, sounding as irritable as ever, though she barely had the energy to speak.

Peter was so overjoyed (and embarrassed) that for several seconds he didn't know what to say. He simply stared down at her, his mouth agape.

'But...I thought you were dead!' he gasped finally. 'I was trying to revive you!'

The Princess glared at him for a moment, then relaxed and smiled weakly.

'I am fine, thank you. Or at least I will be once I get my strength back!'

Meanwhile, the trolls had not been idle. Realising that Peter was distracted, they were silently tip-toeing their way towards the door, hoping they could escape unnoticed. They would have made it too had Crusher paid more attention to where he was going. His eyes fixed on Peter, he didn't notice the sharp metal hook that had fallen out of one of his pockets when he'd been bouncing upside-down until he put his bare foot on it and it sank into his tender flesh. There was a delay of about a second before the pain hit him, then he started to scream. Almost immediately, several trolls clamped their hands over his mouth as they stared at Peter in trepidation. Then, realising the game was up, they made a run for it! With incredible speed for such large creatures, they raced up the stairs and darted through the door, yelping at the top of their gruff voices with Crusher, surprisingly, the fastest of them all.

Dunstable panicked.

'What are we going to do? What are we going to do? They'll raise the guards! *We'll be squashed!*'

Much to his alarm, neither Peter nor the Princess moved. For the moment, neither of them cared. They were just glad to be alive. Ignoring Dunstable as he ran in circles around them, unsure whether to run and hide or stay with them, they finally rose to their feet, the Princess leaning heavily on Peter's arm.

'*We must go! We must go!* We'll be *squashed!*' repeated Dunstable. Encouraged that the Princess was now standing, he tried to pull her towards the door.

'We cannot go yet,' whispered the Princess, pulling away from him feebly. 'There are other Vikings. The Prince is here. We must free them too!'

'The Prince is here?' said Peter in surprise. 'Where is he?'

'In the dungeons below us. I…I think we are losing the battle. The trolls…' she coughed and would have fallen had Peter not reached out to steady her. 'We have not got much time. We must free them. Then we must finish the Quest before it is too late!'

In his determination to find the Princess, Peter had forgotten about their Quest and the uncomfortable fact that they had to steal the Viking Stone from Maledict's crown. Whenever he'd thought about it before, it had always seemed far away in the future, and he'd pushed it to the back of his mind. But now that they were in the Tower and, temporarily at least, free from the trolls, he realised that the time had come to complete the task the Queen had set them.

Just as he began to consider how they could possibly achieve such a seemingly impossible feat, the Princess sagged in his arms. Suddenly the horrible reality of their situation struck him. They were about to attempt a deadly task and the Princess couldn't even stand without his support. There was only one thing he could do, terrible though it was to contemplate. He turned to Dunstable.

'I will go…I will go and complete the Quest alone.' His shaky voice steadied as he grew in determination. 'Dunstable - is there somewhere you two can hide until I return?'

The Princess suddenly pulled herself upright and brushed him aside angrily.

'Do not be stupid! You are not going on your own! Maledict will make mincemeat of you! Dunstable can stay here and free the Prince and the others with Crusher's keys. I am coming with you!'

'Keys?' queried Dunstable, looking confused as he glanced from one to the other. 'What keys?'

The Princess pointed to the ground. In front of them was a large indentation in the stone floor marking the spot where Peter had repeatedly bounced Crusher's head. Just beside it was a bunch of thick metal keys, each over half a foot long. Presumably they had fallen out of Crusher's pocket when he'd been suspended upside-down. In his rush to escape, he'd forgotten all about them. Peter reached down and picked them up.

Seeing them in Peter's hand, Dunstable took a step backwards and glanced nervously towards the door.

'But what about the *trolls?* What about *Crusher?* If he finds out that I've let the prisoners escape, he'll squash me flat!'

'Do not worry, Dunstable!' urged the Princess, trying to sound encouraging. She staggered slightly and pushed Peter's hand away as he reached out to support her. 'All the trolls have gone! All you have to do is free the Prince and give him the keys. He will do the rest!'

Peter wasn't happy with the plan. He stared into the Princess's determined eyes. Despite her stubbornness, she was leaning heavily on his arm again. If he moved she would surely fall.

'You should go with Dunstable. You're too weak. Look! You can hardly stand!'

'I am fine, thank you very much!' she replied irritably, shaking off his arm and standing unaided again, though she was swaying precariously. 'Anyway, you are not ready to face Maledict alone. I do not know how you did whatever you just did with those trolls, but you *need* me. I am going with you, like it or not!'

It was clear from her tone that there was to be no argument; the matter was decided. Reluctantly, Peter nodded.

With the Princess determined to walk by herself, they slowly made their way to the door through which Peter and Dunstable had entered so ingloriously just a few minutes earlier. Pushing it open, they hesitated for a moment. In front of them, the stone staircase led up to the Castle courtyard on the left and down to the dungeons on the right.

Dunstable fidgeted, his eyes wide as he gazed at the staircase nervously.

'Do not worry!' said the Princess, beginning to sound a little stronger as she turned to comfort him. 'You will be fine Dunstable! You overcame your fear of trolls and came back for us. Think what would have happened if you had stayed in the passageway? We would have been lost! I might even have been *eaten* – if I had not been able to escape by myself, of course. If you free the Prince as well, think what everyone will say? You will be a hero!'

Dunstable looked at her blankly for a moment.

'Yes, I did save you both, didn't I? And all by myself too! I suppose I *could* free the Prince? After all, the trolls have all gone now, haven't they? As long as he doesn't expect me to do any fighting, of course!' He tapped his chin thoughtfully with his fingers, his fear temporarily forgotten as he considered what being a 'hero' would feel like. Slowly, a mischievous grin spread across his face and he began to chuckle to himself. 'I wonder what the Prince will say when he sees me with Crusher's keys? That will give him quite a shock, I imagine!' Suddenly he snatched the keys out of Peter's hand. 'Leave it to me! I'll have the Prince out in a jiffy, you know!'

With that, he raced down the staircase to the dungeons, an expression of wild glee on his face as if he couldn't wait to see the Prince's expression when he freed him.

As soon as Dunstable had gone, Peter and the Princess slowly made their way up the steps in silence, each considering the enormity of the task before them. Pushing back the outer door, they stared across the Castle courtyard, the cold night air brushing against their faces. Somewhere close by a bell was ringing frantically. They could hear horns being blown and the sound of heavy iron-shod feet on stone. But they no longer cared about the trolls. They had a far more dangerous matter to attend to.

Raising their heads, they stared at the Tower looming high above them. A red light shone through the thin mist from a solitary window at the top. They glanced at each other knowingly. There was no need for either of them to say it - they both knew that was where they would find Maledict.

But they weren't quite ready yet. For a few more seconds, they simply stood with their backs against the door, preparing themselves for what they were about to do. The sound of marching feet was louder now, echoing across the courtyard. From somewhere hidden within the Castle they could hear the barking of commands as trolls were called to arms. But this was not their battle. Theirs was far more perilous.

Gazing over the Castle battlements towards the sleeping city one final time, Peter felt his heart beating in his chest. Everything they had done before had come to this. He glanced at the Princess, signalling he was ready. She nodded back.

Slowly, they climbed into the air.

Chapter 9

Maledict's Secret Journey

The red light shining from the highest Tower window drew Peter and the Princess hypnotically towards it until they were hovering just outside, a hundred feet above the courtyard.

As they prepared themselves for the challenge they were about to face, the unmistakable sound of battle rose through the thin swirling mist beneath them. Dunstable had freed the Prince and the other Vikings, and they were fighting their way up the staircase, pushing the trolls back in a desperate attempt to escape. But Peter and the Princess took little notice. Their attention was focused solely on the task they were about to attempt. Slowly, without making a sound, they drifted through the open Tower window and passed into the dark room within.

They landed silently. A single candle was flickering dimly on the wall beside the window, leaving the rest of the room in shadow. As their eyes adjusted to the near darkness, a large stone table took shape in the centre of the room. Several enormous wooden chairs were scattered across the floor beside it as if the last meeting held there had ended suddenly. Seemingly confirming this theory, a second wilted candle sat in the centre of the table, its flame long since extinguished. They could both picture the scene of Maledict with his troll commanders gathered around the table, plotting the war against the Vikings. But whoever had been there had gone. The room, it seemed, was deserted. Then, as they crept forward towards the edge of the table, they saw him.

Sitting at the far end of the table at the back of the room, a tall dark figure was outlined in the darkness. He was watching them silently as if he had been waiting for them. A large oval stone was sparkling in the centre of his crown.

Peter froze in fear, his heart racing. He breathed in sharply, suddenly realising that he hadn't taken a breath for several seconds. Beside him, the Princess was crouching cat-like, her eyes fixed on the dark figure, ready for anything. Maledict neither spoke nor moved. He simply regarded them silently from the shadows at the far end of the room with the Viking Stone shining brightly on his forehead, daring them to take it.

The tension was almost unbearable. Peter and the Princess exchanged anxious glances, suspecting a trap. At any moment they expected to be attacked. Still Maledict neither moved nor spoke but continued to watch them, torturing them with his silence.

Perhaps ten seconds passed, though it seemed a lifetime. Peter couldn't stand the suspense! He needed something to happen – *anything* to break the oppressive silence! But it was the Princess who snapped first. Suddenly she raced forward and stood in front of Maledict, her fists clenched by her sides.

'Maledict! We have come for the Viking Stone! We have come to take back what you stole from us long ago! Fight us if you dare!'

Still Maledict didn't respond. He simply sat as still as stone as if he either hadn't heard what the Princess had said or didn't care.

Then the Princess marched up to Maledict and stood directly in front of him. Suddenly she pushed him as hard as she could, the flat of her palms rebounding off his chest. Maledict toppled backwards and crashed to the floor. As he fell his crown flew off his head and smashed beside him, the Viking Stone breaking into a thousand glittering pieces. There he lay, still and lifeless, the broken shards of glass scattered across the floor.

It took the Princess just a second to react. Clapping her hands together, a light suddenly appeared. Only then did Peter realise why the Princess had acted in the way she had. Lying on the ground at her feet was an empty brown coat, a pumpkin they had mistaken for a head and a false crown complete with fake Viking Stone, both shattered.

Peter stared at the Princess in disbelief. In the space of barely a second he had gone from an unbearable level of tension to complete and utter bewilderment.

'I...I don't understand!' he said finally. '*I don't understand!* What does this mean?'

The Princess was several steps ahead of him. Suddenly an expression of alarm spread across her face.

'Oh no! We must go! We must go *now!!!*'

'But...What...*Where?*'

'To the Viking Halls of course!! We have been fooled!'

'I don't under...'

But the Princess was already racing to the window.

'There is no time to explain! *Come on!!!*'

*

Thanks to the bravery of the Prince and the Vikings who had stayed and fought with him, most of his army had escaped and made it safely back to the Viking Halls. But despite their defeat and the capture of their leader, they didn't remain there for long. Immediately the Queen called a second emergency council meeting and desperate new plans were made.

In the course of the night, the trolls had taken the entire city. They were now standing on every street corner looking for Vikings, thinking the battle was already won. They were too many to drive back, of that there was no doubt. The Queen therefore proposed a different strategy. This time they would rely entirely on stealth and surprise. Travelling through the network of invisible snickelways that spread across York, small bands of Vikings would emerge in the dark streets and attack the trolls stationed there, disappearing back into the snickelways before they could react. In this way they hoped to harry the trolls, to make them fear attack at any moment and, eventually, force them to retreat.

It was a bold plan with considerable risk, as smaller bands of Vikings could easily be overwhelmed and cut off from help. The Queen was uneasy giving the order. But it remained their only hope until Peter and the Princess could recover the Viking Stone. At the very least, it would keep the trolls occupied whilst their daring Quest was attempted.

So, barely an hour after they had returned to the Viking Halls in defeat, the Viking army marched to war. Guided by the brave scouts who had been following the trolls, they fanned out along the numerous snickelways, only emerging when they were almost upon the troll battalions. Soon dozens of small battles erupted across the city, the clash of steel against steel echoing across the misty streets.

In the depths of the cold night in the ancient city of York, the fate of the Vikings hung in the balance.

*

Leaping onto the sill of the Tower window, the Princess dropped into the night air then rose as elegantly as a swallow. Peter was right behind her, still puzzling over what had just happened and why she was so alarmed. Side by side, they raced over the trolls and Vikings, whose fighting had spilled onto the Castle courtyard. In seconds they were streaking across the city, where fighting was taking place on every street corner. The whole of York, it seemed, was at arms. But the Princess ignored them all. Diving down, they sped towards the Minster and made a running landing just in front of the hidden entrance to the *MINSTER GATES* snickelway. Once inside, they darted through the golden gates and sprinted across the empty Debating Hall.

The Queen was sat in private council with two elderly Vikings when they burst into her room. She looked up sharply, her eyes briefly turning to Peter before focusing on the Princess. For a second the two of them stared at one another, reading each other's minds. Then the Queen rose to her feet, a look of alarm on her usually serene face.

'Come with me!' she commanded.

With the Queen leading, they raced into the Debating Hall then quickly crossed towards the entrance to the Candle Chamber behind the two thrones, its stone archway melting with a wave of the Queen's hand.

The chamber was quiet, just as it had been when the Queen had shown it to Peter when he had first entered the Viking Halls. The few candles that were still lit cast flickering shadows on the roof high above them. Though it appeared the same, something was inexplicably different. Peter sensed it the moment they entered. A heavy, tense atmosphere hung in the air. Something, or someone, had disturbed the peaceful reverence of the chamber.

Led by the Queen, they swept down the narrow pathway that led through the sea of candles until they finally reached the altar in the middle of the enormous hall. There, once again, Peter beheld the eternal flame of the Vikings. Burning brightly, it was swaying rapidly from side to side as if in distress. At the base of the altar on the far side were the remains of the root of Yggdrasil, a long black scar cut across its withered bark. At its centre, a slender stem drooped where once the tree's fruit had hung before Maledict had cut it and fashioned the Viking Stone.

The Queen strode up the steps of the altar and approached the agitated flame. Suddenly Peter noticed something strange. When he had seen it before, the flame had been a vibrant shade of blue. Though its edges were still flickering with that colour, its heart was now burning black. For a moment, the Queen stood directly in front of it as if looking for something within its burning core. Then she stepped forward and reached into its dark centre with her bare hand.

Both Peter and the Princess stared at her in horror, unable to cry out they were so shocked. The Queen's hand – no her *entire arm* - was now inside the flame! Then, just as they were about to race to her aid, she stepped backwards and withdrew. To their surprise, her arm was untouched. There was no burning, no scarring. It was just as white and smooth as it had been before.

The Queen's hand was clenched into a fist. Slowly, as if dreading what she would find, she opened it. A small metal object was sitting in the centre of her palm. Immediately she gasped and staggered backwards, her eyes wide with disbelief. The Princess held her hand to her mouth in dismay. Even the two Viking elders behind them blanched in shock.

Peter stared at each of them in turn, unable to understand what had caused such a reaction. Then he turned back to the Queen. In her palm was a steel ring. At first he didn't realise what it was, then he recognised it. It was a troll nose ring.

'I…I don't understand!' he stuttered in confusion. 'What does it mean?'

No one replied. Finally the Queen raised her head, her eyes cold and expressionless.

'Maledict has stolen it. Soon Ragnarok will be upon us.'

Peter felt a shadow fall across him at the mention of that word, but he didn't falter. He desperately needed to understand what had happened.

'Stolen…stolen *what?*'

'He has stolen the key. Now we are lost!'

'Key? *What key?*'

The Queen turned towards him, her face drained of colour.

'The key to the chain that binds the wolf Fenrir. Maledict has stolen it! If the Wolf is freed, Ragnarok will begin and our most terrible prophecy will be fulfilled. We have been fooled. We believed he only wanted to drive us out of York, but it seems he always had another more sinister plan in mind. We have been blind!'

Then it all came back to Peter. He remembered what Sigurd had said, seemingly so long ago, and the tomb in the haunted graveyard where the Princess had explained the Viking prophecy of the end of the world. Both times he had barely understood what they were saying, distracted by his fear of a man who had been dead for over a thousand years or his fear of the ghostly graveyard. But now it seemed as if everything that had happened was leading up to this point. Maledict had fooled them all.

Staring at each of them in turn, he implored them not to give up hope with his eyes. But no one returned his gaze. All hope, it seemed, was lost.

*

Precisely two hours earlier, a twelve year-old boy was peering through the bedroom window of a large house beside St Helen's Square in the centre of York. He had been up for some time despite the late hour, sensing that something strange was happening outside. At first, he'd simply gazed down at the streets, peering through the fog uneasily. But for the past twenty minutes he'd been watching the strange man who was standing in a shop doorway on the edge of the Square below him.

The man appeared to be waiting for something, or someone. He hadn't moved since the boy had first noticed him. But that was not the main reason why the boy was so interested in him. It might have been a trick of the dim streetlight or the fog, but the man looked strangely *hazy*. When the boy stared at him he could see nothing but a slightly darker shade against the shop doorway that, under normal circumstances, he would have dismissed as a shadow. But when he focused on the street opposite the Square, he could see the man out of the corner of his eye, seeming to mock his attempts to study him properly.

Beyond even this peculiarity, there was something else about the man, something he couldn't quite put his finger on. There was a strange aura about him of power and fear. He was certainly glad that he was inside his bedroom and not out on the dark foggy streets! Despite his anxiety though, or perhaps because of it, the boy couldn't help staring at him, part wishing he could see him more clearly, and part thankful that he could not.

Meanwhile, across the street on the edge of the Square, Maledict remained perfectly still as he contemplated what he was about to do. The freezing fog did not bother him in the slightest. It had, after all, been his own creation. A spell as old as the hills had created it, and it had served him well, as he knew it would. Now it would be his ally in the great task he was about to undertake.

The foolish Vikings had not guessed his intention, of that he was sure. Otherwise they would not have been so rash. They were only concerned with the battle that was being fought on the city streets. But that concerned him little. It was purely a means to a much more important end. Let them fight! Their cause was hopeless anyway, he would see to that. Tonight he would win the final victory, and it would be far more devastating than they could ever have imagined.

Time passed slowly, but he remained patient. As he waited, he knew that the Vikings would be holding a Council and deciding what actions to take. Their arrogant Prince had walked into a trap and been captured, fool that he was. They had suffered their first defeat. It would not be their last. The time had almost come.

Finally, the signal he had been waiting for came. Just across the Square, a faint light appeared, barely piercing the fog. Suddenly a Viking stepped out of what a moment before had been the brick wall of a bank, closely followed by another and then another. Soon a dozen fully armed Vikings were crowded on the edge of the Square. They crept stealthily away from him as they searched for the trolls they intended to ambush. For a moment, one of them looked in his direction as if sensing his presence, but his dark coat hid him well and the Viking did not see him. Then, one by one, they disappeared into the fog.

Maledict smiled grimly behind the folds of his hood. So, the counter-attack had begun at last! All across the city the Vikings would be making their way through their cursed snickelways, seeking to surprise the trolls and launch their raids before sneaking back and hiding like timid rats! He couldn't help laughing at their foolishness. It was exactly what he had expected.

He waited until the last of them had disappeared into the fog, seeking the band of trolls he had positioned at the opposite end of the Square to bait the trap. Then he casually strolled out of the shop doorway towards the wall through which the Vikings had appeared. Standing before it, he made a sign with his hands and muttered a quiet command. Suddenly the light re-appeared, revealing an entrance into a brightly lit passageway. With a brief glance behind him, he stepped inside and vanished.

In the house across the Square, the boy gasped and almost fell over in shock. He stared at the seemingly normal wall through which the man had disappeared. Was it a trick of the fog, or had he really walked straight through it? He had definitely seen something there: a tall old-fashioned lamp and a brief glimpse of a strange passageway! He was absolutely positive he'd seen something!

A cold sweat formed on his brow. He glanced at his watch. It was past two o'clock in the morning. Perhaps the ghostly stories he'd heard about York were true after all? If there were ghosts in York, it would be on just such a foggy night that they would appear. Retreating from the window, he suddenly paused to listen. There was a strange sound in the air – a faint metallic ring as if an ancient battle was being fought somewhere close by. Then his fear overcame him. Throwing the curtains together to block out the fearful night, he leapt under his bed. Not daring to move, he closed his eyes and prayed for the night to end.

*

As Maledict wound his way through the magic snickelways, dark memories came flooding back to him. It had been over a thousand years since he'd last walked these passageways. The last time had been when he'd set his axe to Yggdrasil and drunk its sap. Since then, he had hunted the Vikings from afar, forcing them to hide in their forsaken halls. Now he would finish what he had begun. Now, at last, he would destroy the Vikings forever.

So far, his plan had worked perfectly. His dramatic entry into the city, his spell to create fog that had allowed his troll army to take the Vikings by surprise, his fooling of the Princess and the City

Dweller Peter. That had particularly amused him. They had sought to thwart him (as if they ever could), but by now the Princess would have died a terrible death at the hands of his troll torturers. And as for Peter, after what had been done to the Princess, he would meet the boy soon enough. He had no doubt about that.

The boy had been much on his mind recently. There was something about him - something he couldn't quite put his finger on. It reminded him of something he'd felt long ago. It had been nagging away at the back of his mind. For a while it had worried him, but not any longer. Now it was too late.

He turned the final corner into the *MINSTER GATES* snickelway and faced the golden gates. Almost immediately a voice spoke out, as if coming from the gates themselves:

Speak your name so I may decide
If I will let you come inside.
If a friend then do not fear
For you will find a welcome here.
But if a foe then please beware.
Viking Magic guards this lair!

He smiled coldly. The Vikings and the pathetic magic they were so proud of! How arrogant they were, thinking they were safe in their underground hovels! Time had passed them by and now they would perish as they should have done long ago. He would see to it personally.

He stood in the bright passageway in front of the gates and closed his eyes. Suddenly the light around him began to pulsate, first brighter then paler. At the same time, a great gust of wind blew up from nowhere. Its force was so strong that a grey cloud of dust was lifted from the ground and walls. It swirled around Maledict as he stood perfectly still, dramatically increasing in force until it spun like a tornado. Then, just when the wind became so strong that the brick walls of the snickelway began to shake, he opened his eyes and reached out to touch the gates.

As soon as his fingers made contact, the whirlwind he had created raced forward. It struck the gates full on with a force so violent that the ground shook beneath his feet. For a moment everything stood still in silent anticipation. Then, as if humbly admitting defeat, the gates swung open in front of him.

Completely undisturbed, Maledict straightened his coat, shook it free of dust, and stepped into the Viking Halls.

The Debating Hall was deserted. Almost all the Vikings were in the city fighting the trolls, just as he had anticipated. Pausing for a moment, he stared at the balconies rising high above him. When he had last been here, there had been enough Vikings to fill the entire hall. But not anymore.

Gazing past the thrones of the Queen and her foolish son in the distance, he turned his eyes towards the stone archway that led to the Candle Chamber.

Within a minute he had made his way across the vast hall, so eager was he to be about his task. He examined the archway for a second, pressing his ear close to the stone as if listening for the spell that would allow him to pass through. Then, with a dismissive gesture of his hand as if the puzzle was too easy for him, the doorway disappeared and he casually strolled into the Vikings' most sacred place.

All was quiet and still as he made his way along the path that led through the candles. Finally he reached the centre of the vast chamber and gazed up at the Eternal Flame. Now, at last, he paused to reflect on what he was about to do. This was the moment - the moment he had so carefully planned. He would either change the world forever as he had vowed, or abandon his plans and return to exile. The world was waiting for his decision.

As he considered his intentions, he stared at the tall blue flame. It represented all he had come to hate: the Vikings and their pathetic magic, their arrogance, and their faith in the City Dwellers who had abandoned them. Had the time finally come to extinguish its light forever? Was he the one destined to be the instrument of the Vikings' most dreadful prophecy? He mounted the steps of the altar until he stood just inches away from the flame. Then he reached into its burning core with his bare arm.

Immediately its colour changed from blue to orange then darkest red. As he gazed up at it, doubt entered his heart over the magnitude of what he was about to do. Then the pain hit him and he began to scream.

No one had ever endured such pain and lived! The flame, the burning heart of the Vikings, fought back against the invasion of evil. No spell could subdue it, hard though he tried to conjure one. Nothing could protect him against the terrible intensity of its fire as it bit deeply into his flesh. But as his screams echoed off the far walls as if mocking his torment, his hand closed around what he was looking for. Then the pain became too much. Unable to stand, he staggered backwards, crashing down the steps to the bottom of the altar, the prize held tightly in his grasp.

For several minutes he lay motionless on the floor. Finally he managed to force himself into a sitting position. Raising his right arm, he stared at it in horror. All the flesh to his shoulder was scorched black. The skin was completely burnt away, leaving a raw weeping wound. Bending his head back, he screamed his agony once more.

Revenge, though, would soon be his. Slowly he opened the burnt fingers of his fist. Sitting in his palm, only a few inches long, was the key - the key to Fenrir the Wolf's chain. For a moment he almost forgot about the pain as crazed elation consumed him. He had done it! He would be the instrument of the Viking prophecy! Once the Wolf was released, Ragnarok would commence. The world of the Vikings would come to a devastating end and, when the dust settled, he alone would remain.

Clutching his burned arm, he rose unsteadily to his feet. The pain was gone now, replaced by an evil madness. He looked at his arm and laughed. What was it anyway but mere flesh and bone? Such a small price to pay for so great a reward! He turned to leave, but almost immediately he stopped. Striding back up the steps of the altar, he stood in front of the flame once more and spat in contempt.

'I have won! I have the key! I have won!' he screamed, his voice echoing across the vast emptiness of the hall. As he spoke, the few remaining burning candles flickered hesitantly, their flames bowing in trepidation. He glared at them, his head turning to survey the hated chamber. 'Behold the token I leave you in my contempt!'

Reaching into his coat pocket, he took out a nose ring which he had removed from a disobedient troll just a few hours earlier. His face a mask of insanity, he reached into the flame once more with his charred hand. Laughing as the pain surged through him again, he placed the ring where the key had rested just moments before.

'I have won!' he repeated weakly as he withdrew his scorched arm. *'I have won!!'*

Barely able to stand, he stumbled down the steps then staggered back down the central path through the candles. As he passed them, his voice echoed into oblivion and the hall fell silent again. But he barely noticed. The decision had been made – the final step taken. Now the consequences would have to be faced, for him and all the Vikings. The Viking prophecy would be fulfilled, and the world was about to dramatically change.

Chapter 10

The Dark Abbey

A deathly silence filled the Candle Chamber. Finally the Queen spoke, her voice so quiet they barely heard her.

'So the prophecy has come true after all. Why has Sigurd not come to our aid? Now more than ever we need him to return!' She raised her head as if suddenly aware that she had been speaking aloud. Her eyes fell on Peter. 'It is sad that you should have come to us at a time such as this. We could have taught you much about our world. It is too late now. Go back to your mother and prepare as best you can. City Dwellers should fear the coming storm as much as us, though they will not realise its significance until it is too late.'

Hardly believing what he was hearing, Peter stared into her eyes, searching for hope. But the Queen looked very different from the regal figure he had first met. Now she appeared tired and forlorn, as if a great burden weighed upon her that she couldn't cast aside.

Then something strange happened. Seeing her looking so sad and weary as if she had already given up, Peter suddenly became angry.

'You can't just…*give in!* Not after all we've been through!' He thought quickly, aware that everyone was staring at him in shock that he had spoken to the Queen in such a manner. 'I mean, there *has* to be a way to stop Maledict! Where is Fenrir chained? Is he in York?'

The Queen regarded him sadly.

'No, he is not in York. But we cannot hope to overtake Maledict and reach the Wolf before he does. Even now he will be nearing his destination.'

But Peter was not willing to admit defeat just yet. Crossing his arms stubbornly, he glared at the Queen. Suddenly an idea occurred to him.

'Your gift! The speed potion! Don't you remember? We haven't used it yet! We could take some and go after him! Who knows how fast we could fly? We might still overtake him if we leave now!'

As he spoke he reached under his coat and jumper for the pouch that contained the Queen's magical gifts, his fingers fumbling in excitement as he frantically untied it. At the same time, the Princess, who had been looking as defeated as the Queen, suddenly came to life. She raced towards him.

'How much is there?'

Peter held up the tiny dark green bottle. There was little more than a mouthful, perhaps two at most.

'Enough for the two of us!' he declared optimistically. He turned back to the Queen. 'Where is Maledict headed for? We can still stop him! I *know* we can!'

Now as excited as he, the Princess reached for the bottle and twisted the top to uncork it.

'Wait!' commanded the Queen, laying her hand on the Princess's. 'Even with the speed potion you may still be too late! And what then? Have you considered what you will face? You will find yourself confronting Maledict *and* the onslaught of Ragnarok - *alone!* The Wolf will be set free! He will hunt you down! The Midgard Serpent will rise against you! The Fire Giants will rain fire upon you! I will *not* have you face such a fate!'

'What other option do we have?' demanded Peter. 'We can't just wait here until it's too late! At least we'll have a chance!'

'A chance? What chance? A chance to be the first to die? You have no comprehension of what you will face! I cannot allow it!'

'We must try!' insisted the Princess, her voice echoing in the vast chamber. She stood by Peter's side, her arms crossed defiantly. 'Peter is right! We can not just *give in!*'

The Queen regarded her, her face twisted with torment and grief.

'Think of what you will face! I cannot allow it! Let us speak no more of this foolishness!'

'*But...!*'

It was a crucial moment. Suddenly Peter knew precisely what to say.

'There is something I need to tell you. Something about the day I met Sigurd in the Viking graveyard. I didn't say anything before

– I don't know why. So much has happened since then. I think I understand it better now.'

All eyes turned towards him. For a moment Peter hesitated, but then he found his confidence again.

'Just before I met Sigurd, I found something. It was on Sigurd's gravestone. I think he put it there for me. Look!' He reached into his pocket and pulled out Sigurd's talisman. The golden dragon face glinted in the candlelight. 'I think it is a sign that he is going to return.'

As soon as they saw it, the Queen and the Princess gasped. When the Queen finally spoke, her voice was breaking with emotion.

'Do you know what you hold in your hand, Peter? It is Sigurd's token…a sign that he has not forgotten us!' She paused to regain her composure and stared into his eyes, trying to judge whether she should reveal a secret the Vikings had kept for more than a thousand years. Peter stared back at her confidently. When she spoke again, her voice was so quiet he could barely hear her.

'Long ago, Sigurd was the greatest Viking warrior. But his power was beyond mere strength in arms. Long before we found Yggdrasil in York, Sigurd was the first Viking to learn magic lore. Some thought his skills were a gift from the Gods and that Odin himself favoured him, though most claimed he gained his abilities through drinking dragon's blood. For many years he ruled us, and we became great under his guidance. We explored further than any had before, finding new lands on the other side of the world. But Sigurd's strength was his downfall. His own family became jealous and plotted against him. They stabbed him in his sleep…'

She paused for a moment and briefly glanced at Peter before continuing.

'Sigurd had many skills. One of them was the ability to see the future. He foresaw his own death. Realising that we would be unprotected when he died, he made a prophecy: when our need was the greatest, he would return from the dead. To remind us that he would return, he created a token. That token…*that token*…is the talisman you now hold in your hand.'

Again she paused and bowed her head as if she could scarcely believe what had transpired.

'Sigurd's promise was made long ago. Many generations of Vikings have lived and died since then, and most have forgotten the man he was. But now, it seems, he may be about to fulfil his vow!'

'Then we must go! We must go *now!*' insisted Peter. 'Don't you see? Sigurd needs us to stop Ragnarok! He is asking us to help him!'

For a few seconds the Queen hesitated, staring first at the Princess and then at Peter, torn by the terrible choices she faced. Both Peter and the Princess met her gaze with renewed confidence, their faces set in determination. Finally she closed her eyes and bowed her head in mournful resignation.

'I see there are mysteries here that I do not understand. I cannot stand in the way of whatever fate is about to unfold. *Go! Go now!* What little hope we have rests in you both! Go before it is lost! You will find the Wolf at the Old Abbey by the shores of the Viking Sea. That is where he was tricked long ago and finally subdued. I pray you find him still chained! He is monstrous!'

They didn't wait a moment longer. Side by side, Peter and the Princess raced through the Candle Chamber and the Debating Hall until, exhausted, they finally reached the golden gates. Passing quickly through them, they took the nearest snickelway exit at *MINSTER GATES*. Moments later they were standing on the cold city street once more, staring up at the Cathedral's twin towers that were looming high into the misty night.

'Let's hope this potion works!' said Peter earnestly as he held the tiny green bottle in his hand and pulled out the cork. Holding it carefully between his fingers, he took a small sip and passed it to the Princess. 'You do know where the 'Old Abbey' is don't you?'

The Princess frowned at him indignantly as she sucked the last drop.

'Of course I know where it is! It is on the coast about fifty miles away.' Passing the empty phial back to him, she gazed into the distance apprehensively as if calculating how long it would take them to fly there. 'I hope this potion works, otherwise we will never get there in time! Right! Are you ready? Let us go!'

Without waiting another second, they spiralled into the air side by side, the ground falling away beneath them alarmingly quickly as the Queen's potion took effect. In a heartbeat they were high above the city, gazing down at the Minster as it shone celestially in the night, a symbol of York and what would be lost if they failed. Then, with the Princess leading, they began the race to the coast.

It took Peter a minute to concentrate above the wind, which was roaring so loudly in his ears he thought they would surely burst. When he did, he was finally able to savour the unique experience of flying faster than a falcon. How fast were they flying? It was impossible to tell. At one point they streaked over a dual carriageway and, for a moment, they were above the cars. Fast though the cars were travelling, Peter and the Princess passed them so quickly that they might as well have been standing still.

It wasn't long before they left the houses and roads of the outskirts of York and reached the open countryside. Soon they were racing over countless patchwork fields, their dull monotony broken only by occasional clusters of grey farm buildings that huddled together as if seeking to escape the cold. Ahead of them, grey electricity pylons strode across the landscape like skeletal giants. Suddenly Peter became alarmed. They were flying so quickly they were in danger of striking the looping cables before they could react. The Princess appeared to share his concern as suddenly she climbed as fast as a rocket. Peter raced after her, revelling in the sensation of his stomach churning. A few moments later they were high above the world, gazing towards the distant horizon.

As they rose still higher, they entered thick grey cloud. Immediately the fields below them disappeared and they were surrounded by wispy fog. For a few seconds Peter was worried that he couldn't see anything except the Princess next to him. Then they broke through the other side of the clouds and he gasped in astonishment. Gone was the grey dreary night and the constant drizzle. Suddenly they were flying through crystal clear skies, whilst beneath them cotton-wool clouds stretched into the endless distance.

Peter was astonished by the sudden transformation. He felt as if they had entered a peaceful haven, far away from the madness of the world below. Everything was incredibly clear and intensely vivid. All around him, the stars were shining far more brightly than he'd ever seen them before. Even more miraculous was their number. The sky was absolutely filled with them! Thousands and thousands of glittering stars spread across the horizon, forming countless shapes and formations!

But the stars didn't rule the vast realms of the sky, magnificent though they were. Directly in front of him, hanging above the clouds like a shining pendant, was the glorious moon. Perfectly circular, it too had changed in this magical world above the clouds. From the ground it appeared small and distant, but here it was huge and intensely bright. It looked so close that Peter almost felt he could fly there and explore it for himself.

It took him several seconds before he was aware of anything other than the awesome sky. Finally, he glanced down to the clouds below them. For a moment he was puzzled. Moments earlier the world had been racing by beneath them at a startling rate, but now they barely appeared to be moving at all. The moon, the stars, even the grey clouds – nothing seemed to change even though he knew from the wind blasting against his face that they were travelling as fast as ever. Here, in the peaceful world above the earth, the distance from York to the sea, which he'd previously thought so great, was totally insignificant.

Too soon their journey approached its end. The Princess slowed in front of him and gestured that they should descend. Reluctantly, Peter followed her. Together they dropped into the grey cloud and out the other side, moving back into the chaotic world Peter knew so well.

In the distance, the lights of a town were shining brightly. Soon they could see rows of houses far below them, looking like fragile matchboxes. Most of them were dark, but in some Peter could see the blinking blue light of a television screen or the steady orange glow of a bedside lamp. Despite the early hour, several people, it seemed, were unable to sleep, forced into wakefulness by dark foreboding dreams.

Within a minute, they were above the town centre. They hovered for a moment and studied the landscape beneath them. The wind had picked up and the Princess's hair was blowing about her face, giving her a wild look. Brushing it aside, she pulled on Peter's flapping coat and pointed down. Just ahead, a grey blanket lay over the land. At first, Peter wasn't sure what it was, then realisation struck him. There, less than a mile away, was the vast expanse of the sea. It was the first time he'd seen it, and for a moment he was shocked. It was just so…*big!* Seemingly endless, it stretched as far as he could see into the distance.

The Princess turned towards it and they began to pick up speed again, diving lower. A large bay curled in a near perfect arc below them, a golden ribbon of sand separating the tall black cliffs that surrounded it from the grey restless water. Soon Peter could hear the waves crashing against the shoreline and smell the salty water and damp sand. Just beneath them, seagulls were spiralling, gazing at them with startled red eyes before dropping back down to their homes in the cliffs, their shrill cries rising above the roar of the waves.

They were directly above the sea now. Peter felt strangely drawn to it, fascinated by its movement and power as it dipped and rose. And now that they were closer, it was clear that something had disturbed it. Roused by the wind, great white tipped waves were crashing onto the shore, tossing the fishing boats moored in the harbour of the bay as if they were toys in a bath.

Turning his attention back to the land, Peter saw something strange in the distance. The Princess was staring at it too. Half a mile away on top of the highest part of the cliff was a dark, crumbling building. Clearly it had once been a great abbey, but something had happened long ago and now it was a pale imitation of its former glory. Yet despite its appearance, it somehow carried a sinister aspect. It was more of a feeling than anything else - a feeling that though the building appeared crumbled and broken, an evil power was lurking within its dark interior, silently waiting.

The Princess indicated that they should descend. Buffeted by the wind, they drifted down until they landed on the grassy cliff just outside the ruins of the abbey. The sea was directly beneath them, the air full of sea-spray as the waves crashed against the rocky shore. The moment they landed, a great shadow fell across the cliff. Far out to sea a storm was brewing. Black clouds were rolling towards the shore, hurled by the gathering wind. In moments they had filled the sky and the night became darker still. Suddenly there came a blinding flash of lightening that lit up the cliff, almost immediately followed by a deep rumbling of thunder that sounded as if it rose from the bowels of the earth rather than from the sky. Then, as the darkness returned, the rain came crashing down.

In seconds they were completely drenched. Sheets of icy rain poured down all around them. The Princess shouted, but her voice was lost in the clamour of the rain pounding the ground and the howling of the wind. Grabbing Peter's arm, she pointed to the abbey, though it was now so dark they could barely see it. Understanding at last, he nodded back and together they raced across the sodden earth towards its ruins.

As they darted inside, the roar of the storm was immediately silenced. Like the Viking church in York, no rain penetrated within the abbey, though most of its roof had long since crashed down to earth. As they gazed upwards they could see black clouds racing across the sky, but inside it was completely dry, and the only sound came from the rainwater dripping from their clothes onto the broken stone floor.

Now that they had escaped the torrent, they were able to study the abbey properly. At first glance it looked similar to the Minster, with its tall sweeping arches, wide nave and (what remained of) a central tower. But whereas the Minster exuded light and peacefulness, the abbey had an entirely different feel. A sinister atmosphere hung in the air that struck fear into their hearts the moment they stepped within its crumbling walls.

Shivering, they crept along the wide nave towards the centre of the ancient church.

'What are we looking for?' Peter whispered, as much to break the dreadful silence as for any other reason.

'Shush!' hissed the Princess. 'Something is wrong! I can feel it in the air!'

Peter could feel it too, though he was trying not to think about it.

'Do you think we got here in time?' he asked, ignoring her request for silence. 'Do you think Maledict is here?'

The Princess cast him an irritated sidelong glance.

'We will know soon enough. The Wolf is chained beneath the pulpit at the far end of the abbey!'

Peter sighed, resigned to his fate. He just wanted to get it over with, and was disheartened to learn they would have to creep to the far end of the abbey before they found out whether the Wolf was still chained. And what if they were too late? Even now, Fenrir could be watching them, hidden in the shadows. A shiver ran through his body. He forced himself to think of something else.

Slowly, cautiously, they crept towards the pulpit. Every few steps they paused and peered fearfully around them. But all remained quiet and still. After what seemed like hours, they reached the end of the nave. The abbey was in better condition here and the roof was intact, cutting out the pale light cast by the sky just when they needed it the most. For a moment they inched forward, unsure which direction to take in the darkness, then the crumbling pulpit reared up in front of them as if it had decided to reveal itself at last. Instantly they froze, holding their breath. They were about to find out if the Wolf was still chained. If he had been released, Ragnarok would soon be upon them. But the Wolf wouldn't be all they would face. If Fenrir was free, Maledict would also be here, and they would finally have to confront the dreaded Necromancer.

Silently, they stepped onto the raised pulpit. Standing completely still, the Princess stared straight ahead, as alert as a stalking cat. All remained quiet and still. Too quiet! Peter couldn't stand it any longer.

'Is he there?' he whispered. 'Is Fenrir there?'

The Princess threw him a furious glance. With a frantic wave of her hand she gestured for him to be quiet, then pointed ahead. For a moment he couldn't see what she was indicating, then he jumped in surprise. Just in front of them, almost hidden in the darkness, was a gigantic hole. Roughly circular, it was about sixty feet wide. It looked as if it had been hewn into the ground long ago. A stale repulsive smell rose from it.

Peter froze, his heart pumping like a train. But the Princess was fearless. As silent as a whisper, she crept forward until she was standing just inches away from the edge. Inspired by her bravery, Peter forced his trembling limbs to follow her.

Now at last they would discover whether they had arrived in time. Everything depended upon this moment. Ignoring the ever-increasing stench, they leant forward and peered over the edge of the pit.

Darkness! To their dismay, they could see nothing but impenetrable darkness, concealing whatever lay below! For a few seconds they simply stared agonisingly down, expecting to see evil eyes staring up at them. But the darkness remained, refusing to give up its secret.

The suspense became too much, even for the Princess. She glanced at Peter, signalling with her eyes what she was about to do. He understood immediately and tensed himself, ready to spring into the air.

With a barely audible clap of her hands, a ball of light appeared.

It blazed in front of her for a fraction of a second, then raced down to the bottom of the pit like a fire bolt.

Peter held his breath as the darkness leapt aside. He was expecting to see a hideous Wolf glaring up at them. But what he saw was worse – far worse.

Beneath them, the vast hole was empty. No wolf lay chained at the bottom. In fact, there was almost nothing there at all. *Almost* nothing, but not quite. Lying discarded in the middle of the pit was an enormous silver chain. It was at least thirty feet long and more than a foot thick. At either end it split into two gigantic manacles, both of which had been snapped open.

'Oh no!' exclaimed the Princess, her voice shaking with horror. '*Quickly!* We must find Fenrir before Ragnarok begins! We must chain him again before it is too late!'

'THAT MIGHT BE A LITTLE DIFFICULT, I THINK YOU'LL FIND,' said a deep, growling voice behind them.

Chapter 11

Fenrir the Wolf

Peter and the Princess spun around, taken completely by surprise. At first they couldn't see anything. Then they froze. Thirty yards away, a pair of enormous red eyes was staring at them scornfully through the darkness.

'Who – Who is there?' whispered the Princess, her voice breaking as even she felt fear.

'*WHO?* LET'S JUST SAY THAT I'LL BE YOUR HOST FOR THE REST OF YOUR LIVES, THOUGH THAT MAY NOT BE VERY LONG I'M AFRAID.'

The voice was incredibly deep, as if it was coming from the bottom of a well. It echoed menacingly across the empty abbey. Full of evil power, it was the voice of an arrogant bully who knew he was stronger than anyone else, and delighted in torturing and teasing his victims.

The red eyes moved slowly closer, but the darkness still concealed the creature they belonged to. Hypnotised by their unblinking intensity, Peter and the Princess retreated towards the edge of the pit. But there was nowhere left for them to go. Only the southern end of the abbey lay beyond the pulpit, its grey wall towering above them. For a moment, Peter wondered whether they could escape by flying through the broken roof, and glanced quickly upwards. But the creature had chosen its ambush well. They were in the only part of the ancient church to have retained its roof. Their only escape route was to fly over the head of the creature and flee the abbey on the other side where they had come in. But judging by the height of the eyes above the ground, whatever they were facing was truly huge.

The stale odour was much stronger now, making them feel sick and weak. Tottering on the edge of the pit, they could retreat no further. Their only choice was to face the menace that approached them.

The red eyes continued to stare at them. They held a strange power. It seemed to drain them of hope. Resistance was pointless. They were already defeated. Soon they would be dead.

As meek and timid as rabbits, they awaited their fate. Then, as if the creature was playing a cruel game, the eyes blinked and the spell was broken.

Furious with herself, the Princess stepped boldly forward.

'Show yourself! Only a weakling hides in the dark!'

'*WEAKLING?* I THINK YOU'LL FIND ME QUITE A HANDFUL, EVEN FOR YOU PRINCESS.'

The Princess took another step towards the burning eyes.

'I know who you are! Show yourself, foul Wolf!'

As soon as she spoke, the two red eyes flashed in anger, their evil intensity so bright that Peter staggered backwards and almost fell into the pit. To his horror, the eyes moved menacingly closer. The smell became so intense he could barely breathe. Then, as he watched in terrified fascination, a gigantic grey shadow began to take shape in the darkness, centred around the fiery eyes. Slowly, the horrifying form of an enormous wolf emerged, its great jaws agape and its white teeth shinning.

'YOU *KNOW ME* PRINCESS? I SHOULD THINK YOU DO! I HAVE KNOWN MANY OF YOUR KIND. FOR A SHORT TIME THAT IS – UNTIL I *DEVOURED* THEM! I AM FENRIR, GREATEST OF THE WOLF BROOD! HARBINGER OF RAGNAROK! SLAYER OF VIKINGS! NOW I HAVE BEEN FREED AT LAST! SOON MY BROTHER THE SERPENT WILL RISE FROM THE GREAT SEA! SOON THE FIRE GIANTS WILL SCORCH THE EARTH! THE END HAS COME FOR ALL VIKINGS! BUT YOU WILL BE THE FIRST TO MEET YOUR DOOM!'

His voice thundered from wall to wall and the ground shuddered as if it too felt fear. Even the Princess was shaken and for a moment she was unsure what to do.

Now horribly revealed in the faint light, Fenrir sat back on his haunches and regarded them nonchalantly. Twice the height of a double-decker bus, his great muscles bunched as he languidly stretched out his front legs like a cat that had just woken from a long rest. The claws in his enormous paws sprang out then withdrew as he flexed them lazily.

'SO, WHAT DO WE HAVE HERE? A CRINGING VIKING PRINCESS AND A BOY! A STRANGE COMBINATION! IS THIS THE BEST THERE IS TO FACE ME NOW THAT I AM FREE AT LAST? STILL, I DO LIKE A LITTLE VARIETY AT MEAL TIMES. TOO MUCH OF ONE THING IS NOT GOOD FOR THE DIGESTION, YOU UNDERSTAND. I HAVE ALREADY DINED ON A FEW TROLLS OF COURSE, BUT THEIR FLESH IS TOO TOUGH FOR MY LIKING. STILL, IT IS FORTUNATE FOR YOU THAT I HAVE JUST HAD A RATHER LARGE MEAL. OTHERWISE YOU WOULD ALREADY BE DEAD.'

He paused for a moment and casually licked his great paws, each of which was the size of a car.

'SHOULD WE TALK FOR A WHILE? I HAVE A FEW MINUTES TO KILL BEFORE THE SERPENT ARRIVES AND WE SET ABOUT OUR WORK. YOU COULD BEG FOR MERCY IF YOU LIKE? OR SCREAM OUT FOR HELP, PERHAPS? THAT ALWAYS AMUSES ME! OR PERHAPS YOU'D LIKE TO RUN AROUND AND TRY TO ESCAPE? A LITTLE LIGHT EXERCISE WILL SOON BRING MY APPETITE BACK!'

The Princess stared at the Wolf with revulsion. Somehow overcoming her fear, she took another step forward.

'Do not flatter yourself, slave of Maledict! We have come here to destroy you and the Serpent, if he dares to appear!'

Lowering his long black snout, Fenrir almost seemed to grin down at them, his sharp white incisor teeth revealed.

'OH VERY GOOD! VERY GOOD INDEED! I DO LIKE THE BOLD ONES! SO VERY RARE YOU KNOW. MOST OF MY VICTIMS ARE TOO TERRIFIED TO PUT UP MUCH OF A FIGHT. SO TERRIBLY DISAPPOINTING! BUT NOW IT SEEMS YOU MUST PROVE YOUR WORTH, PRINCESS, IF YOU ARE TO STOP ME AND THE DESTRUCTION I WILL SHORTLY REAP. LET US SEE IF YOU FARE ANY BETTER THAN THE THOUSANDS OF VIKINGS I HAVE DEVOURED BEFORE YOU!'

Suddenly he rose to his feet and glared down at her, his eyes shining so malevolently that Peter would have cried out if terror hadn't frozen his tongue.

The Princess remained uncovered. Her face set defiantly, she stepped forward until she was standing just yards from the Wolf, who continued to watch her. His enormous snout was raised high above her head and his deadly white teeth were shining. She looked so small with the huge beast towering over her. But now she had regained her poise. Gone was the timid girl the Wolf had surprised. In her place was a Viking Princess in her prime, powerful and awe-inspiring. To Peter, who was crouching a few yards behind her fighting his fear, she seemed to glow with pure white light that shone in the darkness as if no evil could subdue it. As she confronted the Wolf, her eyes focused with deadly intent. She raised her hands in front of her and blue light crackled between them.

'Foul Wolf, you have murdered your last Viking! Prepare to meet your end!'

With an ear-splitting crack, blue light sped from her hands towards the Wolf. It was so bright that for a second the whole abbey was lit in perfect clarity. But half way to its target it suddenly lost its energy and fizzled out into nothing. Once again, darkness descended except for the Wolf's fiery red eyes, burning in amusement.

'PROBLEM PRINCESS? DID YOU REALLY THINK YOUR PUNY MAGIC WOULD WORK AGAINST ME? I AM FENRIR! I AM NOT FEARED BY ALL THE GREAT WHO HAVE WALKED THIS EARTH FOR NOTHING! LONG AGO I WAS CHAINED, BUT NOT BY GREATER STRENGTH WAS I CAPTURED! A TRICK - A FOUL WEAKLING'S TRICK DEVISED BY THOSE WHO FEARED ME! PERHAPS YOU THINK YOU ARE MORE POWERFUL THAN THE OTHERS I HAVE FACED? DEAR PRINCESS, I WAS DEFEATING FAR GREATER OPPONENTS THAN YOU CENTURIES BEFORE YOU WERE BORN! PLEASE FEEL FREE TO TRY AGAIN THOUGH. I DO LIKE A LITTLE ENTERTAINMENT AT MEAL TIMES.'

For the first time since Peter had known her, the Princess looked utterly lost. She took a step backwards and stared at her hands as if she couldn't believe her magic had failed. Then she glared at the Wolf, hatred in her eyes. Suddenly blue light streaked from her finger-tips, cutting through the darkness towards the dark hulking figure opposing her. But before it could reach him it faded into nothing again.

'TUT TUT PRINCESS! THAT WAS EVEN WORSE THAN YOUR FIRST FEEBLE EFFORT! I HOPED YOU WOULD BE BETTER THAN THIS. YOU ARE OF ROYAL BLOOD AFTER ALL. OR PERHAPS I WAS MISINFORMED? MAYBE THE VIKINGS

ARE WEAKER NOW THAN THEY WERE. I WAS WARNED IT MIGHT BE SO! SUCH A PITY AFTER WAITING SO LONG! I AM SO DISAPPOINTED!'

Slowly Fenrir advanced towards her. The Princess took another step backwards. She looked utterly bewildered, unable to understand why her magic hadn't worked. Again Peter thought how very small she looked as the enormous wolf towered over her. With a cry of frustration, blue light sped from her hands and raced towards the Wolf. But Fenrir simply laughed at her efforts.

'IS THAT ALL YOU CAN MUSTER? AND I THOUGHT YOU WOULD BE SPECIAL. A CHALLENGE AT LAST! I SEE THAT I WAS WRONG.'

Enraged by the Wolf's goading, the Princess raised her hands and once more blue light raced towards him. But even Peter could tell it was weaker this time. The Princess was exhausted.

Fenrir regarded her scornfully as she shrank back towards the pit, barely able to stand. She glanced at Peter. The moment their eyes connected seemed to last an eternity. She was asking – no *imploring* – him to help her before it was too late. But Peter was so terrified he couldn't move. All he could do was watch, haunted by her face, as Fenrir advanced upon her, a vast fearful shadow in the darkness.

As Peter fought his fear, desperately trying to force his petrified muscles to move, he suddenly thought about Sigurd's talisman and how it had helped him in the past. But even before he attempted to force his shaking hand to reach for it, a strange sensation began to well up inside him. He could feel it tingling through his body like a cold shiver, only it was warm – warm and comforting like standing in front of a fire on a cold winter's night. A heartbeat passed as he battled with his fear, furious and ashamed of its hold upon him. Then something happened. He felt it distinctly. A source of strength and power rose within him just like he had experienced before. But now it was stronger – much, much stronger. For the first time in his life he felt wonderfully sure of himself. For a moment he thought it odd. He hadn't even touched the talisman. Then he cast his doubt aside. It didn't matter what had caused his transformation. It was the most natural feeling in the world.

Fenrir was now just a few yards away from the Princess, torturing her with his malice. Suddenly he pounced. Before she could react, he pinned her to the ground beneath his great paw.

The Princess tried to fight back, struggling under his weight. But Fenrir was in no hurry. Toying with his defenceless victim, he let her raise herself on one elbow before cruelly pushing down again, crushing her with his terrible strength. For a few seconds longer she struggled against him, determined to confront her enemy, but then Fenrir leant on her fragile body and she fell back lifelessly onto the ground. There she lay, utterly helpless. Fenrir pulled his head back and howled in victory.

But even as the Wolf's triumphant cry was echoing across the abbey, Peter's transformation was complete. As his new awareness consumed him, he was surprised to find that he was huddled on the ground, so great had been his fear. Calmly he rose to his feet and walked towards the Wolf.

Fenrir didn't see him. All his attention was focused upon the Princess. His great jaws were open and his black tongue was dripping with saliva in anticipation of his meal. He was about to bite when a powerful voice spoke behind him.

'Leave her alone foul Wolf! Touch her and I will make you regret it!'

With frightening speed, Fenrir spun around to face him, his piercing red eyes flashing with fury. A part of Peter was terrified when he felt the weight of the Wolf's animosity fall upon him. Somewhere deep inside him, a voice was crying out in fear, astonished that he dared face such a terrifying creature - a creature that had so easily defeated the Princess. But that voice was far away, so deep beneath the surface he was hardly aware of it. The rest of him was calm. He had never felt more sure of himself in his life.

Fenrir spat in disgust.

'YOU *DARE* TO CHALLENGE *ME?* A PUNY HUMAN – WEAKEST OF ALL CREATURES? HOW *DARE YOU* INTERRUPT MY FEASTING?'

For one final time, the timid voice within Peter whispered in terrified amazement, telling him to flee for his life before it was too late. But he easily ignored it. A stronger one urged him on; a voice that was without fear.

Without debate, without wasting time with pointless words, Peter struck out. He raised his right hand and instantly the Wolf was hurled backwards as if he had been hit by a train. He crashed into a stone pillar thirty yards away.

Fenrir was stunned. His body shaking, he leapt to his feet, roaring in fury. Never in all his battles had he been hurt before! Even the most powerful Viking had barely touched him. Now a City Dweller - not even an adult City Dweller - was causing him unbearable pain!

But his astonishment lasted for only a second. Then he attacked. With all the fury of a Great Wolf, the strongest of a breed that had not walked the earth for hundreds of years, he leapt towards Peter in one fearsome bound. No more to tease, no more to toy. First to bite and subdue, then to tear and destroy.

As Peter watched Fenrir rise gracefully into the air, time seemed to slow. As the Wolf descended towards him, he could see his jaws gaping wider. His heart beat once inside him, long and full. Then, just when the Wolf was directly above him, he raised his right hand, his palm pushing forward.

The result was devastating. It was as if Fenrir had struck an invisible wall. Yelping in pain, he crashed to the ground, landing in a crumpled heap in front of Peter. In an instant he was back on his feet. Immediately, he leapt away from the unbelievably powerful opponent he faced.

Now it was Fenrir who was unsure of himself as he paced along the wide nave at the centre of the abbey, forty yards from Peter. Like a tiger who had been defeated by a mouse, he backed away then turned to face his assailant, unsure whether he should fight or run. But Fenrir was not feared for his strength alone. His cunning was also renowned. As he paced, he was alert to any sign of weakness, looking for a way to crush his opponent without further risk to himself. He knew that the Midgard Serpent would soon be coming to shore and the Fire Giants would be gathering. But in his great pride he didn't want to wait, held up by a mere human. He determined to crush this foul creature before they arrived. Gathering himself, he waited for the right moment to attack.

Peter knew little about wolves and their cunning. Even if he had, he wouldn't have wavered. His intention was clear: to defeat Fenrir, chain him again and so, he hoped, stop Ragnarok before it began. He had no fear; he had no doubt.

Stepping forward, Peter was about to attack when he heard a small sound behind him. From the darkness on the edge of the pit, the Princess had whispered his name. For a fraction of a second he hesitated, suddenly unsure again, and glanced towards her as she lay completely still.

That was the moment Fenrir had been waiting for. Instantly he leapt into the air, throwing himself forward from his powerful hind legs, striking as fast as a cobra. With one great swipe of his fearsome paw he planned to be rid of this irksome human once and for all.

As Peter turned from the Princess to see that terrible blow descend upon him, the world of magic and miracle was revealed around him. Suddenly he was surrounded by brilliant radiance. All around him, countless thin strands of golden light appeared, criss-crossing each other in a vast network. Every single thing had a bright strand attached to it - the Wolf leaping towards him, the Princess lying on the ground, the crumbling stones in the abbey walls, the blades of grass creeping through the cracks in the floor. And there, as clear as could be, a thin strand of light was connected to his waist.

He was beginning to understand how magic worked. Nothing existed in isolation. People, animals, plants, stones – all of them were connected. Everything was dependent upon everything else. Limitless energy surrounded him – the energy of life and the universe itself. And he could control it if he wished. To create or enhance. To change the world at its most fundamental level. This was magic. It was so simple, so beautiful.

Fenrir's paw struck him full across the side of his body and he felt himself flung violently into the air. It seemed to last an age. He saw the body of the Princess fall away beneath him. He'd been thrown a hundred feet already. Soon he would be crushed against the wall of the abbey. But he didn't feel any pain. In fact, he'd never felt better in his life.

When he was ready, he simply decided to stop. As effortlessly as standing still, he gently alighted on the ground behind the Wolf, completely unharmed.

Fenrir turned in triumph to witness the destruction of his enemy. But when he saw Peter land so easily, his snarl of victory faded into silent disbelief. Peter smiled. Slowly, with complete assurance, he walked towards the Wolf.

That was too much for Fenrir. The blow should have killed the foul creature! Now he was strolling towards him with a smile on his face as if he hadn't a care in the world! This was not a fight for him. He could wait until Ragnarok after all, then the human would be destroyed sure enough! Gathering himself, he sprang into the air. Scaling the abbey wall, he leapt down the other side with a great rush of wind that was full of his foul stench. As the stones came crashing down behind him, he fled into the night, howling in humiliation.

Peter was about to fly after him, but then he paused and stared at the lifeless body of the Princess lying on the edge of the pit. Immediately his confidence and serenity evaporated as fear swept through him. At the same time, the network of light around him disappeared. Suddenly he was just a normal boy again – a boy alone and frightened in a dark place, far away from home. He shivered and ran over to where she lay.

The Princess was ominously still. Crouching beside her, he stared at the shadowy outline of her face and called out her name. But she didn't stir. Unsure what to do, he took her hand and rubbed it lightly. But still she didn't move. A cold sweat broke out on his forehead. Dreading the worst, he bent over and listened for her heart. Deep within her chest he heard a faint beat. The Princess was alive, but only just. The Wolf and the troll torturers had taken a dreadful toll on her body. She needed to be back in the Viking Halls, not lying on a cold stone floor in the dreadful abbey, surrounded by danger!

Leaning over her, he stared at her pale face. What should he do? He was faced with terrible choices. Should he leave her and try to stop Ragnarok? That would surely be the most sensible thing. But he was alone facing terrifying opponents. It was surely a hopeless task. Should he try to get help? But from where? No City Dweller would be able to see the Princess let alone help her, and the Vikings were far away in York fighting the trolls. He could lift her and try to carry her back to the Viking Halls, but by then it would be too late. Ragnarok would have started and all would be lost. He was faced by a terrible dilemma. *What should he do?*

As despair consumed him, he suddenly felt enormously weary, as if the hopelessness of his situation had exhausted him. He collapsed onto his knees and toppled forward, his forehead touching the cold stone floor beside the Princess. Finally he raised his head and stared over the gloomy heights of the abbey walls to the open sky, watching the dark clouds race by as the storm raged outside. He knew the horrible truth. There was only one option. He had to attempt the impossible: to chain the Wolf, defeat Maledict and stop Ragnarok.

Though he knew there was no time to delay, at that moment he couldn't face what lay ahead. Kneeling beside the Princess, he desperately tried to calm the panic that was building inside him.

Chapter 12

Maledict the Necromancer

Peter rose slowly to his feet. The storm raging outside the abbey had intensified. As he stared up through the broken roof to the sky, lightning flashed, illuminating the wall of rain falling from the black clouds above. At the same time, the earth shuddered as thunder growled overhead.

He gazed down at the Princess lying still and pale on the cold grey stone. He didn't want to leave her but he knew he couldn't wait any longer. He had made his decision. She would be safe in the abbey, sheltered from the driving rain and freezing wind until he came back for her. But he couldn't leave her at the edge of Fenrir's pit where his foul stench still lingered. Bending down, he reached underneath her body and lifted her in his arms. Finding her surprisingly light, he walked back down the nave to the crumbling wall through which they had entered the abbey and gently laid her on the ground against the remains of a pillar. As he stared down at her, there was another flash of lightning, and for a second the darkness fled and he could see her face. He was shocked by what he saw. A large, ugly red bruise had formed beneath her eye, and her lip was oozing blood onto her chin. Her face and neck were covered in long thin scratches and a second, even larger, bruise was forming at the base of her neck. Then the light was gone and she was hidden in the darkness once more, her face no more than a grey outline beneath him.

But now he had to leave her. Rising to his feet, he walked towards the broken wall and stared out at the rain pounding the muddy cliff just beyond the false peacefulness of the abbey. He paused for a moment more, then stepped into the tortured world outside.

Instantly the rain and wind struck him like a thunderbolt,

almost knocking him off his feet. Gritting his teeth, he ducked low to the ground and leaned into the gale, forcing his legs forward one step at a time. He risked a quick glance to see where he was going and was immediately struck full in the face by a wall of sharp hail. But he'd seen what he wanted. The top of the cliff was fifty yards ahead. When he reached it, he would have the best possible view of the layout of the land around the abbey.

As if sensing his purpose, the wind raged against him, trying to force him back. But now that he'd left the Princess safely behind, his resolve was strong again. Ducking his head down, he pushed himself forward until he finally reached the summit of the steep cliff. Only then did he know it for certain. Ragnarok was about to begin.

Far out to sea a great wave was forming. Something truly massive was coming to shore. But it wasn't what was happening in the sea that struck fear into his heart, ominous though it was - it was what was happening in the sky above him. A colossal wall of fire was slowly spreading across the eastern horizon, greedily consuming the black storm clouds in its path. Then, coming from somewhere hidden behind the flames, he heard a fearful sound above the howl of the wind and the crashing of waves upon the rocks below. At first he wasn't sure what it was, then he recognised it. It was the sound of horns – hundreds of war horns being blown wildly. A great army was approaching from the skies, spreading fire and destruction.

'It is the Fire Giants, unless I am very much mistaken,' said a deep voice behind him. 'We won't have long to wait now.'

Peter turned around slowly, already knowing to whom the voice belonged.

'Maledict,' he said simply.

The tall figure standing perfectly still a few yards down the grassy cliff bowed his head in mock acknowledgement.

'I was wondering when you would finally make your appearance. It isn't wise to keep me waiting, boy. Still, I am glad you are here to witness the end of the world with me. It should be quite a show, don't you think?'

Feeling strangely calm now that he faced the dreaded Necromancer at last, Peter regarded him closely, wondering why he hadn't already been attacked. Despite the gathering red light from the burning sky, it was difficult to see him clearly. Wearing a long, brown, waxed coat, his face was almost hidden behind a deep, black hood. Only his black eyes and his cruel smile were visible. The only other thing Peter could see was his crown. It shone brightly in the darkness behind the folds of his hood. In the centre was the Viking Stone, its flawless surface reflecting the red light from the burning sky.

Maledict in turn studied Peter. Seemingly impervious to the wind and the frantic billowing of his long coat behind him, he nodded towards the eastern sky.

'Wonderful isn't it? You should feel fortunate to be here with me to witness such a sight. It has caused me a great deal of pain to bring it about. But even I did not think it would be so spectacular!'

Peter didn't take his eyes of Maledict. He'd been dreading this moment for so long, but now that he faced him at last, he felt a desperate need to understand - to understand why Maledict had committed such evil.

'Why? Why did you do it?'

'*Why?*' Maledict's eyes flashed beneath his hood, though Peter couldn't tell whether it was with malice or amusement. 'You – a City Dweller – a member of a race that has devastated this world - ask me why I wish to bring about its destruction?' He focused on Peter with deadly intent. 'When you start something new, it is best to begin with a clean page. A fresh start, where all that is old and decayed is swept away. Have you ever seen what happens after a fire, boy? Everything that is weak is destroyed, *everything!* But once the flames are exhausted, the world rebuilds itself. After time, life begins again. But this time things are a little different. There is opportunity for new creation, to make things better than they were before. That is why! I intend to build a better world; to sweep aside all that is old and worthless. I seek to create a blank canvas upon which I can create a world that is how it should have been – a world where I will be the principle architect. Think what a glorious place that would be!'

He took a step closer to Peter then turned towards the sea, his long coat whipping in the gale behind him. Peter followed his gaze warily. The great wave he had spotted far out from shore was closer now. Peter could see it clearly – an enormous tidal wave with a foaming white peak, surging to shore. Above it the sky was burning red as vast plumes of flame rolled across it, consuming everything in their path. Meanwhile, the ominous blaring of war horns was gradually getting louder.

Peter couldn't watch any longer. Turning away, his eyes briefly fell on the Viking Stone in Maledict's crown as it glittered in the red light from the sky. For a moment he wondered whether he could reach it before Maledict could react. Before he could hide it though, Maledict realised his intention.

'Ah yes! The Viking Stone! Unfortunately, I cannot give it to you. Still, it has served another purpose. It has brought *you* to me!'

Peter was startled.

'I… I don't understand. You *knew* I was coming?'

'Do you think that I did not know about the Vikings' foolish plan to steal it from me? Did you think that I wouldn't guess that they would ask you to fight their battles for them? They have become so weak that even a City Dweller with a minor talent for magic is stronger than they are. It is no wonder there are so few of them left. Soon they will all be destroyed.'

Peter hesitated for a moment, feeling doubt for the first time since he had left the Princess. Then anger rose within him and he glared at the dark sorcerer. No longer did he want to understand him; now he just wanted to defeat him and find Fenrir. He prepared himself for the inevitable fight, waiting for the moment to strike.

Maledict caught his eye and they stared at each other for a moment in a test of wills, then Maledict turned away and gazed calmly out to sea again, certain of his victory. Several seconds passed before he spoke again.

'So, it has come to this! The Vikings prophecy has been fulfilled at last. I am glad that you are here to witness my final victory over the Vikings. Shame about what happened to the poor Princess. I was hoping my troll torturers would have killed her, but, then again, it would have been a shame to deny Fenrir his sport. After all, she was rather irritating, don't you think?'

That was it. After the slighting of the Vikings and his constant taunting, the insult against the Princess was the final straw. All the anger and frustration that had been building inside Peter suddenly erupted to the surface. In a rage greater than any he had ever felt before, he launched himself at Maledict, seeking to knock him down with the force of his flight.

But nothing happened. He couldn't move. He was rooted to the spot!

Maledict's smile broadened. With a final glance at the sea, he turned towards Peter.

'Shall we have a little chat, you and I? We have a few minutes to spare, I think, before the fun begins and the world comes to a violent end. Aren't you curious about the strange new world you have found yourself in and the magical powers you have developed? I have an offer to make you. I think you should at least hear me out.'

Mocked by Maledict's cynical voice, Peter couldn't move. His body simply refused to respond to his commands. He wondered if he had been paralysed.

'First, I need to explain something to you. Four times you have felt the magic within you. By now, you have guessed where it comes from. It is the energy that flows through every single thing in this world. You know what I speak of. You have seen them, I believe. The golden strands! The energy of creation and destruction flows along them - the force that binds atoms together or tears them apart. Nothing is more powerful!

'You do not yet understand what you have discovered. You have the greatest gift. Somehow you have learned the secret of how to tap into the strands and re-direct the flow of energy. That is no mean feat. If I had not seen it myself just now, I would never have believed it. You are one of the few to have even witnessed the strands, and the first for a thousand years to learn how to use them. That is your gift, boy. That is why you are still alive and standing here with me now, a witness to the beginning of the end of the world.'

Peter's mind was racing, struggling to take in the significance of what he was being told.

'Why are you telling me this?'

'Because the time has come. The time of change. History is being made. Even as we speak, my troll army is fighting the last Vikings in York. The Vikings will be no match for them. Victory will be swift and merciless. At first, that was all I planned. But that is no longer enough. Now I have a much grander design. No one will survive what is to come. Even if a few Vikings live through the battle, they will not survive Ragnarok. Not even my faithful trolls will survive that.

'A new age is about to begin, boy. The time of the Vikings and the ignorant City Dwellers has passed. Soon they will no longer exist.'

He turned to stare at the sea again, then lifted his right hand slightly. Immediately the invisible restraints that had bound Peter fell away and he toppled forward onto the muddy ground.

Jumping to his feet, he leapt towards Maledict, furious that he'd been made to look foolish.

'When Ragnarok starts, you will die too!'

Maledict slowly turned to face him, mocking him with his eyes.

'Do not take me for a fool, boy! Even my abilities have their limits. That is why I need the Viking Stone. The power of life itself is contained within it. With that power, not even Ragnorak can touch me. But fate has taken a hand. Once I thought that only I would live through what is to come. Now I have been delivered a worthy servant to help me in the task I will undertake once the storm has passed. That is why you are here, boy. That is why you are still alive!'

Peter was stunned.

'I will *never* help you!'

'If you do not agree to help me, you will die. Though you have discovered the lines of power, that will not save you from Ragnorak without my help. You have a simple choice. If you do precisely what I say, you will live through the coming storm. In return, you will work with me to re-build the world as I see fit. Think carefully, boy. Only I can save you. Without my help you will die, here, on this cliff.'

Maledict turned and stared out to sea again, his long coat billowing madly around him in the gale. For several seconds he watched the waves crashing against the rocks beneath them. Suddenly he laughed, his voice rising above the storm and the blasting of war horns.

'I do like it when a plan comes together! And the Vikings have played their part so very well! I couldn't have done it without them! The Prince and his foolish attack, the capture of the Princess, the emptying of the Viking Halls just when I needed to steal Fenrir's key. I couldn't have asked for anything more!' He paused for a moment and turned towards Peter. 'Ironic, isn't it? You were sent by the Queen on a foolish Quest to destroy me. Instead, you alone will survive and become my servant whilst all the Vikings perish! I do like a little irony. This is your destiny. The one you were born to fulfil. To stand by my side whilst all the Vikings are destroyed!'

Peter couldn't believe what he was hearing! Maledict had fooled them all – the Princess, the Prince, even the Queen! They had all walked blindly into his trap!

'How long have you been planning this? Did you always know about the Quest?'

'Of course I always knew about your pathetic Quest! The Vikings are so predictable. But I couldn't trust them entirely. I had to give them a little helper to ensure everything went smoothly.'

'A helper? Who?'

'Have you not guessed yet? Have you not wondered about that snivelling companion of yours who claims to have once escaped me?' Maledict laughed at the ridiculousness of the notion. 'Have you not *once* considered that he might not be what he seems?'

'Dunstable?'

'Dunstable! Of course! Who else? A pathetic creature, but a useful one. I let him go the first time so he would do my bidding and spy on the Queen for me. I thought he might prove useful. My mercy has been well rewarded.'

Peter was so shocked he was struck dumb! Finally he managed to speak, forcing the words out one by one.

'Dunstable was working for you all along?'

Maledict was clearly enjoying himself, gloating at his own cunning.

'You really are rather slow, boy. I hoped you would be more intelligent. Dunstable was given a choice. Do my bidding or die. He chose well under the circumstances.'

Peter was completely stunned! He thought back to the time he'd first met Dunstable in the Viking graveyard and their subsequent travels together with the Princess. He had trusted him completely. Yet all the time he had been secretly betraying them!

'Where is he now?' he whispered through clenched teeth.

For a moment, Maledict lost his calm demeanour and looked irritated by the question. He waved his arms dismissively.

'Run away I believe. Who cares? He has served his purpose well enough. If it makes you feel any better, he will not escape Ragnarok.

THE RETURN OF SIGURD THE DRAGON SLAYER

He will die with all the others. I will let Fenrir rip him apart.'

Peter felt utterly defeated. What little hope he had left drained out of him. He had been betrayed by someone he trusted – someone he had considered a friend. What should he do? He glanced upwards. The whole sky was on fire, burning in agony. But now there was something even more sinister. A hole was forming on the eastern horizon - a spiralling black circle set against the red flames. The thunderous blast of war horns was coming from the other side of it. An army was forming there – an army from whatever lay on the other side of the sky. The Fire Giants were coming!

But something else was also happening. The sea had fallen ominously still below him. The waves were no longer crashing onto the rocks, despite the wind that was blasting against the cliffs. As he gazed out to sea he realised why. The great wave was now just a few miles from land. Within it a dark shadow was rising. Something was there, something huge and terrifying. A creature from darkest legend was coming to shore!

Maledict regarded him coldly.

'You have a decision to make and you must make it now. I have an offer to make you: an endless life by my side. I am not a callous master. I will instruct you in the greatest magic. Think of it, boy! I will show you how to use the power you have inside you, power you have barely touched upon! I will show you how to fulfil your every desire, how to control others as you see fit! Never again will you feel pain or disappointment! You will become more powerful than you could ever imagine!'

For a moment, Peter thought about his parents and all the things he would like to do. What if he could change the way they thought about each other? What if he could bring them back together? When he spoke, his voice was barely a whisper.

'And if I refuse?'

Maledict's voice was quiet but deadly.

'Then you will die. You will die here, alone and afraid. That is the choice that faces you. Ragnarok is almost upon us. Decide now!'

As Maledict spoke the last two words, there was a sudden crack of thunder that was so loud the cliff trembled. Peter pictured his parents and how unhappy they had been. Then the image passed. He no longer felt fear or anger. The time for fear and anger had passed. Now he would either stand or fall. He stepped towards Maledict.

'I choose to fight you! I will fight you while I can for what you have done to the Princess!'

The sound of his voice surprised him. Full of confidence and authority, it sounded so unlike his own. It was as if his decision to not give in to temptation had given him strength to defy Maledict to his face.

Maledict's eyes narrowed in fury behind the folds of his hood.

'Know this, boy. If you were anyone else, I would kill you instantly for daring to challenge me! But though I will not kill you, I will cause you suffering beyond your imagination. Soon you will beg me for death, but I will not give it to you. That is what you have chosen for yourself! Defend yourself if you can, for now you will discover what happens to those who dare stand against me!'

Chapter 13

Ragnarok

Perfectly framed against the burning sky, Maledict raised his hands above his head like a conductor in front of an orchestra. A sphere of light the size of a football suddenly appeared in front of him. It spat with raw energy, pulsating from vivid red to darkest black. At the same time, the Viking Stone in his crown shone hypnotically. He extended his arms and the energy sphere slowly moved towards Peter.

'Now is the time for you to prove yourself. Let us see how powerful you have become!'

For a moment, Peter watched like a condemned man as the energy sphere approached him. He knew instinctively that it would cause him unbearable pain if it touched him. He only had one chance. He closed his eyes and forced himself to relax so he could reach the source of power within him. Immediately, he felt the familiar tingling sensation in the pit of his stomach combined with a sudden rush of excitement and adrenaline. He could feel it building inside him. The magic was returning. Perhaps a second passed before he was ready. Then he opened his eyes again.

Once more, the world had become a vast energy field. The golden strands were all around him, millions of tiny lines of light criss-crossing each other as far as he could see. Feeling gloriously composed, he gazed at the strand connected to his stomach, his connection to the vast network. There it was, shining brightly, a thin stream of light flowing through a transparent vein into his waist.

Then he saw something he hadn't noticed before. The flow of pure light did not only flow into him, it also flowed *from* him! The light flowed in *two* directions through the golden strands! There was a constant exchange - a constant two-way connection between him and all other things. But even as this startling realisation struck him, a still greater understanding came to him. It was more than simply a network of energy he was witnessing. The energy that appeared as pure brilliant light didn't just nourish all things – it *was* all things! Form, colour, smell, even feelings and emotions – they were all simply different expressions of energy. And he was part of it too, not simply connected to it. Its energy and his were one and the same. He was both part of the whole field and the whole field itself, just like everything else was.

At last he understood magic.

All this happened in a fraction of a second. Feeling uniquely liberated, he calmly regarded Maledict's red energy sphere as it hissed and spat, now no more than a couple of feet in front of him. Then he noticed something peculiar. The sphere was unstable – somehow out of place in the world of free-flowing energy. Instinctively he realised why. Maledict was not able to draw from all the energy that surrounded him. He could only use negative energy – hatred, despair, loneliness and anger. Though his power was great, it was but a small part of what there was. That was why there was such a disturbance around the sphere. It was stagnant and stale, blocking the flow of energy like a polluted river. The world rejected it, fighting against the imbalance it created.

It took him a moment to see, a moment to understand. Then he raised his right hand and the sphere fizzled and disappeared. Instantly the normal flow was restored as the negative energy washed away.

For a moment, Maledict looked shocked, unable to believe he had been so easily thwarted. Then he smiled, full of cruel confidence again.

'Not bad, boy! Perhaps you are a worthy opponent after all! Do you think you understand the lines of power now? Do you think you are ready to challenge *me?* I who have lived for centuries of your time? Let us see how much you have truly learned!'

Closing his eyes in concentration, Maledict held out his hands, his right scorched and withered from the Eternal Flame. His outstretched fingers pointed towards Peter. He muttered a few words under his breath. Suddenly ten balls of pure energy appeared, each smaller than the first but no less deadly. They bobbed in the air in front of him impatiently, as if eager to be released. Then, as he opened his eyes and stared at Peter in cold hatred, they took off and raced towards their target.

Immediately Peter knew that Maledict had drawn on too much unstable energy. If one of the balls struck him it would cause him suffering beyond belief. If more than one struck him, his death would be certain. There was no time to think, no time to consider his options. His death was imminent.

Somehow he remained calm, his mind focusing in an instant. He closed his eyes and when he opened them again a fraction of a second later, the world was moving in slow motion. Instantly he took in the scene with a heightened awareness. Just a few inches from his face, a single fragile leaf was drifting serenely by, as if in no hurry to reach its destination, whilst countless drops of red tinted rain were falling in front of him, taking an eternity to reach the ground. But for some reason the energy balls were not so greatly affected. Perhaps due to some magic on Maledict's part, they still sped towards him, slower than they had been but still very fast.

Peter reacted instinctively. Just before the first ball reached him, he pushed out his hands with his palms held flat and a barrier of yellow light appeared around them. Using it as a shield, he raised it in front of him. Instantly the first two balls struck it and bounced off harmlessly. The third and fourth were close behind. They ricocheted off its glowing edge and blasted black holes in the walls of the abbey behind Maledict. Moving so quickly his hands were a-blur, Peter raised the shield to deflect the fifth and sixth which were racing towards his head. They disappeared over the cliff behind him with a hiss of dissipated energy that sent a cloud of steam shooting up the cliff-face. With unbelievable speed, he lowered the shield to deflect the seventh and eighth which were racing towards his legs. No human could possibly have moved fast enough to deflect the ninth, which was streaking directly towards his head. Without thinking, he somehow deflected it.

But the tenth and last was the deadliest of all. Arriving at almost the same time as the ninth, it was aimed at his waist. In an instant he moved his shield down to block it, but not quickly enough. The energy ball caught the edge and skimmed across his ribs before striking the ground close to the edge of the cliff. Immediately searing hot pain consumed him, scorching him from the inside. He felt as if his body had been set on fire. Unable to cry out due to the shock, he fell to his knees then collapsed onto the muddy ground, clutching his side. Warm blood seeped through his fingers.

As he lay on the ground in agony, he somehow managed to turn his head and stare at his enemy. So great was his torment that he could barely see Maledict as he loomed above him.

'Now, I will ask you one final time. Agree to my terms and I will take your pain away. Refuse and what you are feeling now is but a fraction of what I will inflict upon you. Do you choose life, or will you die here on this cliff? Think carefully before you answer.'

Peter stared at him in hatred. He longed to strike out but his body was too weak. All he could feel was the intense burning inside him and the cold caress of the mud beneath his body. Then it became too much for him to bear. He felt himself sinking down, drifting into unconsciousness, the only escape from the pain. It was as if the world had suddenly become an alien place. All was dark and distant.

Then, just as he was about to lose consciousness altogether, he heard a familiar voice. At first the words were faint, calling out from somewhere far away, then they became clearer as his dulled mind recognised who was speaking. The voice spoke again.

'Maledict! Step away from him! If you are not the coward I think you are, face me!'

Peter opened his eyes. His face was pressed against the wet earth and, at first, all he could see was black mud and glistening strands of grass. He blinked, and slowly his vision began to clear.

The Princess was standing a few yards further down the cliff. She was facing Maledict, staring at him in utter contempt. Though she was pale and looked as if she could barely stand, her face showed no fear. Then she spoke again, her voice clear and strong.

'Leave him alone and face me! You have not defeated the Vikings yet!'

Maledict turned slowly towards her, his eyes shining with bemusement.

'*Princess?* Well this is a surprise. I had hoped that you would have died by now. I do hate disappointments. Still, every cloud has a silver lining, as the City Dwellers say. I can kill you now just as easily.'

Without warning, a bolt of bright red energy shot from Maledict's fingertips. The Princess tried to duck but she was far too slow. She had barely moved when it struck her full on the chest, hurling her into the air. Screaming in agony, she fell to the ground just a few yards away from where Peter lay desperately watching. Perilously close to the edge of the cliff, she writhed in torment, spinning around in the mud. It seemed certain she would fall, but at the last moment she rolled away. Somehow fighting the pain, she tried to get to her feet only to fall back down again, her legs too weak to support her.

As if he had all the time in the world, Maledict strolled casually towards her. Gazing up at him weakly, the Princess lay perfectly still, awaiting the end. Maledict raised his hands to strike, raw energy crackling between his fingers-tips. Then, seemingly appearing out of nowhere, a small dark figure hurtled towards them. Without being seen by anyone except Peter, he sped across the cliff-top and threw himself over the Princess, shielding her body with his own even though it would mean certain death. Poised to strike, Maledict paused for a moment in surprise. Then he laughed.

'Well! This is a night for surprises! Still, it makes no difference. I will kill you both together!'

He raised his hands to deliver the fatal blow. But it never fell.

Peter had gathered his senses. Forcing his pain aside, he rose unsteadily to his feet behind Maledict. Swaying dangerously on the edge of the cliff, he searched the ground around him, looking for something - anything - to help him. He was vaguely aware that beneath the steep cliff the sea had disappeared, revealing a vast expanse of glistening sand. If he had turned around he would have realised why. The great wave had almost come to shore at last. It had sucked up the sea into one great wall of water, barely concealing the horrifying creature that was rising within it. But he did not turn. Instead, his eyes focused on something pulsating in front of him. There, glowing brightly in the darkness, was the last of Maledict's deadly energy balls, the one that had almost killed him. He felt it as much as saw it, sensing the disturbance it caused in the energy field around him. Forcing himself to relax despite the pain burning through his body, he lifted it with his mind, using its own energy and the friction it caused to aid him in his task. It was so unstable that his work was made easier. It was as if the earth itself wished to be rid of it. The ball hovered for a fraction of a second in front of him, spitting and burning, desperate to be unleashed. Then, using the earth's reaction to the ball as a slingshot to increase the power and speed, he hurled it towards Maledict.

Poised to strike the deathblow to the two helpless creatures sprawled beneath him, Maledict sensed the sphere the moment before it struck. He turned just in time to see it speeding towards him, already knowing that he had no time to react. But it was not the energy ball he focused upon in the instant before impact, it was Peter. At that moment he understood for the first time what he faced, the boy he had scorned moments before. In that last fraction of a second, he realised the mistake he had made. Then the sphere struck him full in the face.

For a moment there was complete silence as Maledict clutched his face. Even the war horns were silenced. Then he screamed in agony. As his cry of despair echoed across the cliff-top, he staggered backwards. For a second he tottered on the edge of the cliff, his arms reaching out blindly as if searching for something to cling to. Then, as the lightning splintered the fiery sky behind him and the war horns blared out anew, he fell, hurtling towards the craggy rocks below.

At the same time, Peter sank to the ground, his last strength exhausted. The excruciating pain in his side was worse than ever. His eyes watering, he gazed over the precipice. Just as Maledict was about to strike the rocks, a large bird arose - a golden eagle. It fought against the gale and was almost smashed against the cliff as it struggled to find the strength to escape. Then, slowly, it began to rise, its great wings beating more powerfully. As it rose above the cliff-face Peter thought he saw something very bright in its claws. It looked like a shining stone. Then, with a searing cry, it disappeared into the night.

That cry echoed in Peter's mind as the world collapsed around him and he fell into unconsciousness.

*

'Peter! Wake-up! *Peter!!!*' cried the voice.

It was so far away Peter could barely hear it. Then he felt himself being shaken by desperate hands. He began to rise back to consciousness once more. For a moment he was confused, wondering where he was and what was going on. He was vaguely aware of a loud blaring noise. Then he was shaken vigorously again.

In an instant he was awake.

A dark figure was leaning over him, frantically trying to pull him to his feet. Fearing an attack, Peter tried to leap away but his legs were unable to support him and he lurched backwards on the muddy ground. Slowly, his eyes began to focus and he realised that the figure in front of him was the person who had dived over the Princess, shielding her from Maledict.

'*Peter!*' exclaimed Dunstable, his face contorted with remorse. 'I'm sorry – *I'm so dreadfully sorry!* I had to do it – I *had* to! He tortured me, you see! The *pain…!* I couldn't bear it! It's all my fault!'

As soon as Peter saw his anguished face, all the anger he'd previously felt towards Dunstable evaporated in an instant. He had been willing to risk his life to protect the Princess. There could be no greater testament. Still struggling to see properly, he placed his hand on Dunstable's shoulder to reassure him.

The sound of war horns was now so loud that Peter could no longer hear the storm. But for the moment he had a more pressing concern.

'Where's the Princess?'

Wincing from the throbbing pain in his side, he let Dunstable lead him to where the Princess was lying on the ground after her battle with Maledict. She looked fast asleep. A peaceful expression was on her face as if all her cares had been cast aside. Her hair was covered in mud and her cheeks were colourless. Unsure what to do, they crouched anxiously beside her. Dunstable shook her shoulder awkwardly with one hand whilst Peter stared at her face, searching for some sign of life. Just as they were beginning to fear the worst, she opened her eyes.

'You two look terrible,' she murmured.

Peter almost laughed, despite the pain in his side. Beside him, Dunstable was blubbering incomprehensibly about how sorry he was and how Maledict had inflicted terrible tortures upon him. But Peter barely heard him. The Princess was going to be all right. At that moment, nothing else mattered.

Eventually, she raised her head wearily.

'Maledict? Has he gone?' She gazed at Peter, her eyes wide as they searched his.

'Yes. He is gone.'

'And the Viking Stone?'

Peter was silent for a moment. The image of the eagle carrying the shining stone in its claws was still strong in his mind.

'I, umm, think it might be at the bottom of the cliff with Maledict.'

The Princess smiled in sad resignation as she gazed over his shoulder.

'It does not matter now. We are too late. Look!'

Peter turned. Immediately he realised what she meant. The whole sky was now on fire. The black clouds had been replaced by spiralling waves of flame. Even the incessant rain had turned red. But there was one part of the sky that was not alight. Directly above them, the black hole he'd seen earlier had now formed into a tunnel in the sky – a tunnel to a world only glimpsed in legend. The clamour of war horns was coming from the other side. They sounded horribly near. Battle was about to commence.

Then something strange happened. For a moment, Peter could hear another sound rising above the uproar – the sound of a cockerel crowing wildly in warning of what was to come. But it was too late. When the din reached its terrible climax, they came at last. Racing through the hole in the sky, the Fire Giants appeared.

Mounted on the backs of enormous black dragons, hundreds of them poured through the torn sky. Blasting on their war horns as they rose up in their red saddles, they glared down at the world below. Their dragon steeds roared and snapped beneath them, their black eyes burning in anticipation of the destruction they were about to reap. Like gigantic vultures above a kill, they circled above the earth. Then the circle of dragons parted and into the centre rode the greatest Fire Giant of them all. Surt he was called, and he was infamous even before he was born when his dreadful coming was foretold centuries ago. More than twice the size of any troll and much more powerful, his face and arms were burnt black and his eyes blazed red. In his right hand was a sword of flame, in his left a golden war horn. So great was his size that it took the greatest of all dragons to support him. Nostramo, Lord of the Dragons, bore him on his back, though he would bear no other.

As Nostramo roared beneath him, Surt surveyed the world below. His time had come at last! The time long awaited when he would set the world on fire! Pulling his head back, he let forth such a blast on his war horn that it burst. Then, as Nostramo blew great plumes of flame beneath him, he descended to earth, leading his terrible host to war.

But terrifying though they were, the Fire Giants and their dragon steeds were not the only horror that was unfolding. As they began their terrible descent, the great wave that had been gathering out to sea finally crashed to shore with a deafening *boom!* that sent violent shock waves reverberating through the cliffs. Peter and Dunstable crashed to the ground beside the Princess, Peter landing painfully on his injured side. Crouching on the grass, they stared out to sea. There, less than a mile from the cliff, they saw him – more horrific even than the Fire Giants. Jormungard, the Midgard Serpent, was coming to shore.

It was a sight beyond any nightmare. Colossal in size, he dwarfed even the largest of marine animals. His malice and ferocity were beyond compare. For centuries he had lain hidden in the depths of the great oceans, growing ever larger as he preyed upon the huge creatures that lived so deep beneath the surface that humans did not even know they existed. Sometimes, in his boredom, he had risen to the surface and attacked a ship, and over the years countless vessels had sunk without trace in calm seas. Occasionally men had survived these tragedies and told all who would listen about the terrifying sea serpent that had shown no mercy. But even in the dark ages, few had believed them, considering them mad, driven insane by their ordeal.

But now the time had come, the moment Jormungard had been waiting for all those dark years he had lived in solitude. He had been far out to sea when he heard Fenrir's call when Maledict had broken his chain and freed him from the abbey pit. He had been resting, coiled like a snake in the perfect darkness at the bottom of the deep ocean. Unravelling his vast bloated body, he had risen slowly out of the depths. When he finally broke through the surface he had reared high above the water, his vast head rising up like a cobra's above the storm waves. Seeing the red sky he had screamed in fury, raging against the world he was intent on destroying. Then he had crashed back down with such force that the water had risen in front of him and created the tidal wave that had heralded his arrival. For almost an hour he had raced it to shore, roaring with rage at the burning sky, driven by fear that the Fire Giants would begin the destruction before he came to land. For his was the greatest fury, fury surpassing that of the Fire Giants, the Wolf and even Maledict himself. Through all the long years he had lain in the great depths at the bottom of the ocean, nursing his hatred of the Vikings. Now at last his time had come, and he would reap such vengeance that the world would never forget his name again.

From the top of the cliff, Peter, Dunstable and the Princess watched as Jormungard came to shore, throwing his great body from side to side in his impatience. Above them the Fire Giants circled in the red sky on their dragons. The terrible reality came to them at the same time. They had failed. The attack was about to commence. There was nothing more they could do.

'This is the end,' whispered the Princess, taking both their hands. 'I never thought it would come to this! If only Sigurd had returned!'

Peter was feeling weak again. The throbbing pain in his side was increasing and he could feel the blood seeping through his shirt into his jumper. But when he heard the name of Sigurd he stirred. There was something he had to do – something he had to do now before it was too late. But his mind was slow to react, dulled by loss of blood and pain. An image of Sigurd standing in the Viking graveyard in York appeared in his mind's eye. What had he said? *'When all seems lost, I will come. You will know how to summon me…'*

Suddenly he knew what to do. He reached into his pocket and pulled out Sigurd's talisman. Dimly aware that both the Princess and Dunstable were staring at him, he dropped it onto the damp grass at the edge of the cliff and stepped back.

As soon as the talisman touched the ground it began to glow. The golden dragon engraving came to life in the metal, roaring at the Fire Giants as they sped overhead. Suddenly a white light shot up from the centre of the talisman towards the burning sky, shining so brightly that Peter had to turn away and cover his eyes.

When he turned back, the talisman was gone. In its place stood a tall Viking warrior wearing golden armour. Peter recognised him instantly. But he was no longer the tired old man he had seen in York. Now he had regained his youth. He stood proud and strong, the Viking warrior of legend. Sigurd the Dragon Slayer, the greatest Viking hero, had returned at last.

Chapter 14

The Battle of York

Fifty miles away in York, there was an eerie silence in the freezing night air.

Since midnight the locals had been restless. Unable to gain more than fleeting moments of sleep, they lay uneasily in their beds, constantly tossing and turning. As always, it was the children who were the most aware. Several could be seen in city centre houses and flats, their noses pressed against the cold glass of their bedroom windows. And there was reason enough for their anxiety. Many of them had seen and heard far more than their parents could ever have imagined.

First there had been the noises: strange shouts and clashes of steel against steel rising from the dark streets outside. Sometimes they were nearer and more distinct, sometimes further away and so faded they wondered whether it was nothing more than their imaginations. But in some parts of York, the most sensitive children saw as well as heard. As they gazed onto the rain drenched streets they caught fleeting glimpses of strange shadowy figures. Some of them were huge – great hulking creatures with long spears and clubs. They were fighting much smaller assailants who looked like warriors of old and moved with incredible speed.

Then the fighting had stopped and there had been silence. For over an hour the children neither saw nor heard a thing. By then it was well into the cold hours between midnight and dawn and their parents had fallen asleep, haunted by strange dreams of other-worldly creatures that they wouldn't remember when they woke. One by one, most of the children also succumbed to their tiredness. But still some remained awake, their faces glued to their bedroom windows, fear and excitement overcoming their fatigue. And for those few, the night suddenly came alive again.

The first thing that happened was spectacular and terrifying in equal measure. As even the most resolute children were finally drifting into sleep, the sky burst into light. A brilliant red glow appeared from the east as if someone had lit a fire on the horizon. Then a faint noise rose through the silence of the night. It sounded like horns being blown far away. The children shivered when they heard it, intuitively sensing it was a signal that something terrible was about to happen.

At about the same time, something began to stir on the streets outside. At first, there was just the sound of marching feet. It continued for about twenty minutes, then everything became strangely still. For most, that was all they were aware of. But for those who lived close to the Castle, an astonishing sight was revealed on the rain-drenched streets. There, suddenly appearing through the fading mist as if the veil that separated their worlds had been swept away, two armies stood facing one another.

It was immediately clear who had the advantage. The army with their backs to the Castle was by far the larger. It was made up of the same enormous muscular figures many of the children had caught glimpses of earlier. But now that they were gathered together, they looked even more terrifying. Facing them was a much smaller army of creatures that would have looked human if many of them had not been floating several feet above the ground. They were positioned across the wide road from the Castle embankment upon which their larger opponents swarmed, so overwhelmed in size and number the battle seemed already lost.

One house was particularly well placed to see what was happening. It was a large house which was slowly falling into disrepair. Close by the river, it was less than a hundred yards from the Castle walls, in front of which the vast troll army was gathered. In a bedroom on the third floor, an eleven year-old boy and his younger sister were peering through the misted glass of a large rectangular window. They had been there for several hours now, watching the events unfold a stone's throw away with a mixture of fear and exhilaration. When the two armies appeared out of the grey mist though, fear temporarily overcame the girl and she slipped off the wide window-ledge and fell noisily onto the wooden floor. For a few seconds they froze, hoping their parents hadn't heard them. Then they heard the familiar sound of floorboards creaking and a bedroom door being opened across the landing. Moments later, their weary-eyed mother shuffled into the room.

'What on earth are you two doing? Do you know what time it is?'

'We're watching the strange people! Look!' replied the girl, pointing to the street below as she quickly re-took her place on the window-ledge beside her brother.

Their mother stared at them blankly, her mind dulled by sleep, then decided to play along for the time being until she could work out what was going on. Tightening her dressing gown around her waist, she trudged to the window and rubbed a small hole on the misted glass with her thumb.

'I don't see anything but fog and wet roads. What *are* you two looking at?'

'The armies!' replied the boy indignantly, not taking his eyes off the strange creatures outside. 'Don't you see them? There! In the road by the Castle! There's hundreds of them! The big ugly ones with the spears and the smaller ones that can fly. I hope the big ones don't win – I don't like the look of them very much!'

His sister nodded in agreement, her eyes fixed on the Castle.

'They're scary!'

Confused, their mother peered through the window again, unsure whether she was being made fun of. She stared at the rain swept road by the Castle but saw only thin wispy mist hanging above the ground, casting strange shapes beneath the street lamps.

'Right. I see,' she said finally, deciding that they must be playing a childish game after all. 'Shall we leave them to get on with their little fight then? I think it's time you two soldiers got back into bed, don't you? Come on now, hurry up!'

She pointed to their bunk-beds and placed her hands on her hips, indicating that she wasn't going to leave until she saw them safely tucked up beneath their blankets.

'But I want to see what happens!' complained the boy.

'I want to see too!' echoed his sister supportively.

But they both knew the argument was already lost.

'I'm sure you'll find out tomorrow,' replied their mother wearily as they reluctantly trailed back to their beds. 'Now, I don't want to hear another squeak out of you two until morning. Is that clear? Good-night then!'

Before she left the room, she paused and gazed out of the window once more. For a moment she thought she saw something moving along the road opposite their house – a massive creature far larger than any man - and her jaw dropped in shock. But when she blinked it was gone and there was nothing but a dark foggy street with the Castle walls looming up beyond. Frowning, she shook her head, blaming her momentary vision on a trick of the night and her tiredness, and turned back towards the door. As she left the room she glanced at her children, now safely tucked up in their beds. 'Kids!' she thought. 'Where do they get such vivid imaginations?'

Outside the house, the two armies faced each other in silence across the wide road that encircled the Castle.

The scene had changed dramatically since the Vikings had first approached the Castle earlier in the night. Then the car-park around it had been flooded and a heavy fog had hung in the air. But after the trolls' surprise attack, the floodwater had strangely subsided, falling back as quickly as it had risen despite the constant rain. The fog had also thinned to little more than a fine damp mist, revealing an ugly muddy smear across the ground left by the retreating water.

Facing the Castle walls, the Viking army stood perfectly still, silently waiting. At the centre of their lines, the Prince studied the endless rows of trolls massing on the Castle bank. It had been a long night for the Viking leader - a night full of changing fortune.

It had begun with the ignominious defeat which had resulted in his capture. But just when he'd resigned himself to a terrible fate at the hands of the troll torturers, a small voice had called out to him from beyond the cell door. Against all odds, he had escaped. Dunstable, of all people, had been his liberator.

Once freed, he had acted quickly. Releasing his fellow captives, he resolved to fight his way out of the Castle, hoping to catch the trolls by surprise. Fortunately, almost all the trolls were in the streets of the city, leaving just a small regiment behind. But the Vikings were still outnumbered, and the alarm was raised even before they were all freed. Arming themselves with an assortment of weapons from the deserted Torture Chamber, they barely reached the top of the staircase when they were attacked. Even as Peter and the Princess began the race to the coast, the battle had hung in the balance. Finally though, the Vikings began to prevail. Pushing the trolls back, they fought their way forward until they reached the centre of the Castle courtyard. Then, before the trolls could react, they leapt into the air, quickly rising high above the Tower and out of range of the troll archers, before speeding back to the Viking Halls, arriving a few minutes after Peter and the Princess had left.

The Vikings were rejuvenated by the unexpected return of their leader. But the Prince didn't rest. Desperate for revenge, he immediately led one of the surprise attacks that were taking place across the city, using the cover of the snickelways to strike at the trolls quickly before returning to safety. The Queen's strategy had proved highly effective. Not knowing where and when they would be attacked next, the trolls became increasingly nervous, squabbling amongst themselves and jumping at every shadow.

But within minutes of the Prince's return, the trolls had disappeared from the narrow city streets. It didn't take long for the Vikings to find them again. The whole troll army had withdrawn to the Castle. But they didn't go inside. Instead they waited, massing around the Castle walls and spilling onto the deserted road and car-park beside it, defying the Vikings to attack them.

By this time, the Vikings could see the red glow on the eastern horizon and knew that Ragnarok would soon be upon them. Once again, the Prince demanded that they attack the trolls in open battle. Finally, the Queen had relented. It wasn't that she had any hope of victory. It was simply that there was no longer any point in waiting for their enemies to find them whilst Ragnarok was unleashed and the world laid to waste. Far better to march out, as in days of old, and make a final glorious stand.

But not all the Vikings had chosen to join the battle.

Dunstable hadn't been seen since he'd freed the Prince from the Castle dungeon. Some of the Vikings suspected he was hiding in some deep hole in the city, and that his seemingly brave act in the Castle was so out of character, it had probably been forced upon him by the Princess. There were also rumours that he'd been seen running frantically along the road that led to the coast. But now it mattered little. His whereabouts were no longer of any consequence. Battle was about to commence.

So, for perhaps the final time, the last Vikings went to war. Led by the Prince, they marched openly through the centre of York as the light in the eastern sky grew ominously, casting a red glow across the city. Upon reaching the Castle, they quickly formed battle lines on the road and pavement opposite the Tower in front of the city's fire station and the tall old buildings and hotels. Then, outnumbered almost five to one, they waited silently for the signal for battle to commence.

Across the road from the Vikings at the top of the Tower mound, Elrock, King of the Mountain Trolls, waited patiently. Over ten feet tall, he had gained his sovereignty in the usual troll tradition. When he was old enough he had challenged the previous King to a fight and had beaten him mercilessly in front of the whole troll army, thereby claiming the crown. Maledict had seen his potential, for he was a troll who was both fearsome in battle and cruelly cunning; an evil leader who provoked fear and respect in equal measure and would therefore be obeyed without question. Maledict had taken him and whispered promises of conquest and greatness in his ear, feeding his lust for battle. It hadn't been difficult, such was his hatred of the Vikings. But neither Elrock nor any of the trolls knew anything about Ragnarok. Maledict had kept that part of his plan secret. And though the strange fire in the eastern sky worried him as he didn't know its cause and whether it was a good or bad omen, his resolve to destroy the Vikings did not waiver.

When Elrock saw the Vikings march openly through the city streets, he'd been pleasantly surprised. He had thought they wouldn't dare meet his challenge and face his vastly superior army across an open battlefield. He smiled confidently, his hands tightening around the hilt of his great axe in anticipation. Instead of spending weeks dragging the Vikings from their cursed hidden passageways one by one, losing half his army in the process, now victory would be swift and decisive. He would obliterate them and erase their hated race once and for all!

For almost half an hour the two armies waited. Then the time for battle finally came. Both sides knew it at the same time. Complete silence fell. The moment seemed to last forever. Then it began.

With a terrifying scream of hatred, the heavily armed centre where the largest trolls were assembled charged across the road, their spears glinting in the pale red light as if they had already tasted blood. Their intention was clear: to knock a hole through the Viking line at the centre where the Prince commanded. If they succeeded, the Vikings would be surrounded and the battle would come to a swift and bloody end.

Elrock had planned the charge as soon as he'd seen the Vikings assemble. He had carefully selected the trolls who would lead it, choosing the most ruthless and battle-hardened, many of whom came from the same desolate mountain range as himself. To his surprise though, the trolls were met head-on. Anticipating the move, the Prince had placed his best soldiers in the front line, the same Vikings who had been captured with him and were desperate to avenge their defeat. Before the trolls had time to raise their spears, the agile Vikings flew towards their attackers at lightning speed and slashed at them with their swords before retreating in an instant, bringing havoc to the troll charge.

Dismayed by this unexpected resistance, the trolls tried to re-group, but almost immediately they were struck by the Vikings again. Finally they broke off their attack and ran back to the safety of the main army, furious that the battle wasn't already won.

Then disaster struck. Elated by their first victory, a hundred younger Vikings raced across the muddy road in pursuit of the retreating trolls, ignoring the Prince who screamed at them to return.

Too late! The first attack had been but a feint to test the strength of the Viking line. Though it had met with greater force than anticipated, the foolish young Vikings had allowed Elrock to achieve his purpose. Suddenly the two flanks of the troll army raced forward and closed around them, cutting off all means of escape.

Finding themselves surrounded and separated from the rest of the Viking army, the young Vikings realised their folly. Desperately, they formed a circle and stood back to back, determined to fight to the last. But they could gain no foothold in the slippery mud. The Mountain Trolls attacked them from all sides whilst the Wood Trolls strung their bows and aimed above their heads, making it impossible for them to fly to safety. Though they fought bravely and well, the trolls were too great in number.

It would have ended there for the young Vikings had the Prince not led the counter-attack. Ignoring their own peril, the rest of the Viking army surged forward and attacked the massed trolls from behind. After several minutes of fierce fighting, they finally reached the beleaguered young Vikings in the centre, and together they made an orderly withdrawal. Once again, the two armies faced each other across the dark road, each battle worn but undefeated.

From his high vantage point on the Tower mound, Elrock surveyed the scene with satisfaction. The Viking army had only just escaped complete destruction. Though they had recovered and shown themselves to be more resilient than he'd expected, that bothered him little. He was content to toy with them a while yet and drag out their suffering until their inevitable defeat. Everything was going to plan. He smiled savagely as he contemplated the reward he would receive when he told his master that the Vikings were utterly defeated. For that was what he intended. No Viking would leave the battlefield alive.

Suddenly a great shout came up from the troll ranks below him followed by screams of pain and fear. The Vikings were attacking!

Unknown to Elrock, a hundred deadly female Viking archers had held back from the fighting and flown behind the Tower mound, hidden by the trees lining the river and the tall old houses. From there they had approached the troll army from the rear, inching their way forward without Elrock being aware. As soon as the Prince had retreated they attacked, darting from the tops of the buildings behind the Tower. They moved with unbelievable speed, taking the ponderous trolls completely by surprise. In seconds a hail of arrows had fallen out of the night sky, each one finding its mark. Darting up and down above the heads of the massed trolls, they shot continuously with unfailing accuracy, not allowing the trolls time to return fire.

A troll's skin is thick and can withstand an arrow tip and even a light sword thrust, but the female Vikings aimed for the face, the throat and the knees, all of which were sensitive areas. Their skill was unsurpassed, and they could unleash a dozen arrows with unerring precision in the blink of an eye. Havoc broke out in the troll ranks as they surged forwards, desperate to escape their tormentors. But the air-born Vikings allowed them no respite, stinging them like deadly wasps.

Meanwhile, a hundred more female Vikings suddenly attacked the trolls from the city side where they had lain hidden in the snickelway in St Mary's Square, less than two hundred yards from the battle. They appeared just when the confusion caused by the archers had reached its peak. As the troll army surged towards them, they lit their arrows from the burning torches they carried and shot down into the heaving throng.

There was magic in the fire. As soon as the arrows struck the ground they burst into flames. Immediately waves of fire swept through the massed troll ranks, rolling across the road and car-park. Tormented by fire and arrow, the trolls raced back and forth in turmoil, screaming in terror.

Then, just when their panic reached its zenith, the Prince attacked. Racing across the road, his army charged straight into the heart of the trolls. Desperate to escape their tormentors, many of the terrified trolls ran straight into them and were immediately hacked down, whilst others fled in the opposite direction, only to come under fire once more from the Viking archers. The enormous commanders tried to force the massed trolls to stand their ground and fight, but most of the trolls had no stomach for a fight like this. They wanted quick bloody victory followed by feasting - not fire, dart and unbearable agony! Troll fought troll in their desperation to find an escape route, causing even greater chaos.

The crucial point in the battle had been reached and the Vikings had the advantage. The troll army was buckling. Many Wood Trolls were fleeing down the road away from the city, casting their weapons aside and screaming as they ran. This time the Vikings didn't give chase but concentrated on those still fighting.

But now the Vikings became victims of their own success. The airborne archers were running out of arrows and the rain was putting out the fires that had been lit. Meanwhile, the remaining trolls, almost all of whom were Mountain Trolls from the desolate mountain ranges far away in the West, were standing firm at the foot of the Tower mound. They still outnumbered the Vikings almost two to one. It was at that moment, just when the outcome of the battle hung in the balance, that Elrock, King of the Mountain Trolls, came down from the Tower mound.

For most of the battle he had been content to issue orders via his commanders, using the height of the mound to oversee the battlefield. But when the tide had turned against him, he could no longer watch from afar. Furious, he leapt down the embankment. Now he wanted to taste blood; to lead his army personally and crush the foul Vikings once and for all.

So great was his reputation and the awe he inspired that when the trolls saw him descend the mound they immediately began to fight with renewed ferocity to gain his approval. But Elrock barely noticed. Pushing his way through the massed troll ranks at the base of the Tower, he leapt on top of a parked car, its roof buckling beneath him. With his enormous axe held aloft, he pointed at the fleeing trolls.

'Stand! Stand and fight! Behold what you run from – a pathetic band of scum from a forgotten race! Any troll who runs from this battlefield I will hunt down and slay! Let us end this battle together! Before this night is over, we will drink the blood of Vikings!'

Raising his axe above his head, he screamed a terrible battle cry. Then he leapt down and raced towards the Vikings, his face twisted with bloodlust.

When he had spoken, the two armies had ceased fighting, so great was the power of his voice. But as soon as he raised his axe, each and every troll was transformed. Fear was replaced by hatred of the Vikings. Those who had been pushed back began to force their way forwards using their incredible strength. Those who were fleeing turned and ran back to join the battle, attacking the Vikings from the rear. In minutes the Vikings were surrounded by a reinvigorated army several times their number.

Facing certain defeat, the Prince ordered a desperate retreat towards the city, though he knew they would never reach it. But just when the Prince had almost given up hope, the night suddenly burst into burning red light. Immediately, all eyes turned towards the east. Fire was spreading across the sky. Vast flames were rolling across the horizon towards them, consuming the grey clouds in their path like some vast gorging monster. At the same time a great din arose, so loud it shook the earth. Horns were being blown wildly - great battle horns blown by creatures from half-forgotten legend, so loud and clear that the Vikings and trolls pressed their hands against their ears and fell to the ground in terror.

Then, far in the distance, they saw the Fire Giants pouring from another world into the burning sky, riding fearsome dragons. They paused for a moment to blow on their horns, then descended to earth. But they were not headed towards York. Far away on the shores of the Viking Sea, a greater battle was being fought, a battle that meant far more than that of the trolls and Vikings.

Ragnarok had begun.

Chapter 15

Sigurd's Battle

Sigurd stood perfectly still with his head bowed in silent contemplation. He towered above them, taller and broader than any man currently living. Framed against the burning sky, his golden armour shone brilliantly, giving him a glowing aura. In his right hand his long sword glinted in the red light. In his left, his shield was emblazoned with a fearsome looking dragon, its jaws agape. The talisman hung around his neck as if it belonged there.

For several long seconds he stood perfectly still as if awakening from a deep slumber. Then, very slowly, he raised his head. Though his face was young, his eyes were the same as those of the old man Peter had met in the graveyard - old and deep beyond reckoning. Raising them skywards, he calmly watched the Fire Giants on their dragon steeds as they circled in the burning sky, blowing their horns wildly. Then, without emotion, he turned towards the sea and gazed at Jormungard, the Midgard Serpent, as he made his way towards the shore.

Suddenly he tilted his head as if listening for something. At that moment, the cry of a cockerel rose above the storm again. This time it wasn't a desperate warning - it was a cry of hope. As it echoed into the distance and was consumed by the blaring horns, Sigurd finally stirred.

But he wasn't ready to fight just yet. Turning away from the sea, he stared into Peter's eyes as he crouched on the muddy cliff before him. Then Sigurd smiled and raised his long sword in salute.

'We meet again Peter! The time has come, I see. Do not fear! You have done enough.' He nodded briefly to the Princess and Dunstable. 'You have all done enough. Rest here. The time of reckoning has come and you cannot help me now. I must face this final battle alone.'

As they watched, unsure what to do or say, he turned and walked towards the edge of the cliff, his golden armour glowing against the burning sky. To their dismay, he carried on walking until he dropped off the edge like a stone. In horror, they scrambled across the cliff and stared over the precipice to the shore below. There was a terrible moment of uncertainty before they saw him directly beneath them, striding calmly across the beach towards the Serpent with sword in hand.

Caught in the moment, the Princess and Dunstable shouted like football supporters roaring on their team. But Peter was silent. As soon as he'd dropped the talisman onto the ground he'd felt horribly different, as if his remaining strength had drained out of him. He was acutely aware of the sharp pain in his side and the blood still seeping from his wound. Blinking to clear his eyes, he tried to ignore the pain as he stared at the scene below.

Sigurd was marching across the beach towards the sea. But the Midgard Serpent had seen him and was thrashing his great body in his eagerness to make the shore, sending vast waves crashing against the rocks. Meanwhile, the Fire Giants continued to circle overhead, their dragon steeds roaring beneath them, filling the air with their flame.

By the time Sigurd was halfway across the beach, Jormungard was almost out of the water. It was only then that Peter realised how enormous he was. Taller than York Minster when he reared up, his bloated body trailed for hundreds of feet into the shallow water behind him. He looked like some sort of gigantic snake, but his skin was black and slimy like a worm's and his head was much bigger compared to his body. As he rose to survey the land he was intent on destroying, his long forked tongue tasted the air, revealing several rows of sharp white teeth, each as large as a giant. But it was his eyes that were the most terrifying. As black as the deepest hole, they never blinked as they stared with such malevolence that Peter wondered how Sigurd dared face him. It was all too much for Dunstable. With a petrified squeak, he buried his face in the grass and covered his head with his arms.

It seemed impossible that Sigurd could defeat such a powerful creature. But then something incredible happened. With every step Sigurd took, he grew larger. In moments he was bigger than a troll, then he was as big as a Fire Giant. Soon he was over fifty feet tall, though still dwarfed by the enormous serpent.

When Jormungard saw him grow, he thrashed frantically in the shallow water as if he suddenly realised who Sigurd was. Then, falling out of the sky with their dragons screaming beneath them, the Fire Giants attacked. Led by Surt, they swept down to the beach like gigantic mosquitoes, their black faces wild with battle lust. As they flew they moulded great balls of fire in their hands like clay and hurled them at Sigurd. The fire darts burst into flames that raced across the beach like waves, burning everything in their path. Steam rose from the sea as the shallow water boiled. The heat was so intense that Peter and the Princess had to turn away or risk being scalded.

But Sigurd was undeterred. Somehow his golden armour protected him. Though the Fire Giants threw endless fire darts and their dragons covered him in flame, neither seemed to affect him. He just kept on walking towards the water's edge as if nothing could stop him from fighting the Serpent.

It seemed as if Sigurd couldn't be harmed. But then Jormungard finally came to shore. As he threw himself out of the shallow water onto the sand in his eagerness to face Sigurd, the Fire Giants reined back and circled in the air above them as if content to let them fight. They flew around and around a hundred feet above the cliffs, their dragons screeching in frustration. Terrified of being seen, Peter and the Princess pressed their faces to the ground. The Fire Giants sounded horribly close. They could hear Surt talking to the other giants. It was clear that he was debating whether to set fire to the city across the bay or wait for Jormungard to defeat Sigurd. Peter glanced at the Princess nervously, keeping his head low. For a moment, their eyes lingered on the city sleeping innocently beneath them, unaware that its fate hung in the balance, but then their attention returned to the beach. Below them, the battle between Sigurd and Jormungard had begun.

It started slowly. For several minutes Jormungard simply swayed back and forth, holding his enormous head high above the ground with his thick black body coiling and uncoiling behind him. Sigurd stood perfectly still thirty yards away from him, his sword held firmly in his outstretched hand as he watched the Serpent calmly. Then, without warning, Jormungard spat at him. A burst of green liquid spurted from his mouth, covering Sigurd completely.

It was so poisonous that the ground around him was immediately scorched black. Sigurd staggered and almost fell. Then Jormungard struck. In a flash, he threw himself forward and snapped at Sigurd whilst he was off balance.

Sigurd didn't flinch. Almost as if he was expecting the attack, he leapt to one side and sent his sword slicing down. Jormungard realised his mistake just in time. With incredible speed for such a vast creature, he threw his body to one side. But not quite quickly enough. The blow that was aimed at his head caught the side of his body and cut deeply into his black skin.

His reaction was terrifying! Screaming and hissing in pain and fury, his enormous body thrashed in every direction, sending rocks crashing all around him. The whole cliff shuddered, and for a moment Peter and the Princess thought they were going to be cast into the sea. When it stopped and they dared raise their heads again, Jormungard had moved away from Sigurd and was watching him from the edge of the sea, his long body swaying in the water like an eel's. Thick black blood was oozing from the cut behind his head.

More cautious now, he began to circle Sigurd, his body weaving from side to side, leaving deep trails in the sand. Sigurd turned and followed him, his sword still wet with Jormungard's blood. For several minutes nothing happened. Above them, some of the Fire Giants became restless. Diving down, they raced over Sigurd's head to distract him, their dragons roaring. Then their patience was finally exhausted. All at once, the Fire Giants attacked. Led by Surt, they swooped down and hurled their fire darts at Sigurd whilst their dragons spewed flame over him. In moments, the whole beach was burning again.

But Sigurd ignored them. Standing absolutely still, all his attention was focused on Jormungard, who was coiled up like a snake across the beach, his terrible black eyes glaring at Sigurd. At first the flames didn't seem to touch Sigurd at all, but as the Fire Giants continued their relentless attack, his golden armour began to burn and darken. The Fire Giants noticed it too. They screamed and hurled even more fire darts, never missing him. Though Sigurd didn't waiver, whatever magic he was using was not quite strong enough to protect him. He was clearly weakening.

Suddenly Surt dived down on his enormous black dragon. Resolving to end the fight once and for all so he could begin the destruction of the world, he raced up behind Sigurd. When he was almost upon him, he rose up on Nostramo's back and shouted a horrible curse. At the same time, he ground his hands together and a gigantic black fireball appeared between them, larger than any that had been cast before. Then, as he flew over Sigurd, he hurled it down.

As soon as it struck Sigurd it exploded into black flames that shot across the beach in a vast wall of fire, melting even the rocks at the bottom of the cliff. Sigurd staggered backwards as if he was dazed. Then he fell to one knee.

Immediately, Jormungard struck. Unwrapping his gigantic coils, he threw himself towards Sigurd with his enormous jaws wide open. Peter and the Princess screamed a warning but it was too late. The Serpent was upon him. But just when they thought he was defenceless, Sigurd suddenly stood upright again and raised his sword. Perhaps he was not quite as helpless as he pretended, or perhaps he found some strength from somewhere, but whatever the reason, Jormungard couldn't react in time. Leaping to one side, Sigurd put his foot on the Serpent's neck as it came crashing down where he had previously stood. Then, with his enormous sword raised high above his head, he cut off Jormungard's head.

For several seconds there was stunned silence. The Fire Giants hung in mid-air as if they couldn't believe what had just happened and didn't know what to do. Then they screamed in fury and their dragons roared. They raced around and around the beach like gigantic moths circling a light, screaming and roaring. Peter and the Princess covered their heads and clamped their hands over their ears. Dunstable whimpered beside them, almost dying of fright.

It was impossible to say how long it lasted, but suddenly it was quiet again. When they looked up, the Fire Giants and their dragons were gone. Then, as they watched in astonishment, the sky changed. The flames began to retreat, burning themselves out as if they were spent. Soon they could see the moon and the stars again. Within a minute it looked just like any other night, except strangely brighter, as if the world had been re-born. Somehow Sigurd had done it! As Peter looked up, he thought he heard a dragon's roar and saw something black moving very quickly far up in the sky, but it disappeared before he could be sure.

Gazing down to the beach, they saw Sigurd walking towards

them. With each step he shrank, until finally he was human size once more. Suddenly he appeared back on the edge of the cliff in front of them. For a moment, he simply stood there in his burnt armour, leaning on his sword as he regarded them each in turn. Then he took off the talisman. Bending down, he fastened it around Peter's neck.

'I return this to you to remember me by. I only borrowed it for a while. Now I will rest again. But if you need me you should seek within, for you have the heart of a Viking warrior of old. You have no need for a talisman now.'

Then he stood up and bowed. Confused, Peter was about to speak when a gust of wind came up from the sea. With a final glance at Peter, Sigurd vanished.

For several seconds, all three of them stared in stunned silence at the cliff where Sigurd had stood, trying to take in all that had happened. Then, as the rain finally stopped and the moon shone brightly above them, Peter began to feel strangely dizzy. Clutching his side, he found that he was still bleeding heavily. Suddenly he could neither hear nor feel. The only sense that remained was his sight, but that too was waning. With blurred vision he glanced at the Princess and Dunstable, who were staring at him with fear in their eyes. Though he tried to fight it, his eyes began to close. The last thing he saw was the Princess leaping towards him. Then he slipped into unconsciousness.

*

Peter woke with a start. He had been dreaming of a hideous fire-breathing dragon circling in the sky above him. Suddenly it had seen him and had dived at fantastic speed, its white teeth shining in its gaping mouth as fire blazed from its nostrils to burn him alive where he hid. Then a voice spoke beside him.

'We were wondering when you would finally come back to life. I thought we were going to have to carry you back to York!'

Twisting his head slightly, his eyes slowly focused on the Princess's face as she knelt over him. She was pretending to be angry but she was clearly pleased to see him awake. Her arm was bandaged and the cuts on her face looked sore, but despite looking like she'd been dragged through a hedge, her eyes were shining with joy as she leant closer to him, her face just inches from his.

Feeling himself blush at her closeness, Peter deliberately avoided her eyes. Raising himself on his elbows, he gazed over her shoulder to gather his bearings. He was lying on the cliff-top where he had fallen unconscious. It was daylight. The sun – the glorious yellow sun – was rising over the calm sea, caressing his face with its warmth and dazzling him with its brightness. Above him, stretching to every horizon, the brilliant blue sky was blemish free. It was as if nothing had happened.

The sound of whispering voices made him turn his attention towards the abbey. Standing amongst the ruins a little way further down the cliff, a small group of Vikings were talking happily and gesticulating to one another as if telling some wonderful tale. He searched their faces, hoping to see Dunstable, but he was nowhere to be seen.

Sitting up, he pushed aside a thick white blanket someone had laid on top of him and turned to the Princess.

'What happened?'

'You passed out, that is what happened!' replied the Princess, pretending to be angry again. Then she softened and gazed intently into his eyes. 'You lost a lot of blood. We were all worried! But the Viking elders have tended to you. You just need to rest now.'

But rest was the last thing Peter had in mind.

'What happened?' he repeated insistently. 'Did Sigurd really win?'

The Princess laughed.

'Yes! He did it!' She gazed at him disapprovingly for a moment, though she couldn't entirely hide her smile. 'You kept very quiet about that talisman! How did you know what to do with it?'

But Peter was too eager to hear everything to attempt an explanation.

'What happened with the battle with the trolls in York? Did the Prince win?'

The Princess raised herself up and glared at him indignantly.

'Of course we won! What sort of question is that?'

'But there were so many trolls! I thought we didn't stand a chance!'

'Well you were wrong!' replied the Princess smiling again, her anger only lasting a few seconds. 'Clearly you underestimated us, just like Maledict did!'

For the next hour, the Princess recounted the Vikings' glorious victory. At great length she explained how the Prince (being her brother after all) had anticipated the trolls' tactics and had lured them into a trap. She spent several minutes extolling the virtues of the Viking archers (all of whom were girls of course), going on to explain how the Prince had kept them hidden in reserve before unleashing them when the trolls least expected it. Sounding like an over-enthusiastic history teacher, she painted a triumphant battle scene on the streets of York in the middle of the night, before explaining how the trolls had panicked and fled when the Prince led the charge. She raced through the part where Elrock led a counter-attack, forcing the Vikings back again. She did, however, take great pains to emphasise that the Prince was not retreating; he was merely re-grouping to assess the situation before the Vikings attacked again.

Finally, she described the vital point in the battle when the Fire Giants had raced through the rift in the sky astride their terrible dragons. At that moment, the fighting had stopped as each side gazed at the burning sky in trepidation. Of course, the Princess explained, the trolls didn't really know what was happening. Maledict had not told them that! But even they sensed the importance of what was taking place and stood with the Vikings in silence, awaiting the final outcome.

For almost an hour the Vikings and trolls stared at the sky, their own battle forgotten. Then they saw bright flashes on the eastern horizon. Though they didn't know it, the Fire Giants were attacking Sigurd as Jormungard looked on, waiting for an opportunity to strike. Then something dramatic had happened.

The first they knew about it was a fearful shriek. It sounded as if a thousand evil voices had suddenly screamed in dismay at the same time. Even the troll commanders shuddered, covering their ears with their hands and cowering on the ground. But the moment the voices faded, the Vikings felt gloriously revived. Then, as they held their breath, the fire in the sky began to disappear! It was as if it was being sucked away, back to where it had come from. In moments it was gone and the sky was clear – clearer than it had been for days. There was a momentary high-pitched screech and something dark flashed against the pale moon, then there was silence.

For a few seconds nothing happened. Then, as one, the Vikings began to cheer, realising that the distant battle upon which all their fates depended had somehow been won. Immediately they turned towards their enemies once more and fighting resumed. By then though, the trolls were already defeated. As soon as the red sky had disappeared, most of the trolls had fled, seeking to return to their distant homes as quickly as they could. They had no desire for a battle such as this, where even the skies turned against them. The largest, most ferocious Mountain Trolls fought on, urged by their desperate leader. But the tide of the battle had changed and there was no denying the invigorated Vikings. They harried and pressed, wearing down the Mountain Trolls until they could barely stand.

Finally, an hour before dawn, what was left of the troll army buckled. One by one the remaining trolls fled, racing along the roads out of York, harried by the Vikings who ceaselessly assailed them from the ground and air. At the last only Elrock remained, wielding his great axe as he stood upon a twisted bench at the base of the Tower mound. But the Vikings hacked at his feet and finally he fell, crashing onto the pavement. Binding him head and foot, they took him to the Viking Halls.

The Princess concluded her account by clapping her hands with excitement, unable to restrain herself over the Vikings' glorious victory. Peter was scarcely less affected. For over an hour he had hung on her every word, and when she finished he sat silently, trying to take in all that had happened in the course of one night. Finally, the Princess spoke again.

'So, what do you make of it all? Of course, I always knew we would win in the end.'

Peter took a deep breath. The truth was that he didn't know what to think! The Fire Giants, the Midgard Serpent, Sigurd - there was so much to take in! He kept thinking about the strange words Sigurd had spoken to him before he disappeared.

The thought of Sigurd reminded him of the talisman. Immediately he reached under his jumper and shirt. Sure enough the talisman was there, hanging around his neck where Sigurd had placed it. The dragon's head glinted up at him, its red eyes shining.

Smiling distantly, he glanced at the Princess, pretending to be tired. Now that he had heard everything, he wanted to be left alone so he could ponder what had happened. There was so much weighing on his mind that he didn't know where to begin.

The Princess got the hint. She nodded knowingly, guessing his thoughts.

'Ok then. We can talk about it later. You had better get some rest! We must travel back to York tonight, so you need to get your strength back!'

Peter lay back on the soft grass as she left him. Gathering the blanket around him, he gazed at the clear blue sky and thought through all the Princess had told him. Soon though, his eyes began to close. Within minutes, he slipped into a peaceful dreamless sleep.

Chapter 16

The Trial of Dunstable

Peter woke suddenly. It was late afternoon and the sun was dipping below the horizon. Somehow he had slept through the whole day!

Sitting up, he winced in pain. Gingerly, he reached underneath his shirt and jumper and touched his ribs where Maledict's energy ball had struck him. He had been bandaged whilst he slept. Though his wound was still sore to the touch, it had stopped bleeding. But despite the constant dull pain, he felt much better after sleeping so long. His energy had returned and he was eager to be up and about again. Pushing the blanket aside, he stood up and gazed around him.

It was a peaceful scene, so different from the night before. Below him the tide was coming in. Foaming waves were gently caressing the shoreline then slowly retreating, revealing perfectly smooth sand that briefly reflected the orange glow of the sunset before the waves tumbled forward once more. Beneath the cliffs, the houses surrounding the harbour were lit up in homely fashion for the night ahead as people returned from work to relax in front of their fires. As he turned his gaze further inland, a long line of cars crept towards him in the distance, their headlamps shinning in the night.

One thing hadn't changed: there was still a cold wind blowing from the sea. Stuffing his hands into his coat pockets, he walked stiffly down the cliff-side to look for the Princess. He eventually found her behind the abbey talking to three solemn looking Vikings he didn't recognise. She was wearing a long flowing blue dress with an elegant brown belt fashioned like a vine, and her face and hair were clean and shining once more. Clearly she had been grooming herself whilst he slept. Peter walked towards her nervously, uncomfortably aware that he was still wearing his shabby old jeans and jumper beneath his black coat – the same filthy clothes he had worn through the sewers the day before. When the Princess saw him though, she smiled brightly. The other Vikings, much to his bemusement, bowed respectfully and turned away.

'What are they bowing for?' he asked, staring at the backs of the quickly retreating Vikings.

The Princess gave him a peculiar look.

'They are bowing to you, of course! Who else? You are famous now, what with everything that happened here. Do not worry! You will soon get used to it.'

Peter had forgotten that the Princess was used to people bowing to her all the time. He was not sure he could though, and hoped they would soon go back to ignoring him again. Keen to change the subject, he peered through the growing darkness for a familiar figure.

'Where's Dunstable? I can't see him anywhere.'

The Princess frowned and brushed her hair awkwardly with the back of her hand.

'He has gone back to York. He left this morning when the first Vikings arrived. He was taken away. Arrested, you would call it.'

Peter started in surprise.

'*Arrested!* Why was he arrested?'

'Because he double-crossed us of course! Do you not remember? He was in league with Maledict all along! We almost *lost* because of what he did!'

Peter couldn't believe his ears!

'He saved our lives! He saved *your* life! *That's* what I remember! If it wasn't for him, both of us would be dead!'

The Princess shook her head sadly.

'But he still betrayed us. We trusted him. The Queen trusted him. It is a serious matter.'

'What will happen to him?'

'He will be tried in the Debating Hall. If he is found innocent, he will be freed.'

'And if he's found guilty?'

'I do not know. We have never had a trial before. He will be banished from York probably.'

Peter gasped in disbelief. Had they all gone mad? He felt his face flush with anger.

'But it isn't fair! After all he did! You should be thanking him, not banishing him!' He thought for a moment, trying to control his outrage. 'I want to go to his trial! I want to defend him!'

'Do not worry. You will be asked to speak. So will I. We are the main witnesses in fact. The Queen will judge once she has heard all the evidence.' She nodded towards the three Vikings waiting patiently for them beside the abbey. 'Come on. We are already late. We need to return to York as quickly as possible. The trial starts at midnight and we have a long journey to make. We cannot risk flying over the cities and towns, not with a full moon and hardly any cloud cover. We will have to walk part of the way.'

Wasting no more time, she signalled to the waiting Vikings and immediately they rose into the air together and headed back across country towards York. As Peter followed them, he gazed down at the crumbling abbey on the cliff with the grey sea looking so calm beyond it. A mile from the shore several fishing boats were dotted on the horizon as they slowly sailed back to harbour. Everything looked so peaceful, as if nothing of consequence had happened. Then, as the sea and cliffs fell away beneath them, they climbed through a pure white cloud and all he could see was the black star-studded sky with the huge white moon shining high above them.

It was a long journey back to York. On the strict instructions of the Princess, they didn't fly the whole way. Every time they approached a city or town they couldn't easily fly around, she insisted they descend and walk in case they were seen. During these landings, Peter felt very peculiar as he flitted through well-lit streets accompanied by a troop of Vikings, dodging out of sight whenever they saw any children as if they were fugitives on the run.

He much preferred it when they could fly, particularly when they were racing over woods and farmlands to make up for lost time. But even then he was distracted and couldn't lose himself in the joy of flight as he had before. There was simply too much on his mind. He knew that the time had almost come for him to return to his old, dull life, so different from the magical world of the Vikings. But how could he return to their tiny flat and go back to school after doing and seeing so many incredible things?

By far his biggest concern, though, was Dunstable - knowing that he was about to go on trial and could be banished from York. He kept picturing in his mind how he had thrown himself over the Princess and saved her life. Whatever he had done before, he had surely redeemed himself with that act of bravery. He wondered how he must be feeling now, knowing how nervous he would be. The more he thought about it, the more his anxiety to return to York increased. Soon he dreaded the sight of city lights ahead, knowing that the Princess would shortly give the command to descend.

Finally, after what seemed like an eternity, they spied the twin towers of the Minster in the distance and dropped down to earth for the final time. They landed in a field close to the river, less than a mile outside the city. Racing along the riverbank, they entered the *FISH LANDING* snickelway and a few minutes later arrived at the Viking Halls just as the Minster bells were striking midnight.

Outside the golden gates they were met by an anxious looking elderly Viking with a long grey beard, who frowned at them impatiently like a headmaster at the school gate.

'You are late! Come quickly. The trial has already begun!'

The moment they entered the Debating Hall, the arguing voices were hushed to silence and hundreds of pairs of eyes stared at them from the balconies at the far end of the vast chamber. But Peter barely noticed them. All his attention was focused on the small figure of Dunstable, who was standing in front of the thrones of the Queen and Prince, his head bowed in shame. Side by side, Peter and the Princess raced across the marble floor towards him.

'I want to speak!' shouted Peter as soon as they were within earshot. 'I want to speak for Dunstable!'

There was a rumbling of protest from the Vikings above them. As they slid to a halt in front of the Queen, the Princess poked her fingers into his ribs and shot him an angry glance. Clearly he had broken some rule about speaking out of place. The Prince in particular looked furious as he swivelled on his throne and would have spoken had the Queen not placed her hand on his arm to restrain him. Perfectly calm, she beckoned them forwards.

'Welcome back Peter! Great deeds have been accomplished! We have much to celebrate. But for the time being, we have serious business to attend to. You will be given your chance to speak in due course. For now, you must sit and listen. Places have been reserved for you and the Princess.'

She motioned towards two seats in the lowest balcony, just a few yards behind Dunstable. Feeling foolish and extremely frustrated, Peter allowed himself to be led away by the Princess and together they sat down to witness the trial.

For the next hour, Peter bit his tongue as Dunstable endured endless questioning by the Prince, whilst the Vikings around him murmured angrily. As the Prince relentlessly bullied him, the extent of Dunstable's treachery was gradually revealed.

It had started after Maledict had captured him two years earlier when he had been on a scouting mission for the Queen. He had not escaped as he had claimed; he had been freed on the condition that he spy for Maledict. But terrible though this revelation was, Dunstable's worst confession was his last. He had deliberately led Peter and the Princess into a trap when they were attempting to secretly enter the Castle to steal the Viking Stone. He had misled the Vikings in the Council. The secret passageways were in fact well known to Maledict. He had instructed Dunstable to lead them to the Castle by the longest route possible whilst he attacked the Prince and planned his secret entry into the Viking Halls to steal Fenrir's key. His treachery had allowed Maledict to unleash Ragnarok, and only Sigurd had saved them.

As the Vikings leapt to their feet in fury, Peter fell back into his seat in shock. He could scarcely believe what he was hearing! He had trusted Dunstable completely. He shuddered to think that he had been so easily misled. Yet it seemed so obvious as each deceit was revealed. How had he not seen it? His sympathy for Dunstable began to evaporate and he had to close his eyes to remind himself how he had saved the Princess.

But when the Prince sat down and the Queen began to question Dunstable, another side of the story was revealed.

Once more it began with his capture by Maledict. As he described what the trolls had done to him in the Black Mountain caves, the whole hall fell silent. Peter began to feel guilty that he'd judged him so quickly, and even the Prince shuffled on his throne uncomfortably. After Dunstable had been tortured, Maledict had given him a choice: either do his bidding or he would be returned to the trolls for more terrible suffering and inevitable death. By that point Dunstable's spirit had broken, and he would have agreed to anything to escape yet more agony being inflicted upon him.

Under the Queen's prompting, Dunstable then explained what had happened after he'd led Peter and the Princess through the secret passageways into the Castle. When they had left him in the tunnel beneath the dungeons, he'd realised they would be captured and most probably tortured, and knew only too well how terrible that would be. His guilt fought with his fear, and finally he'd gathered enough courage to attempt the bravest thing he'd done since Maledict had released him. He decided to creep through the troll stronghold and somehow free them before it was too late.

Fortunately for him, the trolls who remained in the Castle were intent only on their preparations for the battle with the Vikings, and he was small and careful enough to sneak past them unseen. But he'd been unable to find Peter or the Princess. They were not in the prison cells as he'd expected. Nor could he find them in the Torture Chamber, though it was clear that the trolls there were preparing for something dreadful as the furnaces were being lit and the terrible torture instruments he knew so well were being sharpened. The only remaining option was the pit. But though he knew it lay hidden somewhere in the courtyard, he didn't know where, and he dared not search for it in open view of the trolls.

As he huddled in the freezing darkness beneath the Castle walls, unsure what to do next, a Mountain Troll had appeared from the Tower leading a dozen Wood Trolls. They made their way across the courtyard carrying a large steel cage. Curious, he watched as they pulled open a trap door in the ground and lowered the cage inside. He had found the pit! Then, to his horror, the cage was raised with the Princess inside! He was so shocked he barely had the wits to follow them as they carried her to the dreaded Torture Chamber.

But he didn't dare follow them inside, knowing what the trolls did there. Terrified, he huddled in the darkest corner of the courtyard for several hours. His fear increased still further when the Castle gates opened and the Prince and the Vikings who had fought with him were dragged towards the dungeons by an army of enormous trolls, their arms bound and weights tied to their legs to stop them from flying.

Finally, perhaps an hour later, the Castle emptied as the trolls swept through the city streets in search of the Viking army. After waiting to ensure the courtyard was empty, he built up enough courage to creep to the edge of the pit and call out to Peter. Together they had freed the Princess and had gone on to release the Prince and the other Vikings.

But his relief at their escape had been short-lived. When he'd seen Peter and the Princess race from the Tower to the Viking Halls, he had guessed Maledict's plan. He had first suspected something when Maledict had questioned him. When he heard whisperings that Maledict had broken into the Viking Halls and stolen Fenrir's key, his suspicions were confirmed.

Immediately he had set off for the coast on foot, running as fast as his legs would carry him. But he knew he would arrive much too late. Maledict could fly and he could only run, and it was a long way to the abbey. Then his urgency had moved him to do something no Viking had ever done before - he hitched a ride on the back of a City Dweller's lorry! Much to the astonishment of everyone in the Debating Hall, he described how he'd boarded it whilst it waited at traffic lights, and had hidden behind the stack of crates it carried. Peter couldn't help smiling at the thought of Dunstable peering nervously out of the back of the lorry as it raced along the road to the coast!

Though the lorry was fast, by the time it reached the coastal town across the bay from the abbey and he had scampered up the cliffs, Peter and the Princess had already fought Fenrir, and Peter was facing Maledict alone.

Despite his newfound bravery, that had been too much for him. Shaking uncontrollably at the sight of the Necromancer, he had hidden behind a rock further down the cliff-face, not daring to move for fear of being seen. Throughout the fight he had remained there as the skies burned and the war horns sounded, wishing he could help but unable to overcome his terror.

But when Peter had been injured and the Princess appeared, his surprise was so great that he had temporarily forgotten his fear. Thinking she'd been killed by Fenrir, he came out of his hiding place and stared at her in disbelief. When he saw her fall and watched Maledict raise his hands to deliver the final blow, something had snapped within him and he had raced towards her, willing to risk his life to protect her.

When he completed his tale, silence fell in the Debating Hall. Even the Prince was quiet, his head bowed in thought. Then the

Queen invited Peter and the Princess to speak. As Dunstable gazed at them forlornly, they both defended him vehemently, stressing the courage he had shown in freeing Peter from the Castle pit and in saving the Princess's life.

When all had been told, the Queen rose to her feet and stared at Dunstable, her expression unreadable. A nervous silence descended over the Debating Hall. Dunstable bowed his head, unable to meet her gaze as he waited for her judgement.

'Dunstable. You have committed a grave crime. No one in our history save Maledict himself has ever committed such treachery. Your acts almost brought about his victory and the terrible consequences that would have followed. We put our faith in you and you betrayed us all because you feared for your own life above the lives of others. Such a heinous act cannot be ignored.'

Her voice was clear and firm, her face stern and emotionless. No one doubted the seriousness of Dunstable's crimes. Dunstable could barely stand he felt so ashamed and shrank away from her, trying to appear even smaller under the weight of her gaze. The Queen continued.

'But we must also take into account the good deeds you have done. In the end, when all our fates depended upon you, you acted bravely and well. The Princess has told us how you saved her life. Peter has spoken for you also, describing how you freed him from the pit in the Castle. Such pleas cannot be ignored, and I have taken them into account in arriving at my judgement.'

She paused and glanced at the Prince. A silent communication passed between them, then he nodded back, looking uncomfortable, as if he was not sure whether he agreed with her. When she spoke again, her voice reached every corner of the hall.

'You are hereby banished from the Viking Halls! No longer will we allow you entry into our home and you will live outside our protection. Your banishment will last three years from this day. Then, if you have shown good faith, I will consider this judgement again.'

As soon as the Queen said the word '*banished*' there was a collective gasp. Almost everyone believed she would pardon Dunstable, great though his crimes had been. Each knew he would have nowhere to go. Most of the Vikings were now in York. He would wander, homeless and friendless, perhaps never to return.

The effect on Dunstable was even worse. His face turned completely white and his mouth gaped open in shock. He stood, unable to move, staring blankly at the Queen as if he couldn't comprehend the judgement that had been made upon him.

But the Queen hadn't finished. After a pause she spoke again, silencing the astonished Vikings in an instant.

'This judgement will last three years. For three years you will be an outcast. But though you will be banished from our halls, you will not be banished from our hearts. I will give you a task to complete in your absence – a task vital both to Vikings and City Dwellers - a task as great as any Quest. To no other would I trust such an undertaking.

'I have not forgotten that it was you who first found Peter, without whom Maledict would surely have succeeded. I therefore propose that for the three years of your banishment, you will wander amongst the City Dwellers...'

Instantly hundreds of Vikings leapt to their feet in the balconies above her.

'*The City Dwellers? Isn't it forbidden?*'; '*Surely we must uphold our laws?*'

Pausing only to raise a solitary eyebrow (which was enough to instil silence again), the Queen turned her attention back to Dunstable.

'The time has come to reach out to City Dwellers. No longer will we hide from them. Your task will be to seek out those special children who still believe in magic and tell them about us and our world.

'I believe you will find children like Peter. For too long, they have been constrained by their world, unable to achieve their potential. Only a few realise that all things are possible through belief. You will travel across all lands to find them, and when you do, you will tell them about the Vikings and the magical world which their parents have forgotten.

'It is my hope that one day our two worlds will become one. Only then will we be able to leave our underground halls and live amongst the City Dwellers again. Will you accept this task?'

Dunstable's jaw had dropped several inches since the Queen had started speaking and now he was staring at her in complete astonishment, hardly able to believe that she would trust him with such an important task. Slowly he turned towards Peter and the Princess, who grinned back at him, nodding their heads encouragingly.

'Will you accept this task?' repeated the Queen firmly, forcing Dunstable to return her gaze.

'I, err…' He stared into the Queen's piercing blue eyes and slowly became more confident. 'Well, err, I, err…*yes?*'

Instantly every Viking in the hall leapt to their feet and roared their approval. The hall shook as they chanted Dunstable's name.

'Goodness me!' whispered Dunstable, blinking in bemusement as the scale of what he'd just agreed to sunk in. 'Wherever shall I start?'

Chapter 17

Many Partings

After the Council meeting, the Queen announced that a celebratory feast would be prepared. Immediately there was a buzz of excitement as everyone dashed out of the hall to prepare, leaving Peter alone in the lowest balcony, wondering whether he should leave or stay.

Eventually he rose to his feet and wandered down the empty hall, staring up at the wonderful carvings on the ceiling. Soon the two crystal trees rose elegantly in front of him. Suddenly he stopped. Perfectly clear in the crystal, his shocked reflection was staring back at him. He couldn't believe how dirty and scruffy he looked! How could he attend a feast looking like this?

At that moment, there was a polite cough behind him. Spinning around, he was confronted by a pretty Viking girl wearing a long white dress. She was grinning at him as he reddened in embarrassment. Without saying a word, she led him to a stone archway on the side of the hall behind the trees. Tentatively following her through the solid wall, he emerged into a steam filled room. Confused, he stood at the entrance for a moment, then the most wonderful sight was revealed behind the swirling steam. In the centre of the room was an enormous bathtub brimming with hot soapy water!

Immediately he sprinted towards it. It was shaped like a swan with its wings partially folded to encompass the bath within their wide span. Hot foaming water was pouring from the mouth at the end of its long, elegant neck at the centre, whilst excess water was slipping into a narrow channel behind it. It was big enough to have accommodated an elephant! And the smell! He'd never smelt anything like it! It was like his mother's bubble bath only much, much sweeter!

With a final smile, the girl turned to leave. Peter waited until she disappeared through the archway then undressed. He couldn't wait to get clean! He hadn't had a proper wash for days and he'd been in some unspeakably dirty places in that time. In an instant, he threw off his filthy coat, jumper, jeans, trainers and underclothes and leapt straight in.

After feeling so dirty for so long, the joy of immersing himself in gloriously hot soapy water was beyond bliss! For several minutes he rolled and twisted in the enormous bath like an excited otter, pushing off from the sides and ducking his head beneath the surface, luxuriating in the feeling of hot water against his body. Then he began to clean himself in earnest. On a shelf above the bath he found a large yellow sponge and several brightly coloured bottles. Picking the largest – a green bottle the size of a kettle – he popped the cork and poured the thick, sweet smelling liquid over his hands and face. Then, for the next thirty minutes, he scrubbed every inch of himself clean.

He felt gloriously refreshed when he had finished. But he couldn't leave the water just yet, the joy of it was still too great. Allowing himself to float on the surface, he closed his eyes and listened to the gentle melody of the water pouring into the bath from the elegant swan's head. It was so relaxing he couldn't bear to move. As the water gently flowed past him, it caressed his body, soothing away his aches and pains and taking the sting out of the wound in his side.

Suddenly he sat up with a start, sending little waves of soapy water tipping over the sides of the bath. How long had he been here? Had the feast already started without him? Immediately his stomach rumbled in protest at being so neglected!

Tumbling out of the bath, he frantically searched for his clothes and discovered that they had been neatly folded and laid on a chair just a few feet away from him. When he picked them up, he was surprised to find that they too had been cleaned. The girl who had showed him the bathroom must have taken them away whilst he bathed. But he was too hungry to worry about whether she had seen him naked. For the moment, all he could think about was food. Dressing himself in an instant, he raced towards the archway that would take him back to the Debating Hall. Just before he passed through it he paused, wondering whether he would be welcome.

After all, it was a Viking feast and he was the only City Dweller. Then his hunger overcame all doubts. Without another thought, he leapt inside.

The meal that followed was the best Peter had ever eaten. But it was not only the food that made the feast - it was the company of the Vikings. As soon as he walked into the hall and spied the four enormous dining tables set around the sparkling crystal trees, Peter realised that he had no reason to doubt whether his presence would be accepted. A profound change had occurred in the Vikings' attitude towards him since he'd returned to York, and for the first time in his life he was treated with utmost respect. Immediately, several Vikings who were sitting at the nearest table beckoned him towards them. Taking turns to sit beside him, they chatted to him as if he was an old friend, asking him endless questions and listening intently to his every word. Within a few short hours he became aware of a strange sensation rising within him – a sensation he'd never experienced before. It was a feeling of belonging and the joy of being part of a happy family; a feeling that no matter what happened in the future, he would always have friends who respected him and would never let him down.

When the food was finally eaten, the most wonderful thing happened. Suddenly the constant background hum of happy voices and the chinking of cutlery faded, and a deep silence fell across the hall. At the same time, the light from the great trees dimmed and the ceiling was spotlighted. Wondering what was happening, Peter glanced at the faces of the Vikings around him. Several of them winked in response and pointed eagerly upwards. Then he saw it. The wonderfully carved ceiling depicting the Vikings' adventures over the centuries was changing. A new scene was appearing directly above him, a scene that looked strangely familiar. Then, magically, the carvings began to move and he realised what was happening. There, thrashing in the white-crested waves, was the unmistakable figure of the Midgard Serpent, his great body coiling out to sea. On a tall cliff beside him was the crumbling abbey. An enormous wolf was there, howling in humiliation as he fled from two smaller figures, one a young female Viking wearing a crown and the other a boy standing protectively in front of her. Above them the sky was burning red and terrifying creatures were circling, riding on the backs of ferocious dragons. Meanwhile, on the beach below, a tall warrior dressed in golden armour was striding across the sand towards the thrashing serpent, a long sword in his hand.

As he took in the glorious scene, Peter felt emotion overcome him. There he was amongst all the Viking heroes for all to see! Then, as the great trees lit up once more, the Vikings began to applaud.

As everyone turned towards him, Peter shrank down in his seat. He felt himself reddening. Then something very peculiar happened. One by one, the Vikings stood up. But instead of leaving, they walked across the floor and bowed in front of him before making their way out of the hall. Unsure how to react, Peter self-consciously nodded to each in turn, simultaneously wishing he was somewhere far away whilst feeling happier than he'd ever felt in his life.

As the hall emptied, he realised that not all the Vikings greeted him. There was one exception - the Princess. He'd been unable to find her throughout the meal, but when everyone began to leave he spotted her at the far end of the table opposite his, as far away from him as she could possibly be. Soon she was the only one remaining.

Sensing trouble, he walked across the hall and sat down opposite her.

'Not hungry?' he asked cautiously, noticing she had barely touched her food.

'Not really.'

Her reply was sharp and abrupt. He knew her well enough now to know what that meant. He tensed himself for an argument.

'So. You are a big hero now,' she said sullenly, briefly glancing at him before returning her attention to the food on her plate, prodding it with her fork.

'I – I suppose so. Some of them seem to think so anyway. It's a bit embarrassing really. After all, it was Sigurd who did all the work really – and yourself of course.'

The Princess raised her head and stared at him for a moment, her eyes narrowing.

'Yes, I did my own little bit, I suppose. Obviously I am not the hero you are though. After all, *I* did not defeat Fenrir, did I? Sigurd did not give the talisman to *me*, did he?'

Peter winced. He had felt so happy a few moments earlier. The last thing he wanted to do was argue with the Princess, despite how blatantly unfair she was being.

'Sometimes everyone forgets that you are only a City Dweller,' she continued, her voice measured as if she was delivering a pre-prepared speech. 'But I do not. I still remember when you came here. You looked so lost and confused. You could not even fly until *I* taught you.'

Bowing her head once more, she began to push her food around with her fork again. Peter sighed. Clearly she was angry with him about something and was determined to have an argument, but he was equally determined not to rise to the bait.

'Does it really matter that I'm a City Dweller? I didn't know anything about Vikings or Sigurd when I found the talisman…other than what it said on the gravestone, that is. I didn't mean to come here. I was quite happy in the City Dwellers' world.' He said the last sentence quietly, knowing it was a lie.

The Princess raised her head and stared at him.

'Well, you have certainly made yourself comfortable since you arrived! Everyone seems to love you all of a sudden! They have even made a carving of you in the ceiling. Look!'

Without taking her eyes off him, she jabbed her fork towards the carving of him stepping in front of her whilst Fenrir fled howling into the distance.

Despite his best efforts to remain calm, Peter could feel his face flush with anger. This was the most wonderful moment of his life and he wasn't going to let her childish vanity ruin it for him.

'Is that what's upsetting you then? That someone is getting more attention than you for a change? Or are you upset because the other Vikings actually like me now?'

The Princess's eyes flashed with fury.

'How *dare* you talk to me like that! Do you think I even *care* what anyone else thinks?'

'Yes I do! I think that's *all* you care about!'

The Princess leapt to her feet, her fork dropping noisily onto her plate. At the same time, Peter sprang up in front of her. Their eyes locked together as they glared at each other across the table, their faces just inches apart.

'You know what?' spat the Princess, crossing her arms in defiance as she leant back on her heels. 'I really do not like you very much. I never have. I only let you come on the Quest with me because the Queen insisted I took you! I never wanted to take a useless City Dweller! I never wanted to take *you!*'

Peter stared at her numbly for a moment, his anger suddenly replaced by confusion and uncertainty.

'I...? We're friends aren't we? After all we've been through?'

'I do not know – are we? You tell me. I am not so sure we are. You are going back to your silly little City Dweller world now, are you not? I will probably never see you again.'

Suddenly Peter understood what was upsetting her. It wasn't that she was jealous that he was getting more attention than her as he'd originally suspected - it was because she had guessed that he was thinking of leaving. For a moment he was encouraged that her bad mood was caused by the thought of not seeing him again, but then a wave of sadness descended upon him. Though the prospect of returning to his former dull life had been weighing heavily at the back of his mind ever since he'd flown back to York, it was only now that he truly appreciated how much he had enjoyed the past few days. Despite all the dangers he'd faced, they had been the happiest of his life. He had found friends, discovered he could do incredible things, become a hero, even learnt how to fly! How could he go back to his dreary home and school now?

As he thought about returning, he suddenly became angry again. Where exactly was his home anyway? Was it in York or Wales? He'd felt more at home with the Vikings than he'd ever felt with his parents, with their constant arguing! And now he was supposed to simply go back to them? Why *should* he go? Why couldn't he stay here where he'd been so happy?

Then something caught inside him and his anger faded away. The image of his mother sitting alone in their tiny flat formed in his mind and his heart jumped. How must she be feeling? She'd probably think he'd run away or something crazy! As his anger evaporated, a horrible feeling of guilt replaced it.

He gazed at the Princess, meeting her furious eyes.

'I *have* to go. She's my mother,' he said sadly, unable to get the picture of her waiting for him out of his mind. 'She'll think I've been abducted or something. You know what mothers are like.'

The Princess continued to glare at him, her face bright red and her arms crossed tightly in front of her. He had never seen her look so angry. She looked as if she was about to burst. Then, suddenly, she exhaled and slumped into her seat again.

'But…*why?*' she whined. 'Why can you not stay here with us?'

Peter perked up slightly. It was almost the first time the Princess had been nice to him. He sat back down opposite her.

'You want me to stay?'

'Well…' she quickly backtracked, realising her mistake. 'Of course, I *am* a Princess, and I am far too busy to waste my time with you. It is not as if you are really important after all. But I thought we might go flying together, sometime? I have not taught you everything I know yet, and you are still not nearly as good as I am!'

Peter smiled at the thought of flying with the Princess and felt a little better.

'I could come back every few days, maybe? We could fly together then?'

The Princess bowed her head, shaking it sadly.

'You do not understand. Once you return to the City Dwellers' world, you might not be able to come back to us again. You might not be able to see us any more, at least not properly. There is no magic in your world, or no belief in magic, which amounts to the same thing. Once you go back, you might never be able to return.'

Peter stared at her in disbelief.

'But I saw Dunstable before I came here! *And* I saw Sigurd! I will always believe in magic!'

The Princess shook her head sadly.

'If you stay here with us, yes. But if you go back to the City Dwellers? How long will it be before you start to doubt what you have seen and done? How long will it be before you forget us?'

'I will *never* forget you!' insisted Peter, suddenly furious again. 'Anyway, what about Dunstable? The Queen would never have sent him if she didn't think he could find City Dwellers who still believe in magic! There *is* still magic in my world! I know there is!'

'Maybe there is, maybe not. But you are the only City Dweller ever to have left your world and found us. Are you really so sure you could find us again?'

For a moment Peter was about to argue with her, but the words died on his lips. He knew she was right. He had entered the world of the Vikings mysteriously, seemingly by chance. Could he be so sure that he could find his way back again?

Feeling utterly miserable, he contemplated everything he would lose. As well as all the friends he'd made, he would lose something almost as great – the ability to perform magic. Above all else though, he would miss flying, and flying with the Princess was the most wonderful thing he'd ever done. How could he live without the feeling of the wind blasting against his face as he raced across a field or skimmed the surface of a river? Or the sheer rush of excitement of dropping into a sharp dive, and the exultation of rising up again just in time!

But the image of his mother waiting for him still remained, ever present at the back of his mind. He had no choice. He had to go back.

The Princess could tell by his eyes that he had made his choice. There was nothing more to say. Their heads hanging in sadness, they sat in the deserted hall in silence.

*

By the time the Princess led Peter to his bedchamber and said good night, it was well past midnight. Despite the lateness of the hour, Peter couldn't sleep. After tossing and turning for two hours, he finally sat on his bed and propped himself against the wall with a pillow. Staring at the ceiling, he thought through everything that had happened to him and contemplated what he should do next.

As he pondered, he saw something glitter in the darkness. Reaching down, he held up Sigurd's talisman as it hung on its silver chain around his neck. The dragon's red eyes stared back at him, refusing to give up their secret. He dropped it back down the front of his shirt. There was still so much he didn't understand! So many unanswered questions!

Finally, the hour hand on his watch crept round to 6 a.m. He still hadn't slept a wink but he couldn't wait any longer. Jumping out of bed, he quickly dressed. This morning, he resolved, he would speak to the Queen and tell her that he had decided to leave. If he could see her early enough, he would be able to sneak out before the other Vikings woke up. He couldn't face having to say goodbye to them all, and he definitely didn't want to see the Princess again. Far better to creep out of the Viking Halls unnoticed before anyone else was about!

As quiet as a mouse, he crept out of his room and made his way across the Debating Hall to the archway that led to the Queen's private chamber. For a few seconds he stood outside, wondering whether she would be awake and if it was 'proper' that he should call on her so early. Then, just when he was thinking about going back, a clear voice called out to him from the room beyond.

'Come in Peter! I have been waiting for you!'

Slightly embarrassed, he stepped through the magical archway into the Queen's chamber.

The room was barely lit. Just a few candles were dotted around the stone floor, giving a warm glow. The Queen was sitting on a long cushioned couch at the back of the room dressed in a simple green dress. Behind her, sparkling water was trickling down a granite wall to a clear pool beside her feet. As the water flowed, it made a light melody that sounded like a hundred tiny bells gently ringing. As he listened to them, Peter felt his eyes drooping, lulled into sleep by their gentle song. Then the Queen spoke and the spell was broken.

'Come in Peter! Sit beside me for a while. We have much to speak about before you go.'

Jumping out of his stupor, Peter stared at the Queen in surprise.

'But h-how...' he stuttered. 'How did you know I was leaving today?'

The Queen smiled warmly in the light of the flickering candles, slightly amused by his question.

'Your eyes – they told me yesterday. And the Princess also. You are an open book to us. We can read your thoughts on your face before even you realise them.'

Her words did little to ease his nervousness. Awkwardly, Peter crossed the room and sat beside her on the long couch. But the sound of falling water was so gentle and melodic he soon relaxed again.

'Do you...*mind* me leaving?'

'Your bond to your mother is a strong one and I would not ask you to break it. You should act as your heart tells you. You miss her. You need to return to her.'

The Queen regarded him closely from across the couch. The light from the candles illuminated half her face mysteriously whilst casting the other half in shadow.

'You have not only come to tell me you are leaving, I see. You have come seeking answers to your questions. Now at last you will learn the truth. I see you are wearing Sigurd's talisman?' Peter touched the talisman nervously, wondering how the Queen would react to seeing it hanging so blatantly around his neck, but she immediately continued. 'Let us begin the tale with that, as it is a good place to start.'

Taking a deep breath, she leant back on the couch, her eyes far away in the past.

'The talisman was fashioned by Sigurd shortly before he died. Even then, few people believed in magic and our worlds were drifting apart. Sigurd knew that eventually two worlds would be created – a magical one where all things were possible and one full of doubt and fear. He knew that one day the last Vikings would need his help. So he crafted the talisman. Its purpose was to remind us that he will return. But the talisman is not a mere trinket. Great magic went into its crafting.'

'So the talisman *is* magical!' interrupted Peter, speaking aloud his thoughts. Feeling the Queen's eyes upon him, he reddened at speaking out of turn. 'I mean, I assumed it must be. How else could I have done the things I did?'

The Queen regarded him closely.

'You underestimate yourself Peter. It was not by chance that you found the talisman.'

'What do you mean?'

'Let me continue with the tale, then you will understand. When the talisman was made, Sigurd spoke aloud a prophecy. The two are bound together. The talisman was created so that the prophecy could be fulfilled.

'The prophecy was simple. When the greatest need befell the Vikings, Sigurd would come back from the dead. But the magic was only so strong. He could only return when a child who believed in magic appeared. This child had to prove his belief in our world beyond doubt by being willing to defend it against overwhelming danger, just as Sigurd himself had done. Only then could the prophecy be fulfilled.

'When the talisman was fashioned, most people were turning against us and our ways. They were already retreating into their cities and cutting themselves off from nature and the magic of life that surrounds us. But Sigurd had not lost hope. He created a beacon - a device that would only reveal itself to a child whose mind was still open – a child who could enter our world, should he be brave enough. The talisman was created to find one who was almost awake, and then to achieve its second great purpose – to awaken him!'

Peter was silent as he slowly took in her words. He gazed at the sparkling water pouring down the granite wall to the pool behind her.

'So…I found the talisman because I was somehow…*aware* of magic and your world?'

'At a deep subconscious level, yes. Perhaps you felt the magic in the Welsh hills of your home. Only then could you have seen the talisman. No other could, though it lay visible to all. Do you realise now why you are so important? Sigurd could not have returned if it wasn't for you! Only you could make the prophecy come true!

'Of course, once you took the talisman it aided you. To develop enough belief in our world, you had to learn magic yourself. It strengthened your confidence and reinforced your ability to access what lay deep inside you. Slowly you began to realise what you were capable of. When you defeated Fenrir and fought Maledict, you finally understood magic at last. Only then could Sigurd return.'

Peter recalled what Maledict had said to him on the cliff.

'Maledict wanted me to join him. He offered to teach me about magic!' He remembered how tempted he had been. 'I almost helped him!'

The Queen shook her head.

'You are stronger than you think. Maledict knew nothing of the talisman, which in the end proved his undoing. It was not Maledict you helped when you finally believed in yourself – it was the entire Viking race. We have been given another chance, thanks to you.'

Peter was silent as he pondered on what the Queen was saying.

'So, will I still be able to do…' he gestured vaguely with his hands, '*magic things* when I go back? Will I still be able to fly?'

The Queen smiled sadly as if she had been expecting the question.

'What you ask is difficult to answer. All humans have potential within them, potential to do incredible things if they truly believe in themselves. Unfortunately, the environment in which most live makes it almost impossible for them to achieve what they are capable of. They live their lives too quickly. Few can appreciate the magic in each moment and not lose it by thinking ahead to the next. And fewer still have the ability to break through the barriers they and their kind have created.

'That is what the talisman did. Though you were more aware than any other City Dweller, that would still not have been enough. Without it you would never have come to us. Though you might have seen Dunstable – a flickering figure on the edge of your vision that you would later doubt you had witnessed - you would never have been able to follow him into the snickelways and embark upon the great Quest you undertook.'

'Perhaps you will retain your abilities when you return to your world, perhaps not. The talisman no longer has any power to help you, and you are at an age when most City Dweller children begin to doubt what they have always believed and become like their parents. Our world is then lost to them forever. Remember, it is belief that makes all things possible. Here in our world you can see magic all around you and cannot deny it. But when you return to your world, it will not appear to be so. City Dwellers think that everything must obey strict laws which they themselves have created, and think they have no influence on the world around them. Will you still believe so strongly when you live amongst them once more? I do not know.'

Peter bowed his head sadly.

'And what about the other children? Is there any hope for them?'

'If they can break through the mists in their minds that your world has created before it is too late, they may learn to understand what they are capable of. There is a chance, but it is only a small one. Most will grow up too soon and will lose the opportunity to understand magic forever. That is why I am sending Dunstable to find them and tell them about us before it is too late. Perhaps then some may begin to awaken. It is you who has given us this hope!'

There was a long silence as Peter bowed his head in thought. When he looked up again, the Queen was gazing across the room, her face glowing in the candlelight and her eyes far away, pondering on the fate of the Vikings. He was aware of the sweet melody of the water once more. Finally, he spoke again.

'What will happen now? I mean, I know we stopped Ragnarok but...' he remembered seeing the golden eagle rise above the cliff after Maledict had fallen, '...I think Maledict might not be dead. I think he might still be alive.'

The Queen turned her head towards him and smiled sadly.

'Yes, I feared as much. His power is great and he still has the Viking Stone. He may return, though I cannot foresee what he will do. But the Midgard Serpent is gone, and we must draw comfort from that. The great wolf Fenrir is still free though, and even now he runs through the woods and fields with madness in his eyes.'

'Now you must return. Go back to your world and be glad, for you have achieved great things and have learnt much. But I must warn you before you go. When you return, you will find that you are unlike other City Dwellers. You have seen and done things no one else could imagine. You will never be the same as you were before. Many will not understand and will fear you. Beware of them! Do not let their fear affect you. Remember always the great things you have achieved and rise above their ignorance.'

The Queen rose gracefully to her feet. Peter knew that the time had come for him to leave. Suddenly he felt enormously sad. He thought about the Princess.

'Will I see any of you again?'

The Queen leant forward and gazed deeply into his eyes. For several long seconds she held him in her gaze, reading something hidden deep within him, then she smiled enigmatically.

'Perhaps you may come back. There is still a chance. You must try to believe and not forget us! Be alert and wait, and perhaps we may meet again. But for now we must part. Farewell Peter! Your deeds will always be remembered!'

*

It was a long lonely walk through the Debating Hall to the golden gates and a poignant moment when Peter left the Viking Halls and stepped into the snickelway. For a moment he stared at the gates, wishing he could stay. Before he could change his mind, he turned away and jogged around the corner into *STONEGATE*.

As he made his way through the winding passageways he now knew so well, an orange glow spread across the sky above the snickelway walls as dawn came to the city outside. He paused to stare at the brightening sky and slowly his spirits began to rise. He was going home.

Finally, he reached the exit that led to the churchyard where he'd first met Sigurd. On the snickelway wall, illuminated by an elegant lamp, was the sign: '*VIKING GRAVEYARD EXIT*'. Beneath it was the white outline of a door. He knew that just beyond lay his mother's flat where she would be waiting for him. But he couldn't step through it just yet.

For several minutes he stood beside the lamp, reluctant to take the final step back to his old life. He was roused from his daydream by the sound of footsteps coming from the snickelway behind him. For a moment he panicked. The last thing he wanted to do was bump into someone when he was trying to leave as quietly as possible! What if the Princess had come to persuade him to return? Part of him was terrified by the prospect, but he was disturbed to find that another part of him leapt with joy at the thought that she might have come looking for him. Should he dart through the snickelway exit before she saw him or should he wait for her?

His indecision was fatal. It was too late to run or hide. The footsteps were too close. Then, jogging round the corner, Dunstable appeared. Seeing Peter, he slid to a halt and blinked in surprise.

'Well! My, oh my! I never thought I'd bump into you here, you know! How very strange! How very fortunate! I'm about to leave York, you see! *Official* business, you know! On the Queen's specific instructions! But then you know all about that!'

Peter relaxed, feeling both relieved and happy to see his friend again.

'I thought you'd already gone! I couldn't find you in the Viking Halls last night. Why weren't you at the feast?'

As if he had all the time in the world, Dunstable sat on the pavement beneath the lamp and stretched out his legs to make himself comfortable.

'Oh, I don't care much for celebrations, you know! Anyway, I was expelled remember? I could hardly turn up at a feast, could I? In any case, I had a lot of preparations to make. I have a long journey ahead of me!'

Looking completely relaxed, Dunstable took off his glasses and began cleaning them with the handkerchief from his outside blazer pocket. He fixed Peter with a mischievous, slightly out of focus stare.

'So, what are you doing here so early in the morning? Trying to avoid the Princess?'

Peter felt himself turning bright red. He stared at the opposite wall, avoiding Dunstable's inquisitive gaze.

'No, we err, said goodbye last night.'

Dunstable winked hugely, much to Peter's discomfort.

'Oh yes? Take it well, did she? You don't want to get on the wrong side of her, you know. She's got a terrible temper!' Putting his glasses back on, he propped his arms behind him and yawned. 'These early starts – they're really not very good for me, you know.' He squinted at the snickelway sign behind Peter. 'You're going back are you? Back to the City Dwellers?'

Peter nodded sadly. Dunstable gave him a most curious look.

'Things have a funny way of turning out, you know. You never know what's around the corner. Who'd have thought that we'd meet here again just as I'm setting out on an important Quest? Everyone was ever so polite to me, you know! Thought I was a hero, they did! Who'd have thought *that?'*

Peter frowned, not sure what he was getting at. But Dunstable simply grinned at him, looking extremely smug as if he knew something Peter didn't.

'What I am saying is, don't worry too much about it! Going back, I mean. Things never turn out the way you expect them to, you know! You may as well just relax and let it happen. That's my motto! Who knows what the future might bring? All sorts of surprises, I shouldn't wonder!'

Peter couldn't help smiling at Dunstable's simple philosophy, though there was something about the way he was looking at him that made Peter wonder whether there was more to his words than there appeared to be. He was just about to ask him what his plans were when Dunstable suddenly leapt to his feet.

'Oh dear! I must be going! No time to sit here and chat! The Queen has given me a very important Quest, you know! Lots of children to find!'

With that, he immediately raced down the snickelway past Peter. He was ten yards away before Peter could call out to him.

'Goodbye Dunstable! Good luck in your Quest! I'm sure there are lots of children out there who still believe in magic! I'm sure you'll find them!

Dunstable spun around and waved a final farewell.

'Goodbye Peter! We may meet again, you and I! I may come to see you and tell you what I've been up to! You'll be able to see me I'm sure, just like you did before! Goodbye!'

Then he was off again, his footsteps fading rapidly into the distance as he disappeared around a corner.

Peter waved one final time, though by then Dunstable had long since turned the corner. Feeling his spirits lift, he turned back to the snickelway exit. He was glad to have bumped into Dunstable. The thought of returning to his old life no longer held any fear for him. Suddenly he longed to see his mother and father again. With a smile on his face, he stepped through the snickelway wall and instantly appeared back in the church graveyard where his adventures had begun.

The graveyard was deserted. The only sound came from the bright yellow birds singing happily in the branches of the trees beside the church wall. For several seconds he stood on the grass listening to them, feeling the warmth of the bright morning sunlight on his face. Then he stirred. Gathering his bearings, he slowly turned around. He glanced at the church, the overgrown graveyard and the twin-towers of the Minster rising majestically over the rooftops in the distance. And there in front of him was the large old house within which his mother would be waiting for him.

His heart suddenly racing, he sprinted across the graveyard and car-park, opened the front door then leapt up the stairs until he reached the top-floor flat. Barely pausing, he knocked on the door three times. It opened almost immediately.

Standing on the doorstep, his mother and father stared at him in shock, unable to speak they were so overjoyed to see him.

'Mum! Dad!' Peter exclaimed, his voice full of joy at seeing them together. 'I'm back!'